He gathered her closer and found her lips with his.

She had not known it could be like this, and for a little while was lost in a spinning, starry daze of delight before the enormity of what was happening dawned upon her. She uttered a muffled sound of protest and struggled to free herself, pressing her hands against his chest to thrust him away.

"What am I thinking of?" she gasped. "Oh, we must not!" She spoke desperately, but her protest was stifled beneath his kisses, and the hands which had been holding him off relaxed their resistance and crept up around his neck. . . .

MISTRESS OF ASTINGTON

Sylvia Thorpe

FAWCETT CREST • NEW YORK

First published in hardcover in 1983 by
Hutchinson & Co. (Publishers) Ltd.

A Fawcett Crest Book
Published by Ballantine Books
Copyright © 1983 by Sylvia Thorpe

Library of Congress Catalog Card Number: 83-90639

ISBN 0-449-20309-3

This edition published by arrangement with
Hutchinson & Co. (Publishers) Ltd.

Manufactured in the United States of America

First Ballantine Books Edition: November 1983

PART
ONE

WITH A SIGH, Hebe Cullingworth closed the lid of her brother's trunk and sat back on her heels, sadly contemplating the battered receptacle. It seemed pitifully small to contain the sum total of a man's worldly possessions, even one who had set no store by material things. Now, in a little while, another man's servants would carry the box away, and there would be nothing left to mark Felix Cullingworth's twenty-eight years on earth but the simplest of memorials in a foreign graveyard. That, and his sister's memories.

Somewhere in the quiet house a clock chimed the hour, and Hebe roused herself with a start from her unhappy thoughts. She had been kneeling on the floor by the trunk for far longer than she had realized. It was high time she completed her sad task and went to change her dress for dinner, since her host's household was still conducted with the ceremony which had obtained when he was a young man.

Rising with difficulty, for her limbs were numb and cramped, she walked stiffly to pull the bellrope which hung beside the bed. Her brother's room, stripped of his few possessions, had resumed its former impersonal air of a seldom-used guest-chamber. She had opened one of the shutters when she came in, and the strong Italian sunlight thrust a shaft of gold across the bed with its smooth, unwrinkled coverlet and curtains hanging in precise folds, and defined the outlines of the rest of the handsome, old-fashioned furniture. It was a room which spoke silently of wealth; the only discordant note was struck by the shabby trunk and the tall, pale girl in the plainest of black gowns, as devoid of ornamentation as a nun's habit.

Footsteps sounded outside, and the door opened to admit Guiseppe, the butler, a slight, erect man who looked at her with dark eyes brimming with sympathy. Hebe indicated the trunk.

'I have finished, Guiseppe,' she said quietly in her faultless Italian. 'The box may be taken away.'

'At once, signorina!'

He half turned, snapping his fingers like a conjuror performing a tediously simple trick, and two footmen came past him into the room, lifted the trunk and carried it out. Hebe bit her lip, and turned quickly aside to pick up the only remaining mementoes of her brother. The gold watch and enamelled snuff-box which had belonged to their father, and the half dozen particularly precious books which had accompanied Felix everywhere.

'Permit me, signorina.' Guiseppe came forward to relieve her of the books, waited for her to precede him from the room, and then followed her along the corridor to the door of her own bedchamber. As she took his burden from him again he added anxiously, 'Signorina, is there anything—?'

She shook her head. 'Thank you, Guiseppe, but no. There is no more to be done.'

She gave him a small, steady smile and went into the room. The butler closed the door behind her and walked away, shaking his head in perplexity at the composure of this young English lady, bereft of her only relative and so many miles from her own country.

Had Guiseppe but known it, Hebe's calmness was no more than a veneer, a mask instinctively assumed to hide a frightening sense of disorientation. Bereavement had not come unexpectedly, for she had known before they left England that her brother was incurably ill, but though she had faced the fact that she must lose him, she had been unprepared for this feeling of utter emptiness and lack of purpose.

Hebe and Felix were the only offspring of a late marriage,

and though both had been born in Italy, they had grown up in a small house on the fringe of a famous English university, where their scholarly father could surround himself with the learning which to him was the very breath of life. Felix had soon shown signs of extraordinary brilliance, and as the years passed, father and son had immersed themselves so completely in a life of classical study that the world of antiquity held far greater reality for them than the turbulent era in which they lived.

For these were days when Europe was in turmoil. Felix had been born in 1789, in the very month the people of Paris stormed the Bastille; Hebe, four years younger, made her appearance in the world at the time when Britain first found itself at war with revolutionary France. It was this latter event which had prompted Mrs Cullingworth to insist upon removing to England, and though her husband had agreed, the family was no sooner established in Cambridge than he returned thankfully to his studies, indifferent to the great events which were taking place.

It was fortunate that Mrs Cullingworth, the daughter of a Frenchwoman and a Highland gentleman exiled after the Jacobite rebellion of 1745, possessed the practical common sense which her unworldly husband so signally lacked. It was she who managed the family's finances, contriving upon a small independence a life of modest comfort and even a degree of elegance; who saw to it that her daughter was suitably educated, and that her impractical menfolk ate and slept at proper times, which, left to themselves, they would probably have neglected to do. A born home-maker, she would have been happiest with a large brood of children to care for, but being denied this, devoted her considerable domestic talents to creating a little world of peace and tranquillity in which her husband and, later, her son also were able to pursue their studies undisturbed.

Hebe, who apart from a natural vivacity Mrs Cullingworth lacked, resembled her mother as closely as Felix resembled their father, found it the most natural thing in the world that from the earliest age she was expected to play a similar part. A lively child, she learned to curb her exuberance so as not to disturb Papa, and soon resigned herself to the fact that it was useless to look to Felix for any kind of companionship, accepting both these facts without question because it was what Mama expected of her. To Mrs Cullingworth a woman's role in life was clearly defined, and though Hebe, at the Young Ladies' Academy where she was educated, learned what were regarded as the essential polite accomplishments, proficiency at these weighed far less in her mother's eyes than sound knowledge of housekeeping. She had an apt pupil, and when she died, the seventeen-year-old Hebe, newly emancipated from the schoolroom, stepped quietly into her place, and as far as material comforts went, the men of the family were scarcely aware of the change.

Mr Cullingworth survived his wife by barely two years, and though there were certain motherly ladies in Hebe's small circle of acquaintances who were concerned about the girl, and felt that her father had been sadly neglectful in not making sure that she was safely betrothed or married, Hebe herself suffered no such qualms. Naturally, she would continue to keep house for Felix, and to look after him. There was no question in her mind about that, but now, five years later, the delicate, brilliant, beautiful Felix, too, was dead, and for the first time in her life Hebe had no one but herself to consider. It was the loneliest feeling she had ever experienced.

Since early boyhood, Felix had had a burning ambition to visit Italy and Greece, as his father had done in his youth. They had planned to make the journey together, but during the long years of war, travel was difficult and expensive, and the opportunity had never arisen. Mr Cullingworth's sudden death put an end to the dream, and for several years Felix never referred to it, so that Hebe thought he had put it out of his mind altogether. She was not sorry. All his life he had been plagued by ill health, and though he treated it with splendid indifference and loathed being fussed over, it sometimes seemed to her that the fine intellect and formidable degree of learning, housed in the frailest of bodies, were like a flame consuming him from within.

Then, a year ago, he had suddenly announced his intention of making the journey. The wars were over, and English people who had long been confined to their beleaguered island were ranging the Continent like newly liberated prisoners. For the fashionable, the lodestone was Paris, but Felix's eyes were set upon more distant goals. He was determined to visit the source of the culture which was his life's passion; to tread what was to him hallowed ground—Rome and Athens, Pompeii and Delphi.

Hebe, hiding her dismay, ventured to wonder aloud whether he was strong enough to make so protracted a tour. His reaction was precisely what she had expected.

'Oh, nonsense, Hebe! Of course I am strong enough! Nothing ails me but this confounded cough, and that is bound to improve in a warmer climate. I wish you would not fuss so!'

She knew better than to argue with him. He could be excessively obstinate, and she sensed, moreover, a kind of urgency in him, as though he knew that time was growing short and that this might be his last chance to make the longed-for pilgrimage. Fears which she had tried to discount clutched sickeningly at her, but she forced herself to speak calmly.

'Very well, but we cannot dash off at a moment's notice, you know. Arrangements will have to be made to close the house and dismiss the servants, and we—!'

'We?' Felix was startled. 'I thought you could stay with Mrs Hallam while I am away. She would be only too pleased to have you.'

'Very likely, but I have no intention of staying behind.' She saw that he was about to protest, and went on reasonably, 'Be practical, my dear! You will find it far more comfortable if I am there to deal with such prosaic matters as meals and laundry and inn servants, and to look after you if you do not feel quite the thing.'

Considering this aspect of the matter for the first time, he was obliged to admit that she was right. He was so accustomed to being looked after by Hebe that he took it for granted, but now, facing the prospect of being deprived of that care, particularly while travelling in a strange country, he was frankly appalled. So he said magnanimously that of course she should come. Why should he be the only one to experience the pleasures of foreign travel?

'And what pleasure, pray, are *you* likely to derive from trailing after him around Roman villas and Greek temples?' Mrs Hallman demanded indignantly when Hebe, with some amusement, recounted this to her mother's oldest friend. 'I know he is your brother, Hebe, and that you are devoted to him, but there are times when *I* could gladly box his ears.'

'Oh, I expect to enjoy it very well,' Hebe replied tranquilly. 'I have not a fraction of Felix's learning, of course, but I have lived with these subjects all my life and can, I trust, take an intelligent interest in them. Besides, I have often thought that I would like to travel.'

'I do not hold with all this junketing about the world,' Mrs Hallam said severely. 'It is all very well for gentlemen, no doubt, but I *cannot* think it proper for a young, unmarried woman. And though I have the greatest respect for Felix as a scholar, you must admit, my love, that he is really not to be trusted to look after you in a foreign country. Why, let him once become absorbed in some antiquity, and as like as not he will forget altogether that he has you with him.'

'I will not let him forget, I promise you,' Hebe said with a chuckle. 'Dear ma'am, you speak as though I were a piece of luggage which Felix might absentmindedly leave somewhere, but you know as well as I do that it is I who will have the ordering of our journey. Which I am quite capable of, I assure you.'

Mrs Hallam reluctantly admitted this. Hebe was extremely capable, and both she and Felix could converse as fluently in French or Italian as in their native tongue, but Edith Hallam was still uneasy. Since Mrs Cullingworth's death she had been keeping a maternal eye on Hebe, and disliked the notion of the girl accompanying her brother across Europe as much as she would have disliked it for one of her own daughters. There was, moreover, another and more serious aspect of the matter which she was reluctant to refer to, since she was not sure whether or not Hebe herself recognized it.

'You know, my love,' she said carefully after a considerable pause, 'Felix is not strong: If he were to become ill, or—or worse, while you are abroad, you would be left wholly unprotected, with no way of calling upon your friends for assistance. I do not wish to alarm you, but I would be failing in my duty if I did not point out the danger to you.'

'There is no need, ma'am,' Hebe replied sadly. 'When Felix first proposed this journey I consulted Dr Beddoes. He knows how Felix longs to visit Greece, and he advises me that we should set out with the least possible delay. There— there is not a great deal of time. That is why Felix *must* go, and why I must accompany him. Please try to understand.'

'Oh, my dear child, I do understand, believe me,' Mrs Hallam assured her, tears rising to her eyes, 'but you must think a *little* of yourself. If the worst *should* happen, what would become of you?'

'Why, nothing very dreadful, I believe.' Hebe replied gently. 'I am not a young girl, you know, even though *you* may still think of me as one. I am twenty-three years old, and would contrive to get myself home to England without any mishap. Besides, we are bound to make acquaintances on our travels, you know, who would be willing to assist me.'

Hebe's faith had been justified, though exactly how her brother first made the acquaintance of Sir Hugo Roxwell she never did discover, since each gentleman was as vague as the other about practical matters. It was not important. Thanks to Sir Hugo, Felix had been able to realize his life's ambition.

By the time they arrived in Rome, Hebe had begun to entertain grave doubts of their ever being able to journey on to Greece, for her watchful, loving eyes could detect a steady deterioration in her brother's health. The long weeks of travelling, under the conditions which they were able to afford, had taken their inevitable toll. He had lost weight, he tired much more easily, and his cough, far from improving, troubled him more than ever. Nor had she much hope that their proposed stay in Rome would help him to recover, since he intended to cram as much as possible into his time there.

They found lodgings which were clean and reasonably comfortable—anything more luxurious was beyond their means—and set out to explore the historic city, but after a very few days Hebe realized that, to Felix, her company was a liability rather than an asset. Thereafter she resigned herself to occasional expeditions with their elderly widowed landlady, since for all her independence and her excellent command of the language, she could not bring herself to venture out alone in a foreign country. Always accustomed to being busy, she found time heavy on her hands, and was obliged to take herself sharply to task, reminding herself that their travels were for Felix's benefit, not hers.

When Sir Hugo Roxwell's name was first mentioned, and then began to figure prominently in her brother's conversation, she tried to find out something about the gentleman, but Felix, with his customary indifference to such things, could tell her only that Sir Hugo was an elderly bachelor, obviously wealthy, who had lived for a number of years at a villa on the outskirts of the city. These meagre details were tossed off almost impatiently, though Felix was prepared to hold forth at length on the subject of Roxwell's learning, the splendid library of which he had made his young acquaintance free, and his kindness to one whose knowledge lagged so far behind his own.

'You cannot conceive what it means to me, Hebe,' he said earnestly. 'To come here at all is beyond anything wonderful, but to have the privilege of knowing a man like Sir Hugo—! How Papa would have appreciated his acquaintance! Sir Hugo has travelled and studied extensively in Greece, too.'

Seeing her brother's enthusiasm, Hebe felt grateful to the unknown Sir Hugo, even though their friendship meant that she spent even more time on her own. Felix dined almost every day at the villa and stayed on late into the evening, very often arriving home in his host's carriage after Hebe had retired for the night; but even so, she was considerably taken aback when he announced at breakfast one morning that Sir Hugo had invited them to be his guests for the rest of their stay in Rome.

'Felix, you are scarcely acquainted with him, and I have never met him at all,' she protested. 'How in the world can we go and stay in his house?'

'Lord, Hebe, don't be missish!' Felix said impatiently. 'What difference does that make? It will be a capital arrangement, for I waste far too much time going to and fro between this place and the villa. You will find it much more pleasant there, in this hot weather, than being cooped up all the time in these dreary rooms. There is a garden, you know.'

It certainly sounded tempting, the more so since it would undoubtedly be better for Felix to be out of the city. So Hebe stifled her misgivings, packed their trunks and took leave of the widow, though upon arrival at the villa she almost regretted her acquiescence. Sir Hugo's house looked imposing, set on a hillside with formal, terraced gardens around it, but upon closer inspection Hebe was shocked to perceive signs of extravagance and neglect everywhere.

The next few days confirmed her first, unfavourable impression. The villa was staffed by an army of servants, far more, in Hebe's opinion, than were necessary, but the rooms were dusty and untidy, the meals which were served with such ceremony scanty and badly cooked, the gardens untended, while the servants were idle, dishonest and—to the Cullingworths at least—insolent. Hebe's every housewifely instinct was outraged, and she reflected longingly upon the changes which would be made if she were in charge of the household.

She half expected Sir Hugo to be as unkempt as his home, and was relieved to find, when he received them in the drawing room shortly after their arrival, that this was not so. He presented none the less a somewhat odd appearance, for he still dressed in the fashions of his youth, and in contrast to Felix's pantaloons and long-tailed coat, wore the kneebreeches, wig and embroidered waistcoat of the previous century. He was a tall, sparely built man, probably nearer seventy than sixty, with slightly stooping shoulders and a thin, pale, ascetic face, who greeted her with stiff formality. She had the impression that he was neither accustomed to nor much at ease in female company, for his bearing towards Felix was entirely different.

She was able to forgive Sir Hugo his reserve; she found it almost impossible to forgive his indifference to the chaos which prevailed in his household. She soon discovered that his sour-faced, unfriendly English valet, Murslowe, was nominally in charge of all the domestic arrangements, but as he had a profound and abiding contempt for everything 'foreign', and had disdained to acquire more than the most elementary smattering of Italian, he was very much at the mercy of his underlings. She would gladly have offered her assistance, but Murslowe had made it plain from the outset that he resented her presence at the villa. He was, it seemed, an even more confirmed woman-hater than his master.

Hebe endured the situation uncomplainingly for a week, but then, unable to face a repetition of the previous day's uneatable dinner, descended one afternoon to the kitchen to remonstrate with the cook. Her criticism was not well received. The cook, contemptuous of the plainly attired English miss, responded at indignant length, with a torrent of excitable words and a wealth of gesture. She was confident of the kind of easy victory she enjoyed when dealing with Murslowe, and was considerably taken aback when Miss Cullingworth answered her sharply in fluent Italian. Recovering, she became insolent, and Hebe, angry now, proceeded to rake her down so comprehensively that in the end the woman stormed out of the house, taking with her the butler, who was her husband and very much under her thumb; the under-cook (her daughter); and a large proportion of the rest of the staff, all members of her family who for years had been happily feathering their nests at Sir Hugo's expense.

Murslowe, arriving on the scene in time to witness this mass exodus, watched it aghast, and then aggrievedly demanded of Miss Cullingworth what was to be done now, with Sir Hugo expecting his dinner at the usual time. Hebe, choosing to ignore the impertinence of his manner, which she attributed to pardonable dismay, replied calmly, 'There is not the least need to get into a fret. *I* will cook the dinner, and you will see to the serving of it, which I am sure you are very well able to do.'

Murslowe's first impulse was to refuse point-blank, a course from which he was deterred only by the suspicion that Miss Cullingworth, already addressing herself to the few totally bemused servants who remained, would not attend to him. He would have liked to carry the tale of her intolerable interference straight to his employer, but Sir Hugo was closeted with Mr Cullingworth in the library, and Murslowe knew better than to interrupt. In the end he decided to preserve an aloof and disapproving silence, and let the wretched woman pay the price of her own meddling. He would have his revenge when she discovered that it was not as easy as it might seem to produce a dinner fit to be set on a gentleman's table.

He was to be denied this satisfaction. The meal which Hebe cooked was simple (she needed to be able to leave the finishing touches to her underlings while she went to change her dress) but it was both ample and appetizing. Before they were halfway through the first course this fact dawned upon Sir Hugo. He broke off his conversation with Felix long enough to remark upon it to the butler, and so perceived for the first time, and with considerable astonishment, that he was being waited upon by his valet. Seizing her opportunity before Murslowe could speak, Hebe confessed what had happened.

'I must beg your pardon, Sir Hugo, for taking so much upon myself,' she concluded rather guiltily. 'I did not intend to provoke your cook into walking out of the house, but when she did, there was no help for it but to cook the dinner myself.'

He stared at her as though he could not quite believe his ears. '*You* cooked the dinner, Miss Cullingworth? It cannot be possible!'

It was Hebe's turn to stare. 'My dear sir, I was learning to cook almost as soon as I was out of the nursery. My mother was of the opinion that every woman should be capable of undertaking all those tasks which she might order a servant to perform.'

'Extraordinary! Quite extraordinary!' he remarked. 'Pray accept my compliments, ma'am, and my thanks, but I cannot permit a guest in my house to perform so menial a task.'

'Well, no,' Hebe agreed with a smile. 'I am not proposing, sir, to apply for the post of your cook.' She saw that he did not find this amusing, and went on hurriedly, 'What I would be happy to do, if you will permit me, is to find new servants for you, servants who may be depended upon, for you know, those who left today have been cheating and imposing upon you quite shockingly. Pray allow me to do this! It is the only way in which I can make amends.'

He looked dubious, but Felix intervened to assure him carelessly that Hebe liked to be busy, and—with a rare touch of brotherly pride—that she was a capital housekeeper. Sir

Hugo wavered, and Hebe herself clinched the matter by saying earnestly, and with suitable humility, 'I would be so happy, Sir Hugo, to repay your kindness by performing this small task. I am aware that I have very little learning myself, but I *have* been taught to appreciate that those who have ought not to be bothered by tedious domestic matters, and that I have a duty to see that they are made comfortable.'

She had struck exactly the right note. Sir Hugo, presented with a picture of woman as a submissive handmaiden to learning, found it so much to his liking that he had no further hesitation in giving Miss Cullingworth permission to take whatever measures she thought necessary. He even instructed Murslowe to give her whatever information and assistance she might require, thus unwittingly turning the knife in his valet's wounds and transforming him into Hebe's implacable enemy.

The task she had undertaken kept Hebe happily occupied for the next few weeks, and while Felix and Sir Hugo spent all their time immersed in study, or driving out to visit some relic of the antique past, she plunged with enthusiasm into the business of making life comfortable in the Roxwell household. Until the villa was staffed to her satisfaction she acted as housekeeper, keeping the keys, instructing the servants and supervising their work, and reducing to order the chaos of the household accounts. She had her reward in seeing house and gardens gradually lose their unkempt appearance, and thoroughly enjoyed being responsible for a larger household than she had ever had before, but Murslowe, seething with a fury he dared not betray, reflected savagely that 'the English nobody' was behaving as though she were the mistress of the house. Hebe, aware of his resentment but not of its intensity, treated him in the same pleasant but firm manner she used towards the other upper servants, and never suspected that she was storing up trouble for herself in the future.

She had the satisfaction of knowing that she was being useful, and the only thing which clouded her pleasure was the alarming deterioration in her brother's health. As always, he petulantly brushed aside even the most commonplace inquiries, insisting that there was nothing the matter with him, yet she could see him wasting away before her eyes. His clothes hung loose upon him now; the smallest exertion fatigued him; and a savage cough constantly racked his frail body. Yet his spirit was undimmed, and when Sir Hugo, aware of his most consuming ambition, proposed that they should visit Greece, he assented with almost feverish enthusiasm. Hebe, fearing the effect of further travelling, viewed the prospect with dismay, but she knew that such a visit was the thing he most desired, and in his hearing had not the heart to raise any objection.

She did, however, venture to broach the matter privately to Sir Hugo, for she sometimes wondered whether, in his detachment from everyday concerns, he realized how ill Felix really was. He listened with his usual distant courtesy while she tentatively voiced her doubts, and then said gravely, 'I understand your concern, Miss Cullingworth. Perhaps the most prudent course *would* be for Felix to travel no further, but to visit Greece is the thing he desires above all others, and I fear the time has come when prudence is of less urgency than the granting of that desire. Do you not agree? You cannot, I think, be unaware of the incurable nature of his illness?'

Hebe flinched, but continued to meet his eyes steadily. 'I was aware of it, sir, before we left England. Our doctor explained it to me.'

Roxwell inclined his head in acknowledgement. 'Precisely. It is a tragedy, for your brother is an exceptionally brilliant and gifted young man. I have become deeply attached to him.' He broke off, and Hebe realized with astonishment, for she had supposed him incapable of any deep feeling, that he had done so in order to master his emotion. After a few moments he went on, 'You fear that the strain of the journey may be too much for him, but accept my assurance that I shall do everything in my power to lighten that strain. I shall charter a suitable vessel, so that we may be dependent upon no one's convenience but our own and, I trust, with the excellent care which *you*, ma'am, always bestow upon him, Felix will not find the expedition too great a drain upon his strength.'

With that she had to be content, for she knew that Felix himself would choose to go to Greece whatever the consequences. So she hid her fears and set about the preparations for their departure, unobtrusively doing all she could to smooth her brother's path. With this anxiety weighing so heavily upon her she did not expect to enjoy their expedition, but once they reached Greece even she fell under the spell of that storied land; thrilled to the sight of legendary islands rising from the timeless sea, and in imagination peopled the groves and temples with the pagan deities whose names had been familiar to her since childhood; for one of which, indeed, she had been named.

She accompanied the two men on all their excursions, for though she knew that Sir Hugo would have preferred her to remain behind, she had no intention of permitting her brother's enthusiasm to lead him into attempting things which were beyond his strength. She was prepared to do battle with their host on that score, but the need did not arise, and she was obliged to do him the justice of admitting that his regard for Felix was strong enough to outweigh his undoubted dislike of having a woman in the party.

As for Felix himself, a sort of ecstasy seemed to possess him, lifting him for a time above the limitations of his failing body, enabling him to undertake excursions and pilgrimages which even his companions found taxing. Yet he was now skeleton-thin, and the handkerchiefs with which he tried to stifle his coughing were all too often stained with blood.

It could not last, of course. By the time they arrived back in Italy he had to be carried ashore, and once he had reached the villa could no longer find the strength to rise from his bed. Hebe knew that the end could not be far away, and tried to draw what comfort she could from the fact that, thanks to Sir Hugo, the last few months of her brother's life had also been some of the happiest.

Now all was over. The funeral had taken place, Felix's few possessions had been disposed of, and Hebe must look to her own future. Must face the fact that there was no one left who needed her. It was a chilling thought.

She put her brother's watch and snuff-box carefully away, and then changed her dress for the one simple evening gown of black crepe she had felt obliged to purchase. When she was ready she stood for a few moments before the mirror, despondently studying a depressing reflection and thinking, as she had so often done, that Felix had possessed all the good looks in the Cullingworth family as well as the brains. Even in ill health he had remained strikingly handsome, but Hebe's mirror showed her only a drab young woman whose high-waisted, narrow-skirted black gown did nothing to flatter her thin, almost boyish figure and the unusual height she had inherited from her Highland mother. Its colour might have flattered her clear, pale skin, and hair which was neither red nor gold but a coppery tint somewhere between the two, but her face was drawn with the sorrow and strain of the past weeks: hollow-cheeked, with a pinched look about the mouth, and shadows like bruises beneath the defeated, dark blue eyes. Hebe Cullingworth, twenty-four years old, with life stretching empty and purposeless before her. She shivered suddenly and turned away. It was as though a ghost had looked back at her from the glass; a ghost of the lonely years which lay ahead.

Sir Hugo was already in the drawing room. He got up to greet her and civilly inquired how she was feeling. He, too, looked worn and sad, but mutual grief had not drawn them together; if anything, his manner was more cold and distant than before.

'Thank you, Sir Hugo, I am better now.' Hebe took the chair he offered, watched him resume his seat and then, sitting up very straight and steadily regarding him, she continued seriously, 'I know, sir, that you do not like to be thanked, but you must allow me, just once, to tell you how grateful I am for all that you did for Felix. Alone, we could never have visited Greece, for we had not the means to travel in the style which his ill health demanded, and this visit meant so much to him, and so, for his sake, to me.' Roxwell made a slight, dismissive gesture and she added with a faint smile, 'Very well! I will say no more on that head, but assure you instead that I shall relieve you of my presence as soon as I can make arrangements to return to England.'

He looked blank, and a moment passed before he said reprovingly, 'Miss Cullingworth, you are surely not proposing to travel across Europe alone?'

'I would prefer not to, of course,' she replied frankly, 'but you must see, sir, that now Felix is dead it would be out of the question for me to remain under your roof even if I were not imposing upon your hospitality by doing so. I dare say I shall contrive well enough. You must not feel any concern on my account.'

He continued to stare at her from beneath knitted brows. 'And when you reach England, ma'am, what then? Do not think me impertinent. Felix told me once that you are almost entirely without relatives.'

'Yes, that is true. My father had a distant cousin who lives in Yorkshire, but they hardly ever communicated with each other and we are not acquainted. My mother's family I never knew.'

'But you have friends who will look after you?'

She nodded, though without a great deal of enthusiasm. 'Yes, sir, at Cambridge, where I was brought up. There is a particular friend of my mother's, Mrs Hallam, with whom I know I can stay.'

'You will make your home with this lady?'

'I—suppose so.'

Hebe spoke reluctantly. The Hallams would welcome her, she knew, and Mrs Hallam, whose three daughters were all married and settled in homes of their own, would probably be pleased to make the arrangement permanent, but Hebe, fond though she was of the lady, could only view the prospect with a sinking heart. For seven years she had been the mistress of a household, keeping the accounts, taking the decisions, making sure that all went on smoothly; in another woman's house, how would she occupy her time?

Yet she had little choice. By the standards of the day she was long past girlhood, but those same standards demanded that an unmarried woman of gentle birth should not live alone. It was ironic that, though the house at Cambridge now belonged to her, it could no longer be her home. It would have to be sold or rented out, and though this would usefully augment her resources, she would infinitely have preferred to go on living there. She could picture, though, the scandalized outcry this would provoke. Since the death, some years before, of the old Italian woman who had once been the children's nurse, there was not even a family servant to lend respectability to such an arrangement.

Sir Hugo's voice broke in upon these depressing reflections. 'I have the impression, Miss Cullingworth, that the prospect does not appeal to you?'

'No, sir, it does not,' she admitted ruefully. 'Oh, do not misunderstand me! Mrs Hallam is a dear friend and has been very kind to me, but I am accustomed to keeping my own house. I think I am afraid of having nothing to do, and no one to look after.' She tried to smile. 'Perhaps I ought to acquire a pet dog.'

They were interrupted at this point by Guiseppe announcing dinner and, in the presence of the servants, personal topics had to be abandoned. During the meal Sir Hugo made civil conversation, but Hebe had the impression that his thoughts were elsewhere. She could sympathize with him. She could hear herself making the appropriate responses, but the greater part of her mind was occupied with the thought that in a few days' time this ceremonious way of life would be no more than a memory. The villa with its lofty, marble-floored rooms and liveried servants, the terraced gardens dotted with statuary and fountains, would belong to the past, along with the hot Italian sunlight on olive groves and the seven hills of Rome. Her future was the flat fields of Cambridgeshire, under a cool sky, medieval colleges instead of classical temples, and an emptiness of days stretching into infinity.

When dinner was over, Hebe retired punctiliously to the drawing room, leaving Sir Hugo to his wine, but he was an abstemious man and it was not long before he joined her. When he entered the room it occurred to her that he lacked a little of his usual degree of detached composure, for though he came to the chair facing hers he did not sit down, but instead stood behind it with both hands resting on its back while he studied her with the faintest of frowns.

'Miss Cullingworth,' he said abruptly, 'before we dined you honoured me with your confidence, with some of your misgivings regarding the future. I have since been giving the matter a great deal of thought.'

'Oh, that is kind of you, sir,' she exclaimed contritely, 'but

I was only indulging in a fit of the dismals, of which I am now heartily ashamed! I shall do very well, believe me.'

'Before your brother died,' Sir Hugo continued doggedly, ignoring the interjection, 'he spoke to me of his concern that he had never tried to make any provision for you. He felt that he had failed you.'

Hebe caught her breath. 'Oh, poor Felix! How could he be so foolish? I assure you, Sir Hugo, that I am not left destitute. I shall go on very comfortably, believe me!'

'I apprehend that that was not his meaning. He regretted, ma'am, that he had made no attempt to see you creditably established, from which I deduce—forgive me if I appear impertinent—that you have no immediate expectation of being married?'

'No, Sir Hugo.' Hebe was not sure whether she wanted to laugh or cry. 'I have no such expectation, immediate or otherwise.'

There was a tiny pause. Sir Hugo took his hands from the back of the chair and stood erect, steadfastly regarding her.

'Then may I hope, Miss Cullingworth, that you will do me the honour of becoming *my* wife?'

It took her breath away. She felt as though she had been struck hard in the midriff, or plunged into icy water, and could only gasp. Yet somewhere in the far recesses of her mind she heard a voice say, very clearly and with bitter, mocking laughter, 'Your very first proposal, Hebe Cullingworth—from a man old enough to be your grandfather.'

'You are astonished,' her companion stated unnecessarily, 'and I do not expect you to answer me here and now. All I ask is that you will consider what I have said.' He hesitated, looking now not at her, but at a point a few inches above her head. 'In the circumstances, it can scarcely be necessary for me to assure you that what I am proposing is a mere formality. A legal contract, no more.'

She realized with surprise that he was acutely embarrassed, and somehow this helped her to regain her composure. She was still breathless with shock, but managed to say in a tolerably steady voice, 'I am honoured, Sir Hugo, and—and deeply touched by your concern. I do not know what Felix can have said to make you think—! Or whether I said anything earlier this evening to give you the impression—!' She floundered, aware that she was expressing herself badly, and concluded desperately, 'That is, I fear, sir, that in making me this offer you may be prompted by a kindly impulse which you will presently regret.'

'I believe not, ma'am,' he replied seriously. 'I will admit that the thought did not occur to me until you spoke of returning to England, for I had overlooked the fact that it would not be proper for you to remain here now that you are deprived of your brother's protection. Then it occurred to me to offer you mine.'

'And I am honoured, sir, as I have said, but I cannot imagine why—!'

'That is because you have not yet considered the matter, ma'am. Pray do so now. I believe we may be of service to each other. *You* view with repugnance the prospect of being obliged, because of your spinsterhood, to make your home in another woman's house; to have, you say, nothing to do and no one to look after. *I* have found my life a great deal more comfortable since you took charge of my household and I do not wish you to go, but I would not insult a gentlewoman such as yourself by suggesting that she become a paid housekeeper. So if you are to stay, we must, to spare you the censure of the world, submit to the formality of a marriage ceremony. Afterwards, we go on as we do now, except that you will have the authority of the mistress of the house. Think on it, Miss Cullingworth, I beg.'

Think on it she did, far into a wakeful night. Her first, instinctive reaction to Sir Hugo's proposal had been to dismiss the idea as absurd, but the more she thought about it the more forcibly all the practical advantages of accepting it presented themselves to her. She had been dreading a return to England; living in another woman's house; dwindling into 'poor Hebe Cullingworth' who belonged nowhere. Now, suddenly, she was offered an opportunity to be of use to someone, instead of being useless even to herself. It was an opportunity unlikely to occur again. Marriage was every woman's goal, but in England no one had ever shown the slightest inclination to marry her, nor was it likely that anyone would do so in the future, for she was not beautiful and possessed only a very modest independence. Would it not be prudent to accept the only proposal she had ever had, even though the prospective bridegroom was more than forty years her senior?

In some ways, Hebe was entirely unworldly. It did not occur to her that a time might come when she would bitterly regret committing herself to an empty marriage of convenience; that she might some day discover something more urgent and demanding than duty and service, and yearn despairingly for her lost freedom. With her usual practical common sense she considered her one and only proposal; accepted the fact that she might be regarded as mercenary, since it was, in a material sense, a far better offer than she could ever have had any right to hope for; and in the morning told Sir Hugo that she would marry him.

PART
TWO

ANOTHER IDLE DAY was dawdling its languorous course. Hebe Roxwell reached the last page of the novel she was reading, closed the book and put it aside. She yawned, and then leaned back with a sigh against the cushions heaped behind her. What to do now? There was at least an hour to while away before she needed to dress for dinner, even supposing she spun out that process as long as she possibly could. Then the meal, to the accompaniment of Sir Hugo's scholarly discourse, and, later, sitting with him in the drawing room, trying to occupy herself with a piece of embroidery while he read to her from some learned tome.

'I am bored!' she said aloud. 'Bored, bored, bored!'

It was the first time she had dared to put into words a truth which for several months she had been trying to deny, and even though she was alone in her dressing room the sound of her own voice made her start and look guiltily about her. What right had she to complain? She had a beautiful home; her own luxurious suite of apartments; an allowance, to spend entirely upon herself and which was considerably larger than the sum she had kept house with in England; fine clothes; and her own carriage and horses and well-trained servants. Too well trained, she thought sometimes. The household ran so smoothly that she was left with almost nothing to do.

She could find no other way of filling her days. She had no friends, for Sir Hugo held aloof from Roman society, and the only guests to whom she had been required to play hostess were those men, usually of his own generation, who shared his scholarly interests. If they had wives or daughters they were kept firmly in the background, as firmly as Hebe herself was.

She had been Sir Hugo's wife for just over a year, but it had taken far less time than that to discover that her husband was monumentally selfish. He had married her simply to ensure his own continued comfort, and considered that by conferring upon her the coveted status of matron, and the material comfort his wealth could provide, he was amply repaying her. It was a matter of complete indifference to him that she might have preferences and interests of her own. She was there, as Murslowe was, and Guiseppe and his fellow servants, simply to minister to Sir Hugo and anticipate his wishes.

In some ways she was even more closely hedged about than they, for it was not only Sir Hugo's appearance which was old-fashioned. His outlook, too, was set firmly in the formal, ceremonious mould of the eighteenth century, and he expected his wife to live exactly as his mother had done. She must have her personal maid, whose sole function it was to care for my lady's appearance; her own footman to attend her when she drove out; her pageboy to run errands for her. The fact that for most of the time these minions had nothing to do was totally irrelevant.

Hebe thought sometimes that she would have done better to go back to England and Mrs Hallam, for there at least she could have occupied herself with charitable works. As Sir Hugo's wife, even this was denied her. She had made one attempt in that direction, but when her plan to take an active part in providing food, shelter and a measure of education for some orphan children had come to her husband's ears, he had forbidden it with cold disgust. She could give money, he informed her, as generously as she pleased, but it was not fitting for Lady Roxwell to have any direct contact with dirty beggar brats.

With equal finality he had refused to consider a visit to

England, which Hebe ventured to suggest when she discovered, to her astonishment, that he was not after all entirely without family responsibilities there. This surprising information came her way quite by chance, upon the arrival of a communication from England which provoked him to an unwonted display of irritation. They were seated at the breakfast table, and Hebe was avidly devouring the contents of a letter from one of Mrs Hallam's daughters which had just been handed to her, when she was startled by Sir Hugo tossing aside his own letter with an exclamation of annoyance.

'Impertinent puppy! How dare he write to me in this vein!' He encountered Hebe's bewildered glance and added impatiently, 'My great-nephew, ma'am! Clement Roxwell. He has the effrontery to tell me that he needs a more generous allowance.'

'I did not know, sir, that you had a great-nephew!' Hebe exclaimed, and then added in a tone of puzzled inquiry, 'Why does he wrote to *you* about his allowance?'

'Because, ma'am, he is my ward, and my heir. I was obliged to become legal guardian of the whole family when their father died leaving nothing but debts.' He flicked the discarded letter with a contemptuous forefinger. 'Like father, like son, it would seem.'

'Sir Hugo, why did you not tell me that you had young relatives in your charge?' Hebe exclaimed. 'Pray tell me, how many are there, and what are their names?'

'Bless my soul, how should I know?' he relied irritably. 'Clement is the eldest of them. He is up at Oxford. Two of the younger boys are at Winchester. There are several girls. I have only ever seen the two eldest of the brood, and that was when they were in their cradles.'

Hebe's astonishment deepened. 'But, good heavens, sir! How long have they been your responsibility?'

'Their father died five or six years ago. The mother did not survive her last confinement—twins, if my memory serves me correctly.' He looked severely at Hebe over the top of his spectacles. 'Let me make it plain to you that I heartily disapproved of them both. My nephew was totally irresponsible, and his wife a wilful, extravagant, feather-headed creature with not a thought in her mind beyond frivolity and pleasure. He ought never to have married her, for he was master of no more than a respectable competence, but of course, he was *my* heir, and lived upon that expectation.'

There was an acid note in his voice which Hebe had already heard once or twice before, and which revealed a side of his character which had been unknown to her before their marriage. He had seemed so kindly when Felix was alive, but perhaps then she had been too anxious about her brother, and too grateful for everything Sir Hugo was doing for him, to make a clear judgement of their benefactor. After a little she said cautiously, 'Will you agree to Mr Clement Roxwell's request?'

'Certainly not! Let him practise economy, so that he may live upon the perfectly adequate allowance he already has. I have no intention of encouraging his spendthrift ways.' He perceived the doubt in Hebe's eyes, and added impatiently, '*You* have lived in a university city, and must have seen many such expensive young wastrels, blockheads who care nothing for learning and everything for their disreputable pleasures. Now, if Clement had been a true scholar like your poor brother, it would have been a different matter.'

Hebe could not help feeling that if Sir Hugo had not seen his great-nephew since the latter was in the nursery, he was taking a great deal too much for granted, though she knew that in general his strictures upon young men at university were very largely true. So she abandoned that aspect of the matter and instead asked curiously, 'Where do your wards live, Sir Hugo?'

'At Astington.' Astington Park was his family home in Gloucestershire. 'Where no doubt the elder ones are already planning how best to squander the inheritance once Clement is master there.'

Hebe was frowning. 'But who looks after the children?'

'The servants, of course. The house is fully staffed, and there is a governess besides, who was with them during their parents' lifetime. Moreover, I understand that Lord Hendreth, whose lands march with mine, has an eye to them.'

Hebe's heart had immediately gone out to the unknown, orphaned family, to such a degree that she ventured to say, with a hint of reproof in her voice, 'That does not seem to me a very satisfactory arrangement, sir.'

He looked displeased. 'It is one which has answered perfectly well, ma'am, for several years.'

'How do you know it has answered perfectly well, if you have never been there to see for yourself?' she asked reasonably. 'I am sorry, Sir Hugo, but I cannot think it right for a growing family to be left entirely in the charge of servants. Every sensibility is offended.'

'I see what it is!' Sir Hugo made a determined effort to conquer his irritation. 'You are picturing my wards at the mercy of the sort of shiftless, cozening rogues who staffed this house when first you came to it. No such thing, ma'am! These are English servants, remember, and the most senior among them have been at Astington all their lives.'

'Even so, sir—!' Hebe had been doing sums in her head, and was more troubled than ever. 'If Mr Clement Roxwell is up at Oxford, he must be a grown man, and very likely has at least one sister not a great deal younger than himself. What is to become of her, or, indeed, of all the girls in the family, as they pass beyond the authority of their governess? Some provision will have to be made, will it not, for them to be given the chance of establishing themselves?'

He eyed her with displeasure. 'Perhaps, ma'am,' he suggested with icy sarcasm, 'you are of the opinion that I should abandon my studies here, and go back to England to busy myself with the trivial concerns of a troublesome pack of children?'

Hebe quailed inwardly at his tone, but she held her ground sufficiently to say quietly, 'Those children *are* your responsibility, sir.'

'A responsibility which was thrust upon me,' he reminded her angrily. 'Had I desired to be burdened with a family, ma'am, I would have raised one of my own. That prospect did not appeal to me in my youth, and it appeals even less now. I accepted legal guardianship of my nephew's brood because I could not evade it, but I have no intention of allowing it to interfere with my way of life. Do I make myself clear?'

'Very clear, sir! I can appreciate that you do not wish to take the time to visit England, but perhaps *I*!'

'Certainly not!' Her husband's refusal was prompt and

definite. 'Your place is here.' He added cruelly, 'That, you may remember, is why I married you.'

She flushed scarlet, but said in a voice which was only very slightly unsteady, 'I am aware of that, sir, but I cannot flatter myself that you would miss me greatly if I were absent for two or three months, whereas your wards—!'

'No!' Sir Hugo rose to his feet, but paused for a moment to look down at her. 'You had your opportunity to return to England after your brother died. You made your choice, *my lady*, and it is too late to go back upon it now.'

He turned and walked out of the room.

That was a month ago, and Hebe had not dared to broach the matter again, although the family at Astington Park were often in her thoughts, and she yearned, in her loneliness and boredom, for an opportunity to do something for them. It seemed to her unforgivable that she should be in Italy, seeking desperately for trivia to fill her empty days, while in England there were boys and girls, her husband's responsibility, with no one to care what became of them.

She got up from her couch and walked restlessly across to the window, where she stood looking down into the spring-time garden, a very different figure from the drab young woman of a year ago. Paradoxically, she looked younger. Luxurious living and enforced idleness had rounded her figure and filled out the hollows in cheeks and throat, so that though she would always be slender, no one now could have described her as boyish. Her copper-coloured hair was fashionably cut and dressed; Lucia, the skilled and experienced lady's maid, had taught her how to darken brows and lashes to emphasize the blue of her eyes; and she was wearing a gown of fine white silk dotted with tiny pale blue spots, the long sleeves and high neck finished with ruffles of delicate lace and knots of deeper blue satin ribbon.

Her old friends at Cambridge would have found it difficult to recognize Hebe Cullingworth in this graceful, elegant lady of fashion, but her transformed appearance went largely unappreciated. Sir Hugo never commented on it, even though it was he, so insistent that she employ a personal maid, who was indirectly responsible for the change. Partly for something to do, and partly because she felt guilty at having a highly paid servant sitting idle, Hebe had placed herself in the woman's expert hands, with a result which had astonished her. Guided by Lucia, she discovered in herself a flair for choosing becoming clothes, and with money and unlimited time at her disposal had amassed an extensive wardrobe, even though, apart from the occasions when she was driven into the city to shop, she hardly ever left the villa.

Tired of gazing into the empty garden, Hebe sighed and turned away. She walked back to the middle of the room, stood irresolutely by the couch for a moment, and then moved more purposefully towards the door. She would amuse herself for an hour at the pianoforte. Her skill was nothing out of the common, but she loved music, and the drawing room was far enough from Sir Hugo's library for the sound of her playing not to disturb him.

As she reached the head of the staircase, she saw Guiseppe and two attendant footmen crossing the hall in response to a knock on the front door. Hebe had not known that a visitor was expected, but felt little interest in the caller's identity. No doubt it was some elderly professor who had come to discuss an abstruse point of learning with Sir Hugo. She went on down the stairs, but the man who entered the house was so different from anything she had expected that sheer astonishment brought her to a halt midway in her descent.

Slightly built and only moderately tall, he was dressed with an unostentatious excellence of tailoring which marked him unmistakably as English, and extremely fashionable English at that. The dark blue coat which fitted without a wrinkle, the fawn pantaloons and highly polished Hessian boots, the curly-brimmed beaver set at precisely the correct angle on his fair head, comprised a picture of modish elegance completely out of character with Sir Hugo's usual visitors. Most amazing fact of all, this man was young.

Curiosity drew her on down the stairs. She heard him ask for Sir Hugo in formally correct Italian but with an intonation as English as his dress. Saw him hand Guiseppe a visiting card and a letter, and then suddenly become aware of her approach. For an instant he stared, then swept off his hat and bowed, and as he came erect again Hebe found that for the first time in her life a man was looking at her with admiration.

The novelty of it confused her, and when Guiseppe, silently but with a flourish, held out to her the salver on which the card and the letter now lay, she was glad to be able to turn away and pick up the former. 'Mr Geoffrey Fernhurst.' The name meant nothing to her. She replaced the card, saying with a tranquillity she did not entirely feel, 'Inquire whether Sir Hugo is at home, Guiseppe.' She turned to the visitor, adding in English, 'I am Hebe Roxwell, Mr Fernhurst. Forgive me, but I am not yet acquainted with many of my husband's friends.'

The appreciation in his eyes was overwhelmed for a moment by a look almost of disbelief. He said involuntarily, '*You* are Lady Roxwell?' Then, hurriedly recovering, but with his handsome face colouring a little embarrassment, 'I beg your pardon. I have not the pleasure, ma'am, of Sir Hugo's acquaintance, but I bring a letter of introduction from one who has known him for many years. Lady Hendreth.'

This did not do a great deal to enlighten her, but at least the name 'Hendreth' struck a chord of memory. Lord Hendreth was Sir Hugo's neighbour in Gloucestershire, the man who 'had an eye' to the young Roxwells. It was reassuring to know that there was a Lady Hendreth.

'He will, I am sure, be happy to receive it.' They could not stand conversing in the hall, and the stranger came with excellent credentials. She added recklessly, 'Let us go into the drawing room to wait for him to join us.'

Mr Fernhurst professed himself honoured. He handed his hat and gloves to one of the footmen, and with the other preceding them, followed his hostess to the drawing room. Sitting down, and inviting the caller to do likewise, Hebe inquired politely, 'Have you just arrived in Rome, sir?'

'A week ago, ma'am,' he admitted. 'I ought, of course, to have called more promptly upon Sir Hugo.' He hesitated, and then added audaciously, 'Had I foreseen the pleasure of making your ladyship's acquaintance, I would undoubtedly have done so.'

Hebe felt the colour rush into her cheeks. Totally inexperienced in this sort of conversation, she did not know whether she ought to reprove him, acknowledge the compliment, or simply ignore it. She looked uncertainly at him, made the disconcerting discovery that his eyes, as blue as her own, were still warm with admiration, and said rather desperately, 'Your home, I take it, sir, is in Gloucestershire?' She saw that he looked puzzled, and added uncomfortably, 'You said that you bring a letter from Lady Hendreth, and since I know that the Hendreth lands adjoin my husband's estate, Astington Park, I assumed—!'

'Ah, I understand! No, Lady Roxwell, my home is in Devonshire. Lady Hendreth resides permanently at Bath, and I am acquainted with her because she is a close friend of an aunt of mine who also lives there. I visited Bath shortly before coming to Italy, and it was then that her ladyship suggested that I should convey her compliments to Sir Hugo while I was in Rome.'

What her ladyship had actually said was, 'Oblige me by calling upon Sir Hugo Roxwell, Mr Fernhurst! I have been agog with curiosity ever since I heard last year from my son that he has recently married. I was never more astonished in my life, for Sir Hugo is sixty-seven years old and a most determined recluse. I cannot help feeling that he has probably fallen into the toils of some low-bred, scheming harpy, for these men of great learning, you know, seldom have much common sense.'

Common sense or not, Geoffrey Fernhurst reflected now, Sir Hugo had certainly not made the mésalliance Lady Hendreth had suspected, for his astonishingly young and attractive wife was unquestionably a lady. Whether or not she was a schemer remained to be seen, though she certainly did not give that impression.

He saw that she seemed perplexed, and decided that he had not, perhaps, made himself completely clear regarding the Hendreth family. He added a further explanation.

'Lady Hendreth is a widow, ma'am. The mother of the present baron. Hendreth himself is unmarried, so her ladyship is not, strictly speaking, the Dowager.' He added with a smile, 'It *is* confusing, is it not, when one constantly hears references to a set of persons one has never met?'

'Yes, indeed.' It would be too humiliating, she thought, to

let this charming young man know that Sir Hugo never talked to her of such everyday matters; that Hendreth's name had only cropped up by accident, on the day she learned of the existence of her husband's wards. She could only hope that Sir Hugo, when he joined them, would say nothing to betray how woefully ignorant she was regarding such things, or how little patience he himself had with such social niceties.

She found that she need not have worried. Sir Hugo might be displeased at being interrupted, but good breeding would not allow him to betray the fact. He greeted Geoffrey Fernhurst graciously, inquired punctiliously after Lady Hendreth's health, and displayed a courteous interest in the young man's own travels. Finally, when the visitor rose to take his leave, he surprised Hebe by inviting Mr Fernhurst to dine with them the following day, an invitation which was accepted with every appearance of gratification. He later somewhat spoiled the effect of this gesture by saying querulously to Hebe once they were alone that he had felt obliged to issue the invitation, and no doubt the young man had felt equally obliged to accept it. It was hardly to be expected that any of them would enjoy the evening.

Hebe could not agree with him. She woke next morning with an unwonted sense of pleasurable anticipation which she could not immediately identify, for it was a long time since she had felt like this. Then she remembered that Geoffrey Fernhurst was coming to dine that day.

A little spurt of excitement bubbled up within her, and she lay thinking how strange it was that she had not realized until now how greatly she missed the company of people of her own generation. Life at Cambridge had been quiet, but she had had a small circle of friends of about her own age, mostly girlhood companions who were now married with young families. Here in Rome, everyone she had so far encountered seemed to be elderly.

She wondered how old Mr Fernhurst was. Not much more than her own twenty-five years, she imagined, though he obviously moved in far more fashionable circles than she had ever experienced, which, to her, made him seem older. His visit therefore presented something of a challenge, for he must be given no reason to tell Lady Hendreth that her one-time neighbour had married beneath him.

Hebe gave a great deal of thought to all her preparations for the evening, not least to her own appearance, choosing a gown of heavy, ivory-coloured satin with tiny puffed sleeves and a low neck, the skirt padded and ruched at the hem so that it hung stiffly from the high waist. Her hair was dressed in smooth bands and coiled in a heavy knot, bound with narrow black ribbon, on the crown of her head, and a scarf of fine black lace was draped over her arms. It was a striking costume, to which her height lent an almost regal dignity, and the look in Geoffrey Fernhurst's eyes as she greeted him paid tribute to its effect.

He was the only guest. There had been no time to issue other invitations, nor did it seem likely that he would have any more in common with Sir Hugo's scholarly friends than with Sir Hugo himself. As it was, conversation was not easy, but fortunately Mr Fernhurst was able to maintain a flow of pleasant, amusing talk, and after a little while, Hebe found herself able to respond. Sir Hugo took very little part, and Hebe was not in the least surprised when the interval between her own departure from the dinner table and her companions' arrival in the drawing room proved to be very brief. The gentlemen had obviously found little to say to each other.

Too unaccountably restless to sit idle, she was at the pianoforte when they came in, softly playing one of the old Highland airs she had learned from her mother. She stopped at once and would have left the instrument, but Geoffrey said quickly, 'Pray do not stop, Lady Roxwell. That is a charming melody.'

Sir Hugo, perhaps thankful to have an excuse to refrain from talking, agreed and urged her to continue. The two men sat down and Hebe went on playing, while her husband withdrew into some private preoccupation, and their guest, leaning back in his chair, watched her, his gaze wandering from her absorbed face and smooth white throat to the copper-coloured hair that gleamed in the candlelight, and back to her face again. At length she glanced up and encountered that intent regard; her fingers stumbled suddenly; the music ended in a little jangle of discordant notes; and Sir Hugo came to himself with a start, while Hebe, rising quickly from her seat, said with a nervous little laugh, 'Forgive me! I fear I am accustomed to play only for my own amusement. To have an audience makes me uncomfortable.'

She moved away from the instrument into the middle of the room. Geoffrey, who had got up when she did, placed a chair for her, saying as he did so, 'Then it is I who should beg your ladyship's pardon, but I cannot bring myself to apologize for something which has given me a great deal of pleasure.'

She felt her cheeks grow warm, and found it difficult to reply with any degree of composure. 'I think you are prompted more by courtesy than by candour, sir, in saying that. I love music, but am only an indifferent performer.'

He smiled and shook his head, but said, addressing them both now, 'Since you are are fond of music, I venture to hope that I may have found a way to repay your hospitality. I am fortunate enough to have been given the use of a box at the opera while I am in Rome. Will you honour me by being my guests there?'

Hebe looked eagerly at her husband. She longed to attend the opera, but had known beyond doubt that if she made such a request, he would find some reason for refusing it. Surely he would not be so uncivil as to decline Mr Fernhurst's invitation? Then her heart sank, for Sir Hugo was shaking his head.

'Thank you, Fernhurst, but to be frank with you, I have no fondness for such new-fangled forms of entertainment.'

A quick glance at Lady Roxwell showed Geoffrey the eagerness dying out of her face to give way to a look of disappointment. Did this tedious old pedant never consult his wife's wishes? So much the better, if Sir Hugo could on this occasion be persuaded to indulge them at no inconvenience to himself.

'I am sorry to hear that, sir,' he said untruthfully, 'but Lady Roxwell, by her own admission, *is* fond of music. Dare I hope that you will grant me the privilege of escorting *her* to the opera, if you do not care to hear it yourself?'

Sir Hugo was taken aback. He stared at Geoffrey for a moment, as though the suggestion that Hebe might have preferences of her own was too novel to be immediately absorbed, and then turned a look of mildly astonished inquiry towards her. '*Would* you care to hear the opera, my lady?'

'I think I would enjoy it, sir,' she replied cautiously, knowing that it would not do to appear too eager, 'and since Mr Fernhurst is kind enough to invite me, I would like to accept, if you have no objection.'

'Bless my soul!' For a few seconds longer he continued to regard her, as though such a desire was beyond his comprehension. Hebe held her breath, willing him to give his consent, and at last it came. 'Then accept by all means, ma'am. I have no objection at all.'

She did not know whether the emotion uppermost in her mind was anticipation, excitement or sheer nervousness. She knew that she would be stepping into surroundings as strange to her as though they belonged to a different world, where it was of the utmost importance to behave correctly, and yet she was not even sure how she ought to dress.

This problem, however, was easily solved. She consulted her maid, and Lucia, who had spent years in the service of ladies of fashion, rose nobly to the occasion. She had felt for months that her skills were being wasted, and had been obliged to remind herself frequently of the compensations afforded by her present post—the most considerate of mistresses, and no necessity to sit up until all hours to put her lady to bed after a party—to combat the boredom of having so little to do. Now, at last, my lady was going to partake of a social occasion, and not in the company of her dried-up old stick of a husband, either, but escorted by the handsome young *cavaliere* who had just introduced himself into the house. Lucia eyed her mistress with new respect, and accepted with alacrity what she regarded as a challenge.

So when the time came, and Mr Fernhurst handed his charge into the elegant carriage he had contrived to hire or borrow, Hebe could at least feel certain that no fault could be found with her appearance, neither with her primrose-coloured gown of gauze over satin, her apricot velvet cloak, nor the elaborate arrangement of her hair. Mr. Fernhurst certainly found none. He had already paid her a neatly turned compliment, accompanied by a look which said a good deal more than his actual words and brought the colour into her cheeks once more.

She found the opera an unforgettable experience, and while it was in progress sat utterly absorbed, lost to any other consideration, while Geoffrey, to whom the music was no more than a fashionable diversion, divided his time between studying her intent face, and discovering which of his acquaintances occupied the neighbouring boxes.

During the first interval he took the opportunity to present Hebe to the most influential of these, a middle-aged lady of rank who was also a leader of fashion. The Contessa smiled kindly at the younger woman.

'Lady Roxwell? Of course, the wife of the learned English recluse! But you must not permit yourself to be turned into a recluse also, my dear. Not at your age. We should have seen you in company before this.'

'I am only lately out of mourning, ma'am,' Hebe explained. 'My brother died last year, just before I was married to Sir Hugo.'

It was an acceptable explanation, and one which spared her the humiliation of admitting that she had never before had an opportunity to go into company. The Contessa expressed sympathy, and they chatted for a few minutes longer, Hebe being presented to several other people who had come to pay their respects. She noticed that most of them greeted Geoffrey by name, and was so much struck by this fact that she remarked upon it as they returned to their own box.

'You know so many people, Mr Fernhurst, yet you have been in Rome barely two weeks. I, on the other hand, have lived here for nearly two years, and know almost nobody.'

'Only two years, ma'am?' he responded with a smile. 'You speak the language with such fluency I imagined you had lived here all your life.'

'I was born in Italy, sir, and though I was taken to England while still an infant, my nurse was a native of this country,' Hebe explained, and added with a laugh, 'I was chattering in Italian even before I had properly mastered English.'

He was intrigued, and resolved to find out more of her history, but, the curtain going up at that moment, he was obliged to curb his curiosity. When the performance ended,

Hebe expected to be escorted straight home, and was surprised and a little dismayed to find that her companion had arranged a small supper party.

'It is most obliging of you, sir, but I do not know whether—! Sir Hugo gave me leave to attend the opera, but I had no idea—!'

'Oh, come now, Lady Roxwell!' Geoffrey protested laughingly. 'Sir Hugo is your husband, not your gaoler, and to take supper after a visit to the opera or the theatre is so usual as to be almost obligatory. The other guests are quite unexceptionable, I assure you. In fact, you have already been introduced to two of them by the Contessa.'

The colour rushed up again under Hebe's fair skin. Was he jesting, or did he think she suspected him of some improper intention? She said breathlessly, the words stumbling over each other in her anxiety, 'I do not doubt that, sir! It would be discourteous in me, and—and ungrateful, to suggest otherwise. Pray believe that I intended no such thing.' She broke off, biting her lip, feeling that she was behaving like a schoolgirl, and furious with herself for blushing so readily. What was the matter with her, and what had become of her customary composure and common sense?

He was looking at her with a smile in his eyes which just touched the corners of his mouth, but when he spoke his tone was rueful.

'Then I can only assume, ma'am, that your enjoyment of the evening has been nowhere near as great as mine, and that you wish to be delivered from any further tedium. I am excessively sorry.'

'Oh, no!' Hebe spoke earnestly, straight from the heart, and impetuously put out her hand towards him. 'I have never enjoyed myself so much in my life.'

Geoffrey caught the hand before she had time to regret the gesture. She was enchanting, he thought, with the contrast between her appearance of a fashionable young matron, and her frank delight in the simplest of social pleasures. Unawakened, too, in spite of her married status. He had undertaken with reluctance the task of carrying Lady Hendreth's message to Roxwell, but he was beginning to think he had reason to be grateful to her ladyship.

'I am delighted to hear it,' he said with a smile, 'and even more delighted that you are going to grace my supper party. For you will do so, will you not?'

She assented in some confusion, telling herself that she could scarcely do otherwise, that she could not expect him to keep his other guests waiting while he escorted her home, but honest enough to know that she really assented because she wanted more than anything to prolong this delightful evening. He said, 'Capital!' and lifted the hand he held to his lips before releasing it.

Now her confusion was complete. She felt certain that it was no longer the custom, in England at any rate, to kiss a lady's hand, and even if it were, surely such a salute ought to be the merest formality, and not a real kiss such as Geoffrey Fernhurst had just bestowed? She was not wearing gloves, since her gown had long, full, transparent sleeves of gauze over the short, puffed satin ones, and she was intensely aware of the warm, lingering pressure of his lips against her skin.

He was wise enough to make no further advances on that occasion, and throughout supper and the drive back to the villa was once again the courteous host, attentive, amusing and entirely formal. Reassured, Hebe was able to relax and enjoy herself.

It was very late when she arrived home, and only a sleepy porter was there to admit her when Geoffrey escorted her to the front door. In some trepidation, resisting with difficulty an undignified impulse to go on tiptoe, she made her way to her apartments, where Lucia, waiting to undress her, was reassuring. Sir Hugo had retired soon after ten o'clock, apparently unconcerned.

'Thank heaven for that!' Hebe said with relief. 'I did not expect to be so late, but there was a supper party . . .'

She let Lucia divest her of the primrose gown, and sat down for the maid to untie the satin ribbons of her slippers. She said no more, and Lucia, casting a knowledgeable glance at her dreamy face, performed the rest of her duties in silence. She could read the signs, and at that moment understood my lady's state of mind better than my lady did herself.

*   *   *

The next two days seemed to Hebe to be the longest days of her life. To boredom now was added restlessness, and a kind of see-saw of emotion totally foreign to her nature, so that she was elated one moment and despondent the next. She felt a little ashamed of such childishness, yet found it almost impossible to conceal.

Yet from whom did she need to conceal it? Sir Hugo showed his usual lack of interest in what she did, and beyond a politely expressed hope that she had enjoyed the opera, made no reference to it. This was at dinner the following day, for Hebe had slept late that morning, and by the time she emerged from her rooms, Sir Hugo had long since breakfasted and retired to the library. When she apologized rather guiltily for this lapse, he said indifferently, 'I scarcely expected to see you at the breakfast table, ma'am. Murslowe had warned me that you retired late, and would be unlikely to rise at your usual hour.'

Hebe felt a familiar stab of annoyance. Murslowe! She knew that Sir Hugo's English valet disliked her and bitterly resented the fact that she had become the mistress of the house, but since he always accorded her the outward deference due to Sir Hugo's wife it was impossible to make any complaint against him. How did he know that she had been late home? He must have had the impertinence to keep watch for her, for he could scarcely have questioned the porter. His Italian was not equal to it.

'I *was* a good deal later than I expected,' she admitted, and began to explain about the supper party, but in the face of her husband's palpable lack of interest, her words trailed off into silence. After a little, he began to describe in minute detail a difference of opinion he had had with one of his learned colleagues over the exact meaning of an obscure Greek quotation.

Two mornings later there arrived a beautifully engraved card inviting Sir Hugo and Lady Roxwell to hear a recital of music at the Contessa's house. Sir Hugo glanced at it, raised his brows, and passed the card to his wife.

'I was not aware, ma'am, that you are acquainted with this lady.'

Hebe took the invitation and studied it. 'I was presented to her at the opera,' she explained. 'You know her, then, sir?'

'I know her and her husband by repute. A very old family.'

'Then shall I accept her invitation?'

'By all means, if it will amuse you. *I* have no time to waste upon such trivialities.'

She raised a dismayed glance to his face. 'I cannot go there alone!'

'If you wish to go at all, my lady, I fear you will be obliged to.' He saw that she still looked uneasy, and went on with a touch of impatience, 'Surely it is not necessary for me to explain to you that a married woman needs no chaperone? Moreover, the Contessa is a lady of the first rank, and in her house you will meet only those people whom it is proper for you to know.'

Hebe regarded him doubtfully. 'Do you mean, Sir Hugo, that you have no objection, to my going out occasionally, or having friends of my own?'

'Bless my soul! Why *should* I object?' He spoke now with a slightly injured air. 'Such frivolities, I understand, are important to a woman, and I believe I can depend upon you to conduct yourself always in a manner befitting your position as my wife.'

'Indeed, sir, I hope you can!'

'Very well, then! I am not a tyrant, ma'am, and as long as you neither expect *me* to bear any part in such activities, nor to fill my house with guests, I have no objection to you indulging in reasonable diversions, or to receiving occasional callers. All I ask is that you do not pester *me* with such nonsense.'

Hebe was so astonished by this declaration, and so delighted by the permission implicit in it, that she was able to disregard the injustice of his attitude. How could she have known she was free to live a life of her own, when he had never troubled to tell her so?

She thought she knew now what had ailed her for the past two days. She had been given a taste of freedom, and ever since had been hungering for more: for the stimulation of new faces, fresh conversation, company other than her own. It never crossed her mind that the company she desired more than any other was that of Geoffrey Fernhurst, or that her eager anticipation of the Contessa's musical evening was largely inspired by the likelihood of meeting him there. Even when she arrived to find him waiting for her, and her heart gave a great jump and then begin to beat with a hurried uneven rhythm, she thought this was due to relief at finding a friend among so many strangers, and never doubted that he remained at her side simply because he had gauged the depths of her diffidence and out of kindness was offering his support.

Such support was to be offered frequently during the next few weeks. The Contessa's invitation was followed by others, and though Hebe did not dare to accept them all—for in spite of what Sir Hugo had said, she knew he would not take kindly to too many absences from home—whenever she did go into company, Mr Fernhurst was always there, and seemed to be as pleased to see her as she was to see him. She accepted his constant escort without question, and never suspected that it had soon come to be taken for granted by all their fashionable acquaintances that Geoffrey Fernhurst was young Lady Roxwell's chosen *cicisbeo*.

Fernhurst himself, knowing how far this was from the truth, began to regard Hebe as something of a challenge. He was no stranger to modish dalliance, but all the women with whom he had hitherto played the game of love had been as familiar as he with its accepted rules. Hebe Roxwell, although apparently just another fashionable young woman married to an elderly, indifferent husband, not only did not know the rules. She seemed unaware of the existence of the game.

Already, to gratify his curiosity, he had set out to win her confidence and, having overcome an instinctive reticence, led her skilfully to talk about herself more freely than she realized. Thus he learned of the circumstances which had led her to marry Sir Hugo, and even, although she never actually spoke of it, of the boredom and frustration to which the marriage had condemned her. The discovery pleased him. A bored and lonely wife could usually be persuaded to seek a remedy for these ills outside the connubial bonds, though in Hebe's case he was experienced enough to realize that he would have to tread very delicately.

There were unexpected obstacles, he discovered, to the pursuit of a lady so ingenuously innocent of all feminine wiles. The compliments he paid her provoked confusion, but no response which might have led to the opportunity he was seeking; the fact that she knew nothing of the intrigues of fashionable life made her blind to examples among their acquaintances which she might have been tempted to follow. Time passed, and Geoffrey began to wonder whether he would ever succeed in breaching the defences she unconsciously erected against him, yet though he was afraid to force the pace for fear of losing the ground already gained, the uncertainty only made Hebe seem more desirable than ever.

Fortune finally favoured him on an afternoon when he called at the villa on the pretext of bring her a volume of poetry she had expressed a desire to read. She was not expecting him, but Guiseppe, who, like Lucia and one or two of the other upper servants, was taking a benevolent interest in the affair, had no hesitation in conducting him to the garden, where her ladyship was taking the air. The butler, having observed with indulgence the way the colour came and went in her face, and how warmly the visitor kissed the hand she extended to him, discreetly withdrew and went back to the house, casting an appraising glance at its windows as he did so and feeling gratified that the spot where he had left the couple was well out of range of them.

Similar thoughts were passing through Geoffrey's mind, but he was aware of the danger of being too precipitate. He proffered the book which was the excuse for his visit, and Hebe received it with delight.

'How very kind, Mr Fernhurst! I did not intend, when we spoke of this the other day, to put you to the trouble of procuring the volume for me.'

'Any trouble taken on your behalf, my dear Lady Roxwell, becomes a pleasure,' he assured her, 'and there is always satisfaction in passing on something one has read and enjoyed to one who will also find pleasure in it.'

'That is very true,' she agreed, 'and I am particularly grateful to you, sir, for bringing me the book today. I was feeling a trifle low in spirits.'

'Come, this will not do!' he exclaimed. 'Who or what has had the temerity to distress you?'

'Oh, the most nonsensical thing! I received a letter today

from an old friend in England, and it was so full of news of her family and of other friends that it brought home to me how sadly I miss them all.'

He gave her a reproachful look. 'Have you no friends in Rome, then, ma'am? I hoped you had accorded *me* that honour.'

'Oh, yes, indeed!' She laid her hand impulsively on his arm, but withdrew it before he had time to take it in his own. 'But apart from yourself, Mr Fernhurst, I have only *acquaintances*, and that, you know, cannot take the place of associations which reach back into one's childhood. Since my brother died, I have no family of my own, and so old friendships, which are almost like family ties, mean all the more to me.'

'No family at all, Lady Roxwell?'

She shook her head. 'Only a cousin in Yorkshire whom I have never met. That is why I would like so much to concern myself with the well-being of Sir Hugo's wards.' She saw that Fernhurst was totally at a loss, and explained briefly about her husband's great-nephews and nieces, concluding with a rueful little laugh, 'He cannot even recall how many of them there are. Is it not absurd? Yet I cannot help feeling anxious about them, alone at Astington Park with only their governess and the servants, and no one but Lord Hendreth to cast an occasional watchful glance in their direction.'

Geoffrey had been listening with a show of interest he did not really feel, but at this, he stared for a moment and then burst out laughing.

'Hendreth has an eye to these younglings?' he said incredulously. '*Hendreth*?'

'So my husband informs me,' Hebe faltered. 'Have you any reason to suppose him mistaken?'

'My dear ma'am, I cannot imagine Hendreth taking the smallest degree of interest in a parcel of schoolchildren,' Geoffrey replied frankly, adding with another laugh, 'As well if he does not, for I can think of no one more unsuited to such a task.' He saw dismay in his companion's face, and went on quickly, 'I should not have said that! Pay no heed to it.'

Hebe looked narrowly at him, a little frown between her brows, and said with some shrewdness, 'Yet there must be something, sir, in his lordship's character or conduct to prompt such a remark. Pray tell me what it is. I cannot help feeling a responsibility towards these children.'

Geoffrey paused before replying, obviously choosing his words with care. 'Lord Hendreth,' he said at last, 'is a law unto himself. His birth and fortune open all fashionable doors to him, but he seldom honours London with his presence. He travels abroad a great deal, usually, so I have heard, to the most outlandish places. His manner is unamiable in the extreme. He is what is known as a brilliant matrimonial catch, yet apparently he is a confirmed bachelor and I have heard it said that the only woman whom he regards with the least degree of respect or affection is his mother. His father died when he was a schoolboy, so he came early to his inheritance.'

And you do not like him, Hebe reflected. Well, I cannot blame you for that! He sounds a most disagreeable person, and I don't suppose I would like him, either. Aloud, she said, 'Does Lady Hendreth *never* visit Gloucestershire?'

'I believe not. Her health is not good, and she never travels far from Bath.' He paused, studying Hebe's anxious face, and then added remorsefully. 'Now I have given you cause for concern. What a clumsy fool I am!'

'Indeed you are not!' she said indignantly. 'It is not *you*, Mr Fernhurst, who give me cause to worry over these unfortunate children.' It then occurred to her that this was not, perhaps, a proper observation for her to make, and she added hurriedly, 'The thing is that Sir Hugo's studies occupy his mind to such a degree that practical matters which ought, perhaps, to be of some concern to him receive less than his full attention. One cannot wonder at it.'

'Can one not?' Geoffrey's tone was quizzical. 'You can say that, Lady Roxwell, because your father and brother were scholars. I on the other hand, find it almost impossible to appreciate an attitude of mind which rates the study of dead civilizations above the happiness and well-being of those to whom one should be bound by ties of duty and affection.'

'That, sir, is not quite just,' Hebe reproved him seriously. 'There can be no question of *affection* on Sir Hugo's part for his wards, since he is wholly unacquainted with them.'

'No question at all, ma'am, I agree. It was not Sir Hugo's

young relatives of whom I was speaking, or for whom I feel concern.'

This was said with so meaning a look that she could not pretend to misunderstand him. She was shocked and alarmed, yet beneath this very proper reaction she was aware of a leaping elation, a feeling that this was a moment for which she had, all unconsciously, been waiting. When he followed words and look by very gently possessing himself of her hands, and bending his head to press a kiss into the palm of each in turn, she did not try to withdraw them. Feelings such as she had never before experienced and of which she had not known herself to be capable were flooding over her. She did not know how to subdue them, did not even want to try, and when he raised his head, looked for a moment into her eyes and then, still very gently for fear of frightening her, drew her into his arms, she did not repulse him. Emboldened, he gathered her closer and found her lips with his.

Hebe had never been in love, or embraced by a man other than her father or brother. She had not known it could be like this, and for a little while was lost in a spinning, starry daze of delight before the enormity of what was happening dawned upon her. She uttered a muffled sound of protest and struggled to free herself, pressing her hands against his chest to thrust him away.

'What am I thinking of?' she gasped. 'Oh, we must not! Mr Fernhurst—Geoffrey—let me go! You forget—I have a husband—!'

'Have you?' He spoke thickly, his gaze hungrily searching her face. 'You bear an old man's name, an old man who cares nothing for you. Hebe, my lovely Hebe, that is not a marriage!'

'I am Sir Hugo's wife!' She spoke desperately, trying to invoke her married status to strengthen her crumbling defences, but her protest was stifled beneath his kisses, and the hands which had been holding him off relaxed their resistance and crept up around his neck . . .

In a bush on the terrace above them, a bird uttered a harsh, discordant cry and flew up with a flurry of beating wings. Startled, they sprang guiltily apart, both lifting dismayed faces towards the source of the sound. There was nothing to be seen. The shaken leaves were settling back into place, the bird was a diminishing shadow against the blue of the sky, but the spell had been broken. With an incoherent exclamation Hebe turned away, sinking down on to a marble bench and burying her face in her hands. When Geoffrey took a step towards her she shook her head and, still not looking at him, lifted one hand in a gesture of dismissal. He hesitated, and then said in a low voice, 'I love you, Hebe! I will not—cannot give you up, husband or no.'

There was a stifled sob, and then she said in a choking whisper, 'Go now, I beg of you! I do not know—I am so confused! I must have time to think.'

There was a little silence, and then she heard his footsteps going slowly away, but she still crouched on the bench with her face hidden, a prey to such a storm of emotion that she felt it was tearing her apart. 'I love you,' he had said, and she knew now that she loved him, had fallen in love with him at their first meeting. The unthinkable had happened, the possibility of which had never even occurred to her when she made her decision to accept Sir Hugo's proposal. Useless to remind herself that if she had not married him, she and Geoffrey would never have met; useless to wish despairingly that she was still Hebe Cullingworth, and not Lady Roxwell. No amount of wishing would make things other than they were, or spare her the cruel choice she now had to make.

She must not see Geoffrey again. If the past few minutes had taught her anything, they had taught her that. They had shown her with humiliating certainty the extent of her own weakness, so that she knew that unless they parted now, a time would inevitably come when no consideration of honour, no thought of right and wrong, would be strong enough to keep her faithful to her empty marriage vows. Somehow she must find the strength to send him away; to deny the first and only love she had ever known.

Sitting there in her springtime garden, shivering in spite of the warmth of the sun, Hebe faced at last the bitter fact that when she became Sir Hugo's wife, she had walked blindly into a trap, from which she would now give anything in the world to escape.

*   *   *

It was a long time before she felt sufficiently composed to return to the house, and when at length she approached it she heard the sound of a carriage driving slowly away. That, no doubt, was the old professor who had been closeted with Sir Hugo for most of the day. Hebe did not know whether she was glad or sorry that he was not staying to dine. In her present state of mind she scarcely felt capable of entertaining a guest, and yet perhaps it would have helped to have a third person with them at table.

On the way to her rooms she encountered Sir Hugo, going towards his own apartments, and it struck her suddenly how old he had begun to look. Or was it that since this afternoon she was looking at him with new eyes? Although he could know nothing of what had happened between her and Geoffrey, she felt the guilty colour rising to her cheeks, and prayed silently that in his usual unobservant way he would not remark it. It was perhaps fortunate for her that, always self-absorbed, he was at present made even more so by the fact that for a day or two he had been out of sorts, complaining of stomach pains and a feeling of nausea.

'I trust, my lady,' he said querulously as soon as he saw her, 'that you have remembered to order a plain dinner. I am not at all sure I shall be able to eat anything at all, and the mere sight of rich dishes would turn my stomach.'

'There will be nothing of the kind, sir, I promise you,' Hebe replied soothingly. 'I saw the cook myself, and gave her most explicit instructions.' She hesitated, studying him with a little frown. He did not look well. 'Do you not think, though, that it might be prudent to consult a physician?'

'Incompetent quacks, the whole parcel of them,' he said peevishly. 'I will perserve with the soothing draught *you* concocted for me, ma'am—though, to be sure, I have derived no benefit from it as yet.'.

Hebe still looked doubtful. Finding him adamant against seeking medical advice, she had prepared for him a remedy of her mother's with which Mrs Cullingworth had been accustomed to dose her family whenever the occasion demanded it. It had generally proved effective, but Sir Hugo had been swallowing it regularly for two days, and should have observed some beneficial effect by now.

'I do wish you would consent to see a doctor, sir,' she said uneasily. 'It could be that whatever ails you is beyond my skill to cure.'

'We'll see, we'll see!' He spoke impatiently as he turned away. 'I have very little confidence in the medical profession.'

Hebe went on her way feeling more guilty than ever. Lucia, helping her to change into an evening dress, found her preoccupied, and with the tact which helped to make her so excellent an attendant, refrained from intruding upon her thoughts. Guiseppe had mentioned that Mr Fernhurst had called upon her ladyship today . . .

When Hebe was ready, she took her reticule from the maid and was going towards the door when it was thrown open from without and her husband stalked into the room. At first she thought he had become more seriously ill, for his face was a livid grey and his hands were shaking. Then she encountered the cold blaze of fury in his eyes, and realized that it was anger, and not illness, which possessed him. He said curtly to Lucia, 'Leave us! I have something of a private nature to say to your mistress.' Then, as the maid, with an alarmed look from one to the other, reluctantly withdrew, he went on, in English this time and a tone as coldly angry as his look, 'Though no doubt the woman is privy to your shame! No doubt every servant in the house is laughing at me as that most ludicrous of beings, a betrayed husband. Has it amused you, madam, to hold me up to ridicule? You will find now that the time for laughter is past!'

The unexpectedness of the attack stopped Hebe in her tracks; the memory of that afternoon in the garden brought the guilty colour rushing again to her face. Sir Hugo watched the rising scarlet tide with a certain grim satisfaction.

'You blush, my lady? I marvel that you are still capable of it.' There was savage sarcasm in his voice, and he looked her over from head to foot with an expression of profound disgust. 'How I have been deceived in you! I believed that I was marrying a modest and virtuous woman, and now learn that instead I have bestowed my name upon a whore!'

Hebe's face was white now. She cowered before that bitter

denunciation, but when he paused for breath, tried frantically to defend herself.

'Sir Hugo, that is unjust! I have never—! Oh, perhaps I have been indiscreet—!'

'Indiscreet?' he interrupted harshly. 'Is that what you consider it? A mere indiscretion, when you have today been dallying with your seducer within my very gates? Defiling even my home with your lewd amours? Upon my soul, ma'am, you are shameless! Utterly shameless! No!' As Hebe tried to speak again. 'It is useless to lie to me. You were seen, madam, in your lover's arms! There is still, I thank God, one person in this household who remains loyal to me!'

Hebe groped for the nearest chair and sank into it, for she felt suddenly faint and rather sick.. Murslowe! It could be no one else. She remembered a bird flying up with a frightened cry, startling her and Geoffrey out of their increasingly passionate embrace, and she knew beyond doubt that the valet had been there on the upper terrace, creeping and peering, prying with hostile eyes into that precious moment. The thought made her cringe with shame, not because she had been in Geoffrey's arms, but because Murslowe had been spying upon her.

'What, silent now?' her husband jeered. 'It is difficult, is it not, to defend that which is indefensible? Now attend to me! This affair is over! As long as Fernhurst remains in Rome, *you* will not go beyond the boundaries of the garden. You may consider yourself fortunate that I do not confine you to these rooms—which I shall most certainly do if you attempt to disobey me or to communicate with him. Once he has left, whenever it is necessary for you to go abroad, Murslowe will escort you, as a precaution against any further—indiscretions.'

'As my gaoler, you mean!' Hebe was stung into replying. 'Do you think I will submit to such humiliation? I would prefer never to go outside the gardens again!'

'So much the better!' he retorted implacably. 'Stay at home, madam, and look to those duties which were my sole reason for marrying you.' He paused, waiting for some further defiance, but when none came, turned and walked back to the door, where he paused to add coldly, 'To impress upon you the penalties of disobeying me, you will remain here

alone until tomorrow morning. That will afford you an opportunity to reflect upon the wisdom of conducting yourself in
future with rectitude and decorum.'

He went out, closing the door with a quiet deliberation
which to Hebe was more unnerving than violence, and she
heard the key turn in the lock. She was trembling in every
limb, too shocked to weep, to move, even to think. Too
stunned even to resent the humiliation of being locked in.
There was room in her mind for one thing only: a mental
picture of Murslowe lurking among the shrubs and trees of
the upper terrace, peering between the leaves at the couple
below him, eavesdropping upon their talk, watching them
embrace, then seizing the first opportunity to tell Sir Hugo
what he had seen. It could not have been mere coincidence
which brought him there. He must have spied upon her at
other times, waiting his opportunity, hoping that eventually
he would have a tale which could not be denied to carry to his
master. How exultant he must have been when his patience
was finally rewarded, and how triumphantly he must have
poured out to Sir Hugo an account of his wife's indiscretion,
exaggerating it by hints and insinuations into much more than
a single embrace. And Sir Hugo had believed him; had
condemned her unheard upon the word of a resentful servant.

For the remaining hours of that day and throughout a
sleepless night, Hebe plumbed the depths of despair. The
injustice of her situation, when she had already resolved to set
honour and fidelity before her deepest feelings, was like salt
upon an open wound, and she could scarcely bear to contem-
plate the future. Henceforth her every move would be watched,
and she would be no better than a prisoner at the villa, for
nothing would persuade her to submit to Murslowe's escort
when she went out. Nor would she be allowed to forget her
fall from grace, for there was a streak of malice in Sir Hugo's
nature which would delight in casting it up to her whenever
she displeased him. A wife was completely at her husband's
mercy, and she knew him well enough by now to guess that
she would be given none.

This was confirmed as early as the following morning.
Lucia, admitted to her rooms by Murslowe, lost no time in
assuring her earnestly and volubly of her own sympathy and

loyalty, and that of the other servants. Hebe nodded silently and pressed Lucia's hand, but could not bring herself to respond in any other way. They might all be ranged whole-heartedly with her against Sir Hugo, but she had no doubt that they all believed as firmly as he did that Geoffrey was her lover. The only difference was that they saw no reason to condemn her.

Her mirror showed her a haggard countenance, and when she nerved herself to preside as usual at the breakfast table, Sir Hugo studied her critically, with far closer attention than he usually bestowed. A sneer twisted his lips.

'You are not in looks this morning, my lady,' he informed her callously. 'Your gallant would find less to admire in you if he could see you now.'

Hebe's cheeks burned and tears stung her eyes. She hurriedly averted her face in the hope of denying him the satisfaction of seeing them.

'No doubt it is too much to hope,' her tormentor continued, 'that your rest was disturbed by the prickings of conscience, for I fear you have none. Did you lie awake trying to think of means by which you may continue to make a cuckold of me? Abandon such hopes, ma'am! Your race is run.'

Hebe did not reply. If she tried to speak, she thought, staring down at the table, she would burst into tears, and that would be too humiliating to be borne. For a few moments longer her husband regarded her with a speculative expression, as though considering further taunts, but there was little satisfaction to be found in baiting so unresponsive a prey. He abandoned the subject, and instead began to complain about the breakfast set before him, none of which, he declared, was fit to eat. It was no wonder that he still felt unwell.

Hebe forced herself to lift her gaze to his face. He really did look ill, with a faint flush in his usually pale cheeks and a pinched look about his mouth. She said in a low voice, 'You really ought to consult a physician, sir. Pray let me send for the doctor who attended Felix.'

'Your concern is touching, ma'am,' he replied jeeringly. 'Such a devoted wife! I will send for a physician when, and if, I consider it necessary. I do not need your advice.'

It occurred to her, not for the first time, that he was afraid of doctors, of illness and all its attendant unpleasantness. He had even been reluctant to visit Felix towards the end. In other circumstances she might have tried to persuade him, but in the face of his spirit and peevishness she could not bring herself to do so.

The long hours dragged by, weighted with unhappiness, with loneliness, with longing for a joy glimpsed briefly and then lost for ever. With humiliation, too. There were engagements which she would be unable to keep now that Sir Hugo had forbidden her to leave the villa, and she wrote brief notes to the hostesses concerned, pleading as her excuse the fact that Sir Hugo was indisposed. Only later did she learn how closely she was watched. In the drawing room after dinner—a meal which they had both scarcely touched—he said, in that sneering tone she was learning to dread, 'I observe, my lady, that in spite of your indifference to your marriage vows, you still find for me a use of sorts. What excuse, I wonder, would you have made for breaking your engagements had I been enjoying my customary health?' He saw her dismayed, incredulous look and laughed unpleasantly. 'You did not imagine, did you, that I would permit any letter of yours to leave this house unread by me? Let it serve as a warning, in case you are tempted to have a message conveyed to your lover.'

Hebe drew a deep breath, trying to compose herself, to keep her voice steady enough to say, as calmly as she could, 'Would it be any use, Sir Hugo, for me to swear to you that Mr Fernhurst is *not* my lover? That the embrace your spy saw yesterday was the only impropriety of which I have ever been guilty?'

'None whatsoever,' he said grimly. 'Do not perjure yourself to no purpose, madam, for I shall never trust you again, and would not accept your word on anything if you swore it with your hand upon a Bible.'

It was the afternoon of the following day. Hebe was lying on the couch in her dressing room, staring desolately at the ceiling, when a knock sounded on the door. Wearily she gave permission to enter, only to regret it a moment later when Murslowe walked into the room. Indignation jerked her into a sitting position, and gave her the spirit to say angrily, 'This is intolerable! Am I to have no privacy even in my own apartments? What do you want?'

The valet closed the door and came across the room towards her. There was open satisfaction in his sour countenance, and for a moment she wondered if he had merely come to gloat, and what would happen if she summoned Guiseppe and the footmen to eject him. The Italian servants, she felt sure, would still obey her.

'I have something to show you, my lady.' Murslowe lifted his hand, and she saw that he held some scraps of torn paper. 'This was a letter from Mr Fernhurst. I caught one of the grooms trying to smuggle it into the house to give to your maid.'

Hebe caught her breath and put out her hand, then, sensing a trap, snatched it back again.

'If you had done that, Murslowe, you would have taken it straight to Sir Hugo.'

'Naturally, my lady! Sir Hugo read it, then tore it into pieces and ordered me to take it away and burn it.'

Hebe looked longingly at the scraps of paper. She wanted more than anything in the world to reach out and take them, but felt certain that this was merely some refinement of cruelty conceived by her husband and gleefully carried out by his valet. She said with assumed indifference, 'Then you had better obey those orders. I cannot imagine why you have not already done so.'

'Because, my lady, it occurred to me that it might be possible to piece the letter together sufficiently to decipher it. I am sure your ladyship will be interested to know that it is. Fortunately, Mr Fernhurst writes a very clear hand.'

Hebe flushed scarlet with mingled anger and embarrassment. '*You* have had the impertinence to read it? Oh, this is beyond everything! I cannot believe that even Sir Hugo would permit such licence to you, or such humiliation to me!'

'Sir Hugo, my lady, believes that the letter is safely burned and that you are ignorant of its very existence. I think, though, that when you know what it contains, you will be grateful that I did take the liberty of reading it. Permit me!'

Without waiting for her consent, he walked across to the writing-table by the window and began to arrange the scraps of paper on it. Hebe sat watching him, torn between her desire to know what Geoffrey had written, and the conviction that, if she yielded to that desire, she would later regret it. The resolve endured until the valet slid the last piece into place and then stood aside, inviting her, with a slight bow and a wave of his hand, to inspect his handiwork. Temptation was too strong to resist. She got up from the couch and walked slowly across the room.

The letter was not difficult to read.

My love,

What can I, dare I say to you? I would give my life to spare you the least hurt, but Sir Hugo's message forbidding me his house makes it plain that you have already felt the weight of his anger. I cannot forgive myself, but if *you* can forgive me, will you not grant me the inestimable privilege of protecting and cherishing you henceforth? If you love me, my darling, as I love you, entrust your dear self to my care.

I will have a carriage waiting tonight at the crossroads below the villa. Come to me there, and by the time your flight is discovered we shall be far away. I will be there by midnight, and stay until you come.

Ever your devoted

G.

Hebe read it through twice, and such a wave of longing swept over her that her surroundings spun madly round her and she was obliged to clutch at the back of the chair which stood at the desk. For a few moments it seemed that everything she had ever wanted lay within her reach, but then sanity and caution reasserted themselves. She drew a long, steadying breath and looked at Murslowe. He was narrowly regarding her.

'I think Sir Hugo is very well aware that you have shown me this letter,' she said coldly. 'This is to punish me further, is it not? He hopes I *will* try to leave the house tonight, and so suffer the added humiliation of being dragged back to him by you.'

Murslowe shook his head. 'That is not so, my lady. If you do not believe me, take the letter to him and tell him how you came by it. You will know then whether or not I am speaking the truth. Then—when it is too late!'

Hebe was silent for a little while, looking down at the letter and pushing the pieces of it more closely together with one fingertip. She did not really need to read it again; every word of it was already branded on her memory.

'What does it matter?' she said bitterly at length. 'We both know that even if I wanted to leave, I would have no hope of doing so.'

'On the contrary.' Murslowe's tone was matter of fact. 'At the end of this corridor, a staircase leads down to a passage with a door giving on to the garden. At the far end of the lowest terrace, a gate in the garden wall leads to the meadow which lies between the villa and the road. Nothing could be simpler.'

Hebe's thoughts were racing. What Murslowe said was true. The door at the foot of the staircase was secured only by a bolt; she often went in and out of the garden by that way. Sir Hugo's rooms were on other side of the house. There would be a full moon. Escape would be easy, except for one thing.

'The gate,' she remarked, trying to keep all expression out of her voice, 'is always kept locked.'

'That is true.' Murslowe's voice was even more indifferent than her own; he appeared to be gazing absently through the window. 'At midnight tonight, however, it could be found unlocked—if your ladyship so wishes.'

Hebe found that she was trembling. She pulled out the chair and sat down, and from the top of the desk the words of Geoffrey's letter leapt at her again. 'If you love me . . . entrust your dear self to my care.' Oh, she loved him, sure enough. Trusted him, too. Longed more than anything in the world to go to him. Yet it was a terrible step to take, and an irrevocable one, which would cut her off for ever from respectable society. A runaway wife; an adulteress! Never in her wildest imaginings had she pictured herself in such a role.

Murslowe, watching her sidelong without appearing to do so, read the uncertainty in her face and guessed how sorely she was tempted. Guessed, too, the considerations which were holding her back, though he attributed these to mercenary reasons rather than moral ones. Impatience with her was seething within him but he forced it back, certain that if he played the part of devil's advocate a little longer he could persuade her into taking the fatal step which would rid him of her for ever. He said softly, his face still discreetly averted, 'Your ladyship is, of course, aware that both the law and the Church recognize that a marriage such as yours to Sir Hugo is, in fact, no marriage at all. It can very easily be annulled, and you would then be free to wed elsewhere.'

She had not known it. It put a somewhat different complexion on the affair, making it seem marginally less disgraceful. In any event, what was the alternative? To remain a virtual prisoner at the villa, at the mercy of Sir Hugo's spite? His was an unforgiving nature; she would never be trusted again, never be allowed the smallest degree of liberty. To escape, to find happiness with the man she loved, was that not worth the sacrifice of her reputation?

Yet did escape really beckon? Had not her first instinct been correct, to distrust Murslowe and see in his actions a trap which would subject her to even greater humiliation and harsher punishment? She looked at him, studying the sallow, humourless face with its small, mean mouth and sly expression.

'No,' she said abruptly. 'I do not trust you, Murslowe. You must be mad to think I would believe you willing to help me.'

'To help *you*?' He looked her full in the face at last, and she realized with a sense of shock that there was hatred in his eyes. He no longer made any pretence of respect, but studied her with insolent contempt. 'What fools women are! You thought you could have everything, didn't you? Money and position and an old husband whom it would be easy to deceive. It never even occurred to you that you would have to reckon with me, yet I knew that if I was patient my chance would come. Now Sir Hugo no longer trusts you, but he does trust *me*. He will believe whatever I tell him, and no denials from you will make the slightest difference. It is in my power now to make life intolerable for you. That letter offers you the only chance of escape you are ever likely to have.'

Hebe covered her eyes with her hand. Now she had plumbed the very depths of humiliation, yet, by a curious paradox, she was convinced that Murslowe was speaking the truth. He hated her enough to help her leave the villa, to take the step which would ruin her for ever in the eyes of her husband and of the world.

His next words confirmed it. 'The gate will be unlocked tonight,' he said insolently. 'You can go to your lover, my fine lady, or to the devil. It is all one to me, as long as you go from here.'

'The gate will be unlocked tonight.' The words repeated themselves over and over again in Hebe's mind like an incantation, conjuring up pictures of what the future could hold, and what it would undoubtedly hold if she remained at the villa. She had been given fair warning. Murslowe was offering her this one opportunity to escape, but if she refused it, she would be condeming herself to a life of persecution, not only from her husband, but also from his servant. She could not face that. No matter what disgrace her flight brought down upon her, she would go to Geoffrey tonight.

Once the decision had been taken, she forced herself to think only of practical details and not let her mind dwell on the implications of what she was doing. She would have liked to take nothing from the villa that she had not brought into it, to leave Lady Roxwell behind and revert as far as possible to being Hebe Cullingworth, but since this was not possible she would carry with her only the barest necessities. A bandbox should suffice to hold them, but all her preparations must wait until after Lucia had left her for the night. She did not think that the maid would either betray her to Sir Hugo or try to dissuade her, but it would be better, for her sake, if she could later deny all knowledge of her mistress's intention.

Hebe contemplated with misgiving the prospect of sitting down to dinner with her husband, for in her present state of mind it did not seem beyond the bounds of possibility that she might somehow betray herself. But in the event she was spared this ordeal. Later in the afternoon, Guiseppe came to tell her that Sir Hugo would not be dining that day. He still felt unwell, and intended to remain in his rooms. The thought immediately flashed into Hebe's mind that this deviation from the normal was in some way connected with Murslowe's visit to her and boded her no good, but a little reflection convinced her that if Sir Hugo had really sent his valet with Geoffrey's letter for some obscure purpose of his own he would have done nothing to put her on her guard. A guilty conscience, she thought wretchedly, was an uncomfortable thing to have.

'Sir Hugo has been out of sorts for far too long,' she said. 'Has nothing been said about sending for a doctor?'

Guiseppe shook his head and spread out his hands in a gesture of helplessness. 'Nothing, my lady. When Signor Murslowe gave me that message I asked if Sir Hugo desired a physician to be summoned, and he said no.'

Hebe sighed. 'Then I suppose we must not, though I fear it is most imprudent. Very well, Guiseppe. I will not come down to dinner, either, but instead have something served to me here.'

Not that she was likely to have much appetite, she reflected when the butler had gone. Excitement and apprehension, mingled with shame at what she was planning to do, were already churning within her, and she did not feel that she would be able to swallow a single mouthful of food. When the meal was brought to her she did her best, but it was a feeble effort and she could only be thankful that after the events of the past two days, the servants would find little to wonder at in her lack of appetite.

At ten o'clock she rang for Lucia to help her prepare for bed, but had done no more than take off her dress when there was an urgent knocking at the door. The maid went to answer it, and Hebe heard Guiseppe's voice, staccato with alarm.

'Tell her ladyship that Sir Hugo has suddenly become very much worse. He is delirious and in the greatest pain. Signor Murslowe begs that she will go to him.'

Hebe snatched up the discarded gown and began to struggle into it again.

'I will come at once, Guiseppe,' she called. 'Lucia, come here and do up my dress.'

A minute or two later, as she hurried through the house with Guseppe at her heels, she reflected that Sir Hugo's condition must be serious indeed if his valet was appealing to her for support, and this was confirmed as soon as she crossed the threshold of her husband's room. Sir Hugo lay writhing and groaning in the big bed, while Murslowe tried to bathe his face. He had been vomiting, and the stench of sickness was heavy in the air, while when Hebe went quickly to the bedside she saw that he was flushed with fever and did not recognize her. After one look, she flung a command over her shoulder to the butler.

'A doctor, Guiseppe, as fast as you can! Send for the one who attended my brother.' The butler went off at a run, and Hebe looked sharply at Murslowe. 'How long has he been like this?'

'He took a sudden turn for the worse about two hours ago. I did not know what to do. He had forbidden me to send for a doctor.'

'You should have informed me at once, Murslowe,' Hebe said angrily. 'Sir Hugo is in no state to make such a decision.' She then saw with surprise that the valet was genuinely distressed, and added in a milder tone, 'No doubt you felt that your first duty was to him. Come, let us try to make him more comfortable.'

Nothing they could do, however, seemed to afford the sufferer any relief. His fever worsened, he muttered unintelligibly or lay moaning, his body rigid with pain. More than an hour passed before the doctor arrived, and when he saw his patient he looked grave and shook his head. Hebe was not surprised, for it was obvious that Sir Hugo was now much worse than he had been when she first entered the room.

The doctor sent her into the dressing room while he examined the sick man, and when he came to her afterwards, he could hold out little hope. The condition had been left untreated far too long; Sir Hugo was elderly, and not particularly robust; in the doctor's opinion, her ladyship should prepare herself for the worst.

For Hebe, the ensuing hours took on the quality of a nightmare. The doctor stayed at the bedside, leaving her with no choice but to do likewise; nor could she have been heartless enough to leave even if it had been possible for her to do so. As the hideous night dragged by, emotional stress and physical fatigue combined to make her feel lightheaded, so strangely divorced from reality that it was as though she stood outside herself and had no real part in what was going on. Only when at last it was over, when the moaning and the laboured breathing were silenced at last and the doctor drew the sheet up over Sir Hugo's face, did feeling begin to return, like life coming back slowly and painfully to a numbed limb. Hebe's gaze lifted wearily from her husband's deathbed to the window, and she saw that the light of the morning sun was bright around and between the closed curtains and shutters.

'I will stay until you come,' Geoffrey had written, but the day had come before she could, and the night which was to have cloaked her flight had brought her freedom of an unexpected and very different kind. Had it been her salvation, or the end of her one chance of happiness?

How long, she wondered wistfully, had Geoffrey waited for her? How long before eagerness gave way to anxiety, and then to—what? Disappointment? Anger? The fear that their intention had been discovered? Surely he would not think that her failure to keep their assignation indicated unwillingness or indifference! He could not even know for certain whether or not his letter had reached her.

She was too exhausted, too drained by conflicting emotions and by the events of the night, to reach any rational conclusion. The doctor studied her with sympathy and concern, desired Guiseppe to summon her ladyship's woman, and prescribed a small dose of laudanum. Hebe could not find the energy to refuse. She submitted meekly to Lucia's ministrations, dropped wearily into bed and slept until evening.

Even then Lucia, taking upon herself the role of benevolent tyrant, refused to let her get up. There was nothing, she said firmly, that my lady could do until the morrow. The doctor had inquired the name of Sir Hugo's lawyer in Rome and undertaken to inform him of his client's death, and the lawyer himself had already visited the villa. The necessary arrangements were being made.

Lucia had logic on her side, and Hebe followed herself to be persuaded. The situation would have to be faced soon, but it was a relief to be able to defer it for a few hours longer. She ate a little of the food the maid brought her, and then slept again.

This time, however, her rest was disturbed by unpleasant dreams, in which she fled secretly from her home by night to find the trysting place deserted and the villa, when she tried to return to it, barred against her. Or she hastened gladly towards Geoffrey, only to discover with horror, as she reached him, that he had somehow been transformed into Sir Hugo. Then she dreamed that it was her wedding day, hers and Geoffrey's, but that as they stood together before the altar she was clad, not in a bridal gown, but in widow's weeds and veil.

She started awake then to face a new day, and the knowledge that she must indeed put on a widow's black. Lucia had already unpacked, from the trunks where they had not long been laid away, some of the mourning clothes she had worn for Felix, and contrived for her a cap with a veil of fine black crepe, and when Hebe was dressed, she found the sombre reflection in her mirror a disturbing reminder of her dreams. These had been prompted, she decided, by an uneasy conscience, and that conscience was troubling her still, though in a more rational way. It was true that she had done her husband no actual wrong, but the intent had been there; she had betrayed him in thought and desire as she had meant to betray him in fact; to expose him to the ridicule he dreaded.

Yes, conscience pricked, but she could not completely banish the thought that now she was free, and would in time be able to turn to Geoffrey openly and without shame. This seemed so much more than she deserved that she was troubled by a superstitious, nagging fear that something might yet come between them. Some misunderstanding, perhaps, born of her failure to keep their assignation. She had sent him away, told him that she was uncertain of her feelings, and he did not know that she had been prepared to sacrifice home and position and reputation for his sake. No doubt he would soon hear of Sir Hugo's death, but Hebe knew she would not be easy in her mind until she had explained to him what had happened, and assured him of her love. More than anything she longed for the reassurance of his presence, the comfort of his arms about her, but a meeting at present was out of the question. Newly bereaved, she would be expected to deny herself to callers at least until after the funeral.

Presently Guiseppe came to tell her that the lawyer had called to inform her ladyship of the arrangements which had been made. Hebe said that she would see him, which did not greatly surprise the butler, who recalled her composure at the time of her brother's death, a composure which did not really meet with his approval. He fetched the lawyer, who respectfully expressed his sympathy, told her when the funeral would take place, and begged her to furnish him with the names of those persons whom she wished to be informed.

Hebe shook her head. 'Thank you, but I will attend to that myself.' She saw that he looked astonished and slightly disapproving, and added firmly, 'I feel the need to keep myself occupied. Sir Hugo's death was a very great shock to me, and I would rather be busy than sit brooding over what has occurred.'

As soon as the lawyer had gone, Hebe sat down at her desk and wrote first of all to Geoffrey, pouring into a long letter all that she would have said to him had they been able to meet, and finding that simply to express those thoughts and feelings brought an immediate relief of tension. For the first time in her life she cast off all reserve, and wrote as she would have spoken to him, straight from the heart.

Afterwards she wrote briefly to the old professor, and certain other scholars who had been Sir Hugo's closest associates; to the British ambassador, with whom he was slightly acquainted; to the Contessa, and to one or two other ladies whom she had met during the past few weeks. She put all the letters together and gave them to Guiseppe, with orders that they were to be carried immediately to their various destinations. He would notice, of course, that the one addressed to Mr Fernhurst was considerably thicker than the rest, but neither he nor any of the other servants were likely to think that remarkable. She did not know how soon she might look for a reply from Geoffrey, but the time until she received one would seem long indeed.

The days passed. In the virtual seclusion of the newly widowed, with little else to occupy her time or her thoughts, Hebe was possessed by a growing fever of impatience. Each time a letter was brought to her—and these became frequent as expressions of condolence arrived—her hopes went leaping, only to be dashed when she saw that the writing was not Geoffrey's.

The funeral took place, and Sir Hugo was laid to rest in the English cemetery in Rome, though since it was not the custom for women to attend funerals. Hebe was spared the ordeal of being present. The lawyer returned, to acquaint her with the terms of her husband's will, and she was aware of brief disquiet when she learned that Lord Hendreth had been appointed guardian of the young people at Astington Park. The Roxwell estate and the bulk of the fortune passed to young Clement Roxwell—Sir Clement, now—but at the time of their marriage Sir Hugo had made provision for Hebe, and conscience troubled her again when she found how generously she had been treated. With her own modest income in addition to an ample jointure she would find herself a woman of considerable means, but at the time, that fact made only a passing impression upon her. Geoffrey had not yet replied to her letter, and she could think of nothing else.

At last, when her nerves had been frayed to screaming point, she received a visit from the Contessa. This was in itself remarkable, for the villa lay outside the city and the Contessa had never before exerted herself to call there. When she was shown into the drawing room and Hebe came forward to greet her, she took both the younger woman's hands in her own and looked searchingly at her.

'My poor child, this is a sad time for you,' she said gently. 'So lately out of mourning for your brother, and now a widow. I feel most deeply for you.'

'And I am most grateful to *you*, ma'am, for having the kindness to visit me,' Hebe replied earnestly. 'It is at times such as these that one has greatest need of friends.'

'Partiularly when one is alone in a foreign land,' the Contessa agreed understandingly. 'I have come to tell you, my child, that if you are in need of help in settling your late husband's affairs, or in any other way, my husband will be happy to assist you. It is not fitting that a young woman in your sad situation should be obliged to deal with such matters herself.'

Hebe thanked her with sincere gratitude, and they talked for a little while of Sir Hugo's illness and the circumstances of his death, but all the while Hebe was trying to think of a way to introduce Geoffrey's name naturally into the conversation. The Contessa would surely know if any mischance had befallen him, since they had many acquaintances in common, but, desperate though she was for news of him, Hebe was too self-conscious to broach the subject. However she mentioned Geoffrey, she thought, she would be bound to betray her anxiety to this perceptive and experienced woman.

In the end, it was the Contessa herself who spoke of him, and Hebe never guessed, either then or at any future time, that this was the real reason for her visit. She had risen to take her leave, and was drawing on her gloves as she said casually, 'No doubt, my dear Lady Roxwell, you will now be thinking of returning to your native land. It is best to have old friends and familiar places around us in time of bereavement, and though so many of your compatriots come to Rome, few seem to remain here for long. Our friend, Fernhurst, as you may perhaps have heard, is the most recent to depart.'

Hebe felt the floor lurch beneath her feet, and clutched at the back of the chair from which she had just risen. Geoffrey gone? It could not be true! She had misheard, or the Contessa was mistaken—! As though from a great way off, she heard herself say unsteadily, 'Are you sure? Mr Fernhurst called here only two days before Sir Hugo died, and he said nothing then of leaving Rome. When—when did he go?'

'It must have been four—no, five days after you last saw him.' The Contessa was kind-hearted as well as worldly-wise, and concentrated on smoothing the fine kid gloves over her fingers so that she did not look at her hostess as she spoke. 'A quite sudden decision, I understand. Something occurred—I do not know what—which persuaded him it was time to leave our city.'

Hebe did not reply. She could not. She did not even fully understand. The Contessa was telling her something important, she realized that. Something more than the mere fact of Geoffrey's departure, but she could not quite comprehend what it was. After a moment she felt the other woman's hand on her shoulder; heard the kind, concerned voice say quietly, 'Go home, my dear child, back to the friends you know you can trust. This is not the end of the world, or of life or of happiness. You are young enough still to recognize one day the truth of what I say.'

Hebe felt the pressure of the kindly hand increase for a moment before it was withdrawn. The Contessa moved away, the door opened and then closed, and she was left alone, still standing rigidly by the chair while the real meaning of what the other woman had said dawned inexorably upon her. Geoffrey had deliberately and callously deserted her. He was a mere philanderer, prepared only to amuse himself for a while with a woman safely married.

Very slowly and carefully Hebe unclasped her fingers from their support, and with the same careful deliberation walked out of the drawing room and up the stairs to her own apartments. Lucia was in the dressing room, busy with some sewing, and Hebe said in a level voice, 'I am going to bed, Lucia. I am not unwell, but I do not wish to be disturbed until I send for you again. Not disturbed upon any account, you understand.'

The maid studied her anxiously. My lady was very pale, and though she seemed quite composed, there was a curiously blind look in her eyes. Lucia felt impelled to make some protest.

'My lady, I beg of you, let me—!'

'No, Lucia! I desire only to be left alone. I will ring for you when I need you, and you are not to disturb me until then, even if that is not until tomorrow morning.'

She turned away without waiting for an answer and went through to her bedroom. The door closed, and Lucia heard the key turn in the lock.

Hebe walked across the bedroom to the windows and closed both the shutters and the curtains, shutting out the daylight, enclosing herself in the protection of near darkness, and only then did she relax her desperate self-control. With a little moan she threw herself prone upon the bed, burying her face in the pillows as the tears came at last. Tears such as she had never shed in her life. Tears of loneliness, of grief for a lost first love which had been all the more precious because it had come to her late. Tears of humiliation, too, since she knew what even the Contessa did not know. It had been not only her sudden widowhood which had driven Geoffrey away, but also the letter she had written to him, the letter in which she had laid bare her deepest feelings, and in her innocence envisaged a shared future for them which he had never intended.

She moaned with shame at the memory, and burrowed more closely into the pillows as though trying to hide even from herself, feeling that she had stripped herself naked before him and been contemptuously brushed aside. There was not even consolation in the thought of the disaster from which she had been saved, though if she had eloped with him, how long would it have been before he tired of her and she found herself discarded, ruined and disgraced? Not long, that was certain. She should be thankful, yet somewhere at the very back of her mind the rebellious thought was stirring that even that would be preferable to her present situation. For a little while at least she would have known what it was to be desired, if not loved; to be needed, even for the briefest time. Not rejected, as she felt now, and, almost worse than that, pitied, because others must have seen what the Contessa had seen. A foolish, inexperienced woman losing her heart to a libertine.

For hours she remained sunk in an abyss of misery and humiliation so profound that she felt she would never find the courage to face the world again. She wept until no tears were left, and then lay in a stupor of wretchedness until at last sheer exhaustion caused her to fall asleep. When she awoke it was early morning, and she rolled over on to her back and lay with throbbing head and burning eyes, trying to come to terms with what had happened.

What was she to do? 'Go home,' the Contessa had said, and Hebe supposed that was the only thing she could do. Go home to Cambridge, where as a widow she could at least live alone in her own house. Alone! She shivered at the thought. The wheel had turned full circle, and once more her life was without purpose or direction, emptier now by far than it had been at the time of her brother's death.

It was then, as she reached the very nadir of despair, that a fresh thought came, like the tiniest glimmer of light in the blackness of her mood. She was still Lady Roxwell, and at her late husband's house in Gloucestershire his wards were left to the dubious guardianship of Lord Hendreth. There, surely, she was needed. There she could be of use, and perhaps, in caring for the family, would be able in time to remember her recent folly without this agony of loss, this searing shame and self-disgust. Might even, if she were fortunate, regain a measure of contentment and peace of mind.

PART
THREE

It WAS RAINING in Gloucestershire on the day Hebe arrived there, and the whole world looked grey. Grey skies, grey hills, grey stone houses and villages and little market towns. The Cotswold landscape seemed as alien to her eyes, accustomed all her life to the very different Cambridgeshire countryside, as it must have done to Lucia, seated beside her in the post chaise. This was not England as she remembered it. This prospect of bare, rolling hills dotted with sheep, of half-hidden houses enfolded in wooded valleys, of walls of weathered stone instead of living hedgerows, did not speak to her of home. Her mood was as gray as the weather. The journey from Rome seemed to have gone on for ever, and now, approaching her destination, she was growing increasingly certain that it had been a mistake to come.

Four months had passed since Sir Hugo's death, for the process of settling his affairs in Italy had been tediously slow. Hebe, outwardly composed after her one surrender to despair, had coped efficiently with the various problems, but it had been a relief to bid farewell to a city which had brought her nothing but heartache. She had been very lonely towards the end. In the seclusion of widowhood and mourning she had soon been forgotten by the people she had met during her brief venture into society, and no one but the Contessa showed any concern for her. Only the servants, she thought, had been sorry to see her go, and Lucia, offered the choice, had elected without hesitation to accompany her mistress to England.

One small satisfaction Hebe had enjoyed during that period, and that was ridding herself of Murslowe without loss of time. He had been left a small legacy by Sir Hugo, and Hebe herself had made all the arrangements for his journey back to England, at her expense and with excellent references, so he had nothing of which to complain, but she knew that he would always be her implacable enemy. He resented her position as Sir Hugo's widow as greatly as he had resented her as his wife; more so, in fact, since he had come so near to seeing her lose everything. For her part, Hebe was deeply thankful to see him go; to be rid of the one person who shared her shaming secret. His presence was a constant reminder of her folly, but now, perhaps, she could begin to put it out of her mind.

She found, however, that even without this tangible reminder, she could not forget, and as time passed doubts and questions began to torment her. Suppose she had misjudged Geoffrey? Suppose some quite different reason—an urgent summons home, perhaps—had caused him to leave Rome so suddenly? Suppose he had written to tell her of it, and the letter had somehow gone astray? Or had reached the villa, and Murslowe, recognizing Geoffrey's writing, out of vindictiveness withheld it from her? He was more than capable of such treachery. If that had happened, and the letter remained unanswered, Geoffrey might be thinking of her as harshly as she had of him.

There were many times when she almost succeeded in convincing herself that this was mere self-delusion, but hope was as tenacious as memory, though for what she was hoping, Hebe was not sure. Even if she were right, there was no way to remedy the harm, and would it be any less painful to know that they had been robbed of happiness by malice than it was to believe Geoffrey faithless? She would never know, for although she was now in England again, it was in the highest degree unlikely that they would ever meet.

They must be nearing their destination by now, she thought wearily. It was stuffy in the post chaise, for it was June and

the air was warm in spite of the rain, so that the windows
were misted with condensation on the inside, which, combin-
ing with the moisture without, rendered the glass opaque. It
was like travelling through fog. Hebe, unable to endure the
claustrophobic atmosphere any longer, let down the window
nearest to her and looked out, drawing in deep breaths of the
mild, damp, summer-scented air.

She was sitting on the off side, and on her right, beyond a
stretch of rough grass, the road was bordered by a stone wall
some eight feet above which the thick foliage of a belt of
trees hung dripping and heavy. Leaning forward, she saw that
a short way ahead, where the road bore to the left, the wall
was broken by an impressive entrance, sweeping back in a
graceful, semicircular curve to a pair of wrought iron gates
flanked by pillars crowned with heraldic beasts. Just inside
the gates identical neat lodges stood sentinel at the beginning
of an avenue of splendid trees which drove, arrow-straight,
up a gentle rise, to drop out of sight beyond the crest of it.
For a moment of fleeting panic Hebe wondered if these were
the gates of Astington Park, in which case it was a far more
magnificent place than she had imagined, but to her relief the
chaise passed on and began to descend a long hill into one of
the tree-scattered valleys, where a narrow river wound its
serpentine course. She was to discover later that the imposing
gateway was the main entrance of Abbotswood, Lord Hendreth's principal seat.

They passed through a village, two rows of grey stone
cottages, facing each other across a narrow street, with the
square tower of a church on one side and the faded signboard
of an inn on the other; crossed the river by means of a grey
stone bridge; and began to climb the opposite side of the
valley. Halfway up the hill, the chaise bore to the left and
stopped. There was a short delay, they moved forward again
through a gateway, with a brief glimpse of a lodge and a
curiously peering gatekeeper, and drove on through parkland
dotted with fine trees. Clearly, they had arrived at last at Sir
Hugo's family home.

Now the moment of truth was almost at hand, and Hebe's
misgivings had crystallized into a cold knot of apprehension
somewhere about her midriff. She had been a fool to come!

What reason had Sir Hugo's wards, or his servants, to welcome her? They were more likely to regard her as an impertinent interloper.

In an attempt to steady herself, she tried to recall everything she knew about the young Roxwells. It was not much. She had broken her journey for a few days in London, where she had summoned Sir Hugo's family lawyer to her at Fenton's Hotel and sought enlightenment from him, but Mr Benchley was more concerned to discuss legal and financial matters, and to hand over to his reluctant client the Roxwell family jewels, which had been in his care ever since Sir Hugo went abroad. Hebe, glancing with dismay through an impressive inventory, and eyeing with misgiving the sizable casket in which these were contained, begged him to retain them, but the lawyer was adamant. The jewels were her ladyship's property, to wear if and when she chose, and would remain so until such time as Sir Clement took a wife. Defeated, Hebe accepted the charge, and begged him again to tell her all about the children.

This Mr Benchley was unable to do. Apart from Sir Clement, whom he had travelled to Oxford to see when the news of Sir Hugo's death reached England, he had met none of them, and the most he could do was to give her ladyship a list of their names and ages. The eldest, next to Sir Clement, was Miss Barbara, who was just eighteen; then came Miss Sybilla, aged sixteen; Hugo and Charles, fifteen and thirteen respectively, pupils at Winchester; eleven-year-old James; and finally Katharine and Jane, who were twins aged ten. When Hebe inquired also about the children's present guardian, the lawyer shook his head. Lord Hendreth was abroad, had left England some time before Sir Hugo's death, and no one seemed to know when he was likely to return.

Perhaps, Hebe had thought indignantly then, it was just as well she had decided to come home, since no one else seemed to care what became of the Roxwell family. Poor children, finding themselves yet again the responsibility of a guardian totally indifferent to them. At least she would do what she could to befriend them.

Next day she went out and bought presents for them, or rather, for the five she would find at Astington Park. She had

enjoyed choosing the gifts, but now, with her first encounter
with the young people an immediate reality, her generous
impulse seemed suddenly an impertinence. There was no
reason in the world why they should be pleased to receive
presents from her, or even make her welcome. She ought to
have gone home to Cambridge! If she had not written to the
housekeeper at Astington, announcing her imminent arrival,
she would, even at this point, order the postboy to turn back . . .

Stop it! she told herself firmly. You are behaving like a
schoolgirl yourself instead of a sensible woman. You have
not only a right to be here, but a duty. There is not much you
can do for the boys, for they have an elder brother to whom
they can turn and a guardian, too, if he ever troubles himself
to notice them. The girls have no one, except their governess,
and to them you can be of real use. A friend to the older
ones, a mother to the little twins.

Comforted by these reflections, she leaned forward again in
the hope of catching a glimpse of the house, but her attention
was caught instead by swift movement in the middle distance,
veiled though it was by the rain which by this time had
become a steady downpour. As Hebe stared, a female figure
on a light-coloured horse flashed at a gallop across the undu-
lating turf, cleared a wandering stream in one soaring leap
and vanished behind a clump of trees, leaving behind a
startling impression of vitality and wildness. It seemed incredible to Hebe that any woman would choose to ride in such
weather, and she wondered uneasily if the intrepid horsewoman were one of the Roxwell girls.

The drive dropped into a hollow, and hooves and wheels
splashed through water as they forded the stream; climbed the
further slope, ran level for a few hundred yards and then
began another, more gradual ascent. The chaise passed through
a second gateway, crunching on to gravel and then, as it
swept in a wide semicircle to bring up before the door, Hebe
had her first sight of her future home.

A big, rambling house built of the ubiquitous grey stone, it
was a place of steep pitched roofs, of many gables, of windows with small, square panes. For nearly two hundred years
it had stood there in its quiet fold of the hills, until it seemed
a natural part of the landscape. The passing seasons had

weathered its stone and almost obliterated the coat-of-arms carved above the massive oak front door, but the place did not look neglected in spite of its late master's long absence. The gravel was smoothly raked and free of weeds, and the rain-soaked gardens beyond it were well tended and filled with flowers, while the house itself had an equally prosperous and well-maintained appearance.

This much Hebe noted with relief in those first, brief moments before the chaise came to a halt, and then she drew down the veil of fine black lace which had been turned back from the brim of her bonnet. She had chosen the headgear deliberately, for she had experienced some qualms at the prospect of facing for the first time Sir Hugo's family servants, who must surely have been wondering what manner of woman their master had married, and she had felt it would give her an advantage, as well as added confidence, if during the initial encounter she could see without being seen.

Since her arrival was expected, the chaise had barely come to a halt before a footman hurried forward to open the door and let down the steps. He cast a quick, curious glance at her as he assisted her to alight, and Hebe was immediately glad of her veiled face. An elderly butler then bowed her into the house, and she found herself in a dim, lofty hall with a stone-flagged floor, panelled walls and a huge, hooded fireplace. Through an archway at the far end could be seen the first flight of a fine, seventeenth-century staircase.

After a quick glance around, Hebe turned to the butler. 'Your name, I believe, is Danforth?' she said pleasantly, and saw the tiniest flicker of surprise cross the man's impassive features, as though her voice was not quite as he had expected.

He bowed. 'Yes, my lady, and this, if you will permit me, is Mrs Danforth, the housekeeper.'

His wife came forward and curtsied. She was small and round and rosy-cheeked, in almost comical contrast to her tall, thin spouse with his cadaverous cast of countenance, but she looked a comfortable sort of person, one who might well have been happy to mother a brood of orphans. Hebe felt relieved.

'I hope I've done right, my lady, in having her late ladyship's rooms made ready for you,' Mrs Danforth said anxiously.

'Not having any instructions, I wasn't certain what your ladyship would wish.'

'Thank you. I am sure the rooms will suit me very well.' Now that the first encounter was over, and the Danforths had proved less intimidating than she had feared, Hebe found she had the confidence to face them. She lifted black-gloved hands to her veil and put it back, smiling rather shyly at the servants.

There was a moment of stunned silence. The Danforths frankly stared, exchanged a disbelieving glance, and stared again. Hebe looked questioningly back at them.

'Is something wrong?'

It was Mrs Danforth who recovered first. She bobbed another curtsy.

'Begging your 'ladyship's pardon, and hoping you'll forgive the impertinence, but we were expecting—! That is, we had no notion your ladyship was so young, Sir Hugo being—!'

Her words trailed into silence and she continued to study her new mistress, but with compassion now. Hebe could almost read the thoughts passing through her mind. 'Poor thing! So young, and widowed after only a year! Poor young thing!' She thought it very likely that before long Mrs Danforth would be trying to mother *her*.

'Perhaps you will be good enough to show me my rooms, Mrs Danforth, while the baggage is being carried in,' she suggested, and indicated Lucia, standing silent and watchful a few paces behind her with the jewel-case clasped in her arms. 'Lucia, my maid, is Italian, of course, and speaks very little English, though she can understand it to a certain degree as long as you take care to speak slowly. I am sure you will do your best to make her feel comfortable.'

'To be sure we will, my lady,' Mrs Danforth assured her, nodding and beaming towards the unresponsive Lucia. 'Now, if your ladyship will come this way—!'

As she led them towards the staircase there was the sound of quick, light footsteps approaching from another direction, and as Hebe followed the housekeeper through the archway they came face to face with a slightly built young girl. Hebe realized at once that this was the horsewoman she had seen in the park, for the shabby, dark green riding-habit was soaking wet, and so was the black hair which clung in dripping curls to forehead and neck. She carried a sodden hat in one hand and had the skirt of her habit looped up over the other arm, and her face would have been enchantingly pretty had it not worn so sullen and mutinous an expression. She had been hurrying towards the stairs, but checked when she saw the newcomers and stood staring at Hebe with hostile, appraising eyes of smoky grey. Hebe was taken aback, but said with a smile, 'How do you do? I am Hebe Roxwell, and you, I think, must be Barbara?'

'No,' the girl replied curtly, 'I'm not! My name is Barbary, and I detest being called Barbara.'

'Miss Barbary!' Mrs Danforth said reprovingly. 'That's no way to speak to her ladyship, and her but just set foot in the house. What will she think of you, looking like a gipsy? Yes, *and* soaked to the skin, I'll be bound!'

'Oh, stop fussing, Danny! As for her ladyship, I'll be hanged if I care *what* she thinks of me!'

'Indeed, why should you?' Hebe put in coolly before Mrs Danforth could reply. 'After all, we are not even acquainted, are we? Pray do not let me detain you, Miss Roxwell. I am sure you must be uncomfortable in those wet clothes.'

Barbary's jaw dropped and she stared blankly at Hebe, completely at a loss. Hebe smiled pleasantly at her, and made a gesture inviting the younger woman to precede her. Barbary glared, appeared to grind her small, white teeth, and then with a distinct flounce turned away and ran off up the stairs.

The housekeeper was eyeing Hebe with considerable respect, but Hebe herself was dismayed by her own swift, angry reaction to Barbary's impertinence. This was not, she thought, a very favourable beginning.

Mrs Danforth seemed undecided whether or not to offer apologies or excuses for Barbary, and appeared to be arguing silently with herself as she led the way up the stairs, along a wide corridor with a window at each end, turned left-handed into another, shorter passage and threw open the door at its far end, standing aside for Hebe to go through.

She did so, and gave an exclamation of surprise and pleasure. The room was at the very end of one wing of the house and had windows in three of its walls, so that even on that grey day it was full of light, while the fourth wall, which contained the door by which they had entered, was occupied also by a handsomely carved fireplace. A dais in the middle of the room bore the bed, a graceful seventeenth-century fourposter with slender, soaring columns and curtains of softly faded, rose-coloured brocade. The windows were curtains with similar material, and the rest of the furniture was of the same fine walnut as the bed.

'This room's not been used since her late ladyship died,' Mrs Danforth explained, 'and that's close on thirty years ago.' She went to a door on the far side of the fireplace and threw it open. 'Your ladyship's dressing room is here, and there's a bed in it for your maid. Her late ladyship liked to have her woman close at hand, but if your ladyship prefers it, I can find a room for her somewhere else in the house.'

'Thank you, Mrs Danforth, this arrangement will serve very well,' Hebe assured her, and turned to Lucia, translating for her benefit what the housekeeper had said.

The maid started to reply, but at that moment there was the sound of baggage being carried into the dressing room, and with an exclamation she hurried off to supervise its bestowal. Hebe sank rather wearily into a chair and took off her bonnet, and Mrs Danforth, who had listened with lively curiosity to the flow of Italian, bustled forward to take it from her.

'Your ladyship's tired out, and no wonder, after all that travelling,' she said severely. 'Just you rest quietly here, and I'll send up a tea tray. Dinner is usually served at six o'clock, and while Sir Clement is away, the young ladies and Miss Piltbury have been taking theirs in the breakfast parlour, but perhaps your ladyship would wish Miss Barbary and Miss Sybilla to join you in the dining room this evening?'

'By all means!' Hebe was not sure that she found the prospect of sitting down to dinner with Barbary Roxwell an agreeable one, but it was unthinkable that she should dine in solitary state while the girls were relegated to the breakfast parlour. That would indeed offer cause for resentment. 'Is Miss Piltbury the governess? Ask her to give me the pleasure of her company also at dinner, if the younger children do not need her.'

Mrs Danforth withdrew, looking gratified, and Hebe, drawing off her gloves, let her gaze wander slowly over her surroundings. Already she was beginning to relax. The quietness and faded beauty of the room was exerting a soothing effect on her taut and quivering nerves, easing away the strain of endless days spent in a jolting chaise, of a rough Channel crossing, of noisy, crowded cities, even of the brief, antagonistic encounter with Barbary Roxwell. Tonight, she thought, staring at the graceful bed, I really believe I shall be able to sleep.

Without warning, the peace was shattered by a commotion in the passage outside the room. Children shrieked, there was the sound of scampering feet, a thud, and something struck so heavily against the door that it flew open. As Hebe sprang up, a small, black kitten tore into the room, shot past her and made a flying leap for the bed-curtain, up which it scrambled to the top of the tester, to crouch there wild-eyed and spitting, while on the floor in the doorway heaved and writhed a heap of pale pink muslin, black curls, and childish arms and legs apparently locked in mortal combat.

For a moment, shock and astonishment held Hebe motionless, and then she plunged forward and pried the combatants forcibly apart, resolving them into two small girls who, hauled unceremoniously to their feet and held each by a firm hand on a shoulder, continued the dispute verbally and with unabated vigour.

'It was your fault!'

'It wasn't!'

'It was! I should have carried him—!'

'You made me let go!'

'Children, be quiet!' Hebe's voice was not loud, but there was a note in it which brought the quarrel to an abrupt end, and two small, flushed faces, so alike that each could have been a reflection of the other, jerked up to stare at her in astonishment. Whether the truce would have endured, or hostilities have been resumed once the twins had recovered from their surprise, was never known, since at that moment Lucia erupted from the dressing room, demanding in her native tongue to be told what manner of household this was, where children behaved like wild animals, and animals—she had just caught sight of the kitten—ran wild in my lady's bedchamber.

The twins stared open-mouthed, exchanged a look, and drew a little closer together as though for mutual protection. One of them said in a half-frightened, half-excited whisper, '*That* must be the witch!'

Her sister seemed not to agree. 'It can't be, silly! *She's* only the maid. It's that one!'

'Perhaps they both are!'

Two pairs of wide eyes, smoky grey and fringed by short, thick black lashes, slightly apprehensive and decidedly speculative, looked from Hebe to Lucia and back again. Hebe, thankful that her maid's command of English was too limited for her to understand what the children were saying, said soothingly in Italian, 'It is no matter, Lucia. I will deal with this. You may go.'

Lucia, with a look of foreboding at the twins and a remark which compared the behaviour of English children unfavourably with Italian ones, withdrew to the dressing room, while the girls exchanged a nervous glance, as though wondering whether the words were some kind of incantation. Hebe released one of her prisoners, saying quietly, 'Close the door, if you please.'

The child hesitated, but seeing that her twin was still, as it were, held hostage for her obedience, reluctantly did as she was told. Hebe resumed her seat, motioning both girls to stand before her.

'Now,' she said, 'I know that one of you is named Katharine, and one Jane, but which is which?'

There was a moment's hesitation, and then the child who had closed the door said sulkily, 'I'm Katharine, but everyone calls me Kitty.'

'Then I shall call you Kitty, too,' Hebe said with a smile. 'That is, if I can be sure that you *are* Kitty, and not Jane. How in the world does one tell which is which?'

'Not many people can,' Kitty informed her with a touch of pride. 'Barbary can, and Sybilla and James, but even our other brothers get mixed up. Pilty knows, of course, but sometimes she makes us wear different-coloured sashes, so that other people can tell.'

Hebe frowned. 'Pilty?'

'Miss Piltbury, our governess,' Jane explained. 'Please, ma'am, may we fetch our kitten down?'

Hebe glanced up at the errant feline, still perched on top of the bed and regarding them with its head on one side.

'In a moment. It can come to no harm where it is.' She looked from one to the other, somewhat perplexed. 'You know who I am, do you not?'

'Yes, ma'am.' It was Kitty who replied. 'You are Lady Roxwell. You were married to Great-Uncle Hugo.'

'Yes, I was,' Hebe agreed, 'so what is all this nonsense about witches?'

Once again the twins exchanged glances. She was to learn that they had this trick of silently consulting each other in moments of difficulty. Finally Jane said with a touch of defiance, 'When we first heard you were coming here, Barbary said, "Well, the old witch need not think she can come here to interfere and overset the way we go on".' She paused, frowning. 'But you are not old, ma'am, are you?'

'No, and I am not a witch, either,' Hebe assured her, taking care not to betray the annoyance Jane's artless revelation had provoked. 'Neither is my maid, but she speaks very little English, so you must not be alarmed if she addresses you in her own tongue.'

'Barbary says,' stated Kitty, determined not to be outdone, 'that this is our brother's house now and you have no right to come here.'

'I think,' Hebe remarked with a calmness she was far from feeling, 'that we have heard enough for the present of what Barbary says. Shall we see if we can coax your kitten down? What is his name?'

'We call him Fluffy,' Kitty replied. 'James says it is a silly name, but he is not James's cat, after all.'

'Very true,' Hebe agreed with a smile, getting up and going across to the bed. 'Come, Fluffy! Come down!'

Fluffy at first turned a deaf ear both to her blandishments and to the shrill commands of his small owners, but when Hebe had the happy idea of drawing her glove across the curtain below him, he could not resist the temptation to pounce on it, and so found himself captured. She returned him to the twins, recommending them to take him back to the schoolroom.

When they had gone, she walked slowly across to one of the windows and stood looking out at the rain-veiled park, for the children had unwittingly given her food for thought. It was plain that their eldest sister exerted a strong influence over them, and equally plain that Barbary herself had made up her mind, long before they had met, to dislike her great-uncle's widow. Was this because she had fallen into the habit of thinking of herself as mistress of the house, and so bitterly resented the arrival of an older woman whose authority must inevitably take precedence over hers? Yet she must realize, unless she were completely stupid, that though Astington Park now belonged to her brother, Sir Hugo's widow was its present mistress. Realizing it was one thing, however, and accepting it was quite another. Hebe foresaw battles ahead, and wished that she could have deferred her next meeting with Miss Roxwell until she had refreshed herself with a night's rest, but not to appear at dinner that evening would yield the first victory to Barbary.

She took some pains with her appearance, and went down to the drawing room stately in heavy black silk, with black lace draped over her arms and her coppery hair fashionably dressed under her widow's cap and veil. Since she was Lady Roxwell of Astington Park, it gave her confidence to know that she looked the part.

The drawing room had the same slightly faded, old-world elegance as her bedchamber, and Hebe discovered later that this was true of the whole house. Astington was meticulously kept, but with no concession to the current mode, and to enter it was like stepping back half a century, for its late owner had lived there so little, and had been so indifferent to his surroundings, that no innovation had ever been made. Everything was still as it had been in his mother's day, and to Hebe that gave the whole place a slightly unreal charm.

On that first occasion, however, the drawing room made only a fleeting impression upon her, since her whole attention was focused on its three occupants, and her first thought was that she herself was ridiculously overdressed. Barbary, standing before the fireplace, occupied as of right the centre of the stage. Her muslin dress, plain and unadorned, was that of a schoolgirl, and her abundant black hair, twisted into a knot on the crown of her head and curling naturally about forehead and temples, gave the impression of having been coiled up hastily without the aid of a mirror, but neither fact detracted in the least from her beauty. Small though she was—Hebe, with her five feet nine inches, felt like a giantess beside her—her figure was excellent, and she was blessed with a perfect complexion.

In both these respects she differed sharply from her sister, who was seated on a sofa beside a white-haired old lady who must be the governess. Sybilla was obviously taller and of larger build than her sister, and she was disastrously plump; it would not be altogether unfair, Hebe decided regretfully, to call her fat. She had the black curls and grey eyes which appeared to be common to all the family, but her skin was not good, and where Barbary looked rebellious, Sybilla's expression was merely unhappy and defensive. She got up when Hebe came into the room, and bent to help Miss Piltbury to her feet, the seams of her somewhat outgrown muslin dress straining perilously, but Hebe, seeing that in addition to Sybilla's help on her left, the governess was also leaning heavily on the stick held in her right hand, went quickly forward.

'Pray do not trouble yourself to rise, ma'am,' she said kindly, and sank gracefully into the seat lately occupied by Sybilla. 'I collect that you are Miss Piltbury?'

The old lady admitted it, her faded blue eyes anxiously searching Hebe's face. She looked frightened, and Hebe could not wonder at it. Miss Piltbury was far older than she had expected, and she must be fearful for her position now that Lady Roxwell had come home. Hebe felt sorry for her, and smiled reassuringly before turning to the two girls.

'Miss Roxwell and I have already met,' she remarked pleasantly, 'so you must be Miss Sybilla. How do you do?'

'Yes, ma'am. How do you do?' Sybilla spoke nervously, dropping a slight curtsy and then looking uneasily at her sister as though afraid that even this small civility would meet with disapproval. Hebe, intercepting both this glance and the vengeful glare which answered it, added smilingly, but with fell intent, 'So, since Kitty and Jane have already presented themselves, the only one of you I have yet to meet is James. I look forward to having that pleasure tomorrow.'

'Your ladyship may find that less of a pleasure than you suppose,' Barbary retorted, emphasizing the title so that it sounded faintly insulting. 'James can be very forthright.'

'James is a dear, intelligent boy,' Miss Piltbury put in hastily, with an apologetic glance at Hebe. 'I do not deny that he is high-spirited, but I am sure that Lady Roxwell will agree that that cannot be regarded as a serious fault.'

'Quite so,' Hebe agreed, wondering as she spoke just what Miss Piltbury meant by 'high-spirited'. 'Is he solely in your charge?'

'Oh no! Mr Villiers, our rector, has been acting as his tutor, ma'am,' Miss Piltbury explained anxiously. 'James goes to the rectory every day, but he will be joining his brothers at Winchester after the summer holidays. Mr Roxwell was educated there, you understand, and wished his sons to follow his example.'

'Have you had charge of the children long, Miss Piltbury?'

'Pilty was Mama's governess,' Barbary put in before her preceptress could reply. 'She was with Mama until she married, and then came back when Clement was four years old. She has looked after us ever since.'

'Dear Mrs Roxwell was only seventeen at the time of her marriage,' Miss Piltbury explained nervously, 'and Clement was born within the year. Your ladyship will not find it wonderful that I cannot help regarding the children almost as my own family.'

'You *are* one of the family, Pilty,' Barbary assured her,' and you always will be. How should we go on without you? Besides, the twins will need a governess for years yet.'

This was said in a challenging tone, and with a defiant look in Hebe's direction, but Hebe, who found this spirited defence of the old governess admirable, refused to rise to the bait, and merely said with a smile, 'It would be wonderful, ma'am, if you did *not* regard them as your own. Your presence must have been a great comfort and support to them when their mother died.'

'*And* when we had to come live here, after Papa's death,'

Sybilla put in earnestly. 'We could not have *borne* it if dear Pilty had not come with us.'

'I am sure you could not,' Hebe agreed sympathetically. 'Was your own home very far from here?'

'We lived in Kent.' Barbary, answering for her sister, spoke in a dismissive tone, and it was plain that she had no intention of elaborating on this information, or of allowing Sybilla to do so. There was an uncomfortable pause, and at least three of the four ladies were glad that Danforth chose that moment to announce dinner.

The dining room, which could have accommodated a score of persons with room to spare, seemed to Hebe a trifle overpowering for a party of four, and she realized why her companions had hitherto preferred to use the breakfast parlour. The meal was ample and well cooked and the service excellent, but she was conscious of a constraint which made conversation difficult. Miss Piltbury expressed the hope that her lady-ship had not found the journey from Rome too wearisome, and Hebe was able to describe some of the incidents which had occurred, but the two girls contributed neither remark nor question, Barbary out of spite, and Sybilla because her whole attention was upon the food. It was no wonder, Hebe reflected, seeing the enormous amount she ate, that the child was fat, and she wondered why Miss Piltbury made no attempt to teach her moderation.

When they returned to the drawing room, the sight of a pianoforte there prompted Hebe to inquire whether the young ladies were interested in music. Barbary tossed her head.

'Not in the least,' she said ungraciously, and directed towards her sister so quelling a look that Sybilla, who had opened her lips to reply, closed them again without speaking.

For once, however, Miss Piltbury was blind to the wishes of her eldest charge, and said with some eagerness, 'Sybilla delights in it, Lady Roxwell. She plays well, and has an excellent voice.' She turned to the girl. 'Come, my dear, let her ladyship hear the song you have just learned.'

Sybilla hesitated, casting an anguished look at her sister, but when Hebe, with more kindness than truth, expressed a keen desire to hear her sing, she seated herself reluctantly at the instrument. With a shrug, Barbary picked up a book and began turning the pages, disassociating herself from the others, but for the first time Hebe saw Sybilla indifferent to the other girl's displeasure. She began to play softly, and then to sing.

Music was regarded as an indispensable accomplishment, and every girl with the least pretension to gentility was expected to acquire it, but Hebe recognized at once that Sybilla was really gifted. Her voice soared effortlessly, pure and true, and when the song ended there was no need to feign appreciation. Sybilla blushed with mingled embarrassment and pleasure, and Miss Piltbury said triumphantly, 'Now, my dear Sybilla, perhaps you will believe me when I tell you that your voice is something quite out of the common way. Remember, Lady Roxwell has lived in Italy, the home of opera, and must have heard some of the finest singers of the day.'

Hebe continued to smile encouragingly at Sybilla, but it was an effort to do so, for at the governess's words she felt as though a knife had turned cruelly in her breast. Lately, changing scenes and fresh experiences had enabled her to push the thought of her unhappy love affair to the back of her mind, but Miss Piltbury's innocent remark brought memory rushing back. Her first visit to the opera; the glorious music; Geoffrey beside her, and the world transformed suddenly into a place of enchantment. Would she ever forget him, or be able to forgive herself for her folly?

Abruptly she realized that she could endure no more that night. She felt tired to death, the beginning of a headache was throbbing behind her eyes, and the thought of her rose-draped bed in its quiet room had become irresistible. She got up, saying apologetically, 'I think I must beg you to excuse me, for I am more tired than I realized. It is strange, is it not, that to reach the end of a long journey seems more fatiguing than the journey itself?' She looked at Sybilla. 'Thank you for singing to us, my dear. You possess a true gift, and I look forward to hearing you again.'

She inclined her head to Miss Piltbury, who uttered a flustered good night, and hesitantly expressed the hope that her ladyship would find herself restored on the morrow. Sybilla got up and curtsied. It seemed for a moment that Barbary was not going to look up from her book, but when the governess spoke her name in an imploring whisper she laid it aside and got up. She said good night with grudging civility, but Hebe, encountering the smouldering hostility in those grey eyes, guessed that the battle was by no means over.

This assumption was soon confirmed. It needed only a few days at Astington Park to convince Hebe that not only had her decision to live there been the right one, but also that the task she had undertaken would be far from easy. Confronted by reality, the hazy and, as she ruefully admitted to herself, rather sentimental picture she had formed of the orphaned family was soon dispelled, but that she was needed there was no doubt; the only difference was that she was going to have to help the young Roxwells against their will, at least in the first instance.

Little help was to be looked for from Miss Piltbury. Though not ill disposed, the old governess was too much aware of her own shortcomings, and of the failings of her charges, to be other than terrified of the new mistress of the house, and her manner towards Hebe hovered between the conciliatory and the apprehensive. When Barbary was impertinent, or the younger ones naughty, she would beg them in an anguished way to behave themselves, but if they obeyed her at all it was out of affection, and not out of respect for her authority.

Barbary, of course, was the root cause of Hebe's difficulties. She was accustomed to having everything her own way, and it seemed to Hebe that this state of affairs must have obtained long before her emancipation from the schoolroom, for Miss Piltbury appeared to exercise very little control over her conduct. Her influence over her younger sisters and brother was strong, not because she was particularly kind or affectionate towards them—Hebe thought sometimes that there was a streak of her great-uncle's selfishness in Barbary—but because they all looked up to her as their natural leader. Barbary had decreed that Lady Roxwell was an interloper at Astington, and so as an interloper she must be regarded.

Hebe herself was at a loss to understand this determined antagonism. Barbary had neither interest in nor knowledge of the conduct of the household and had never regarded herself as its mistress in the way Hebe would have done at her age, so her hostility was not due to a feeling of having been supplanted. Nor was she envious of the newcomer's stylish clothes, for she was totally indifferent to her own appearance and spent most of the day in a shabby riding-habit, only exchanging it with the utmost reluctance for one of her skimpy schoolgirl muslins in time for dinner. Hebe's fashionable gowns moved her to undisguised contempt, and any hope Hebe might have cherished of finding in such matters a common interest did not survive the first twenty-four hours of their acquaintance.

Sybilla, closest to Barbary in age and very much in awe of her far stronger personality, copied her slavishly, but where Barbary was headstrong, Sybilla was shy and withdrawn, seeming to find happiness only in her singing. At first Hebe had hopes of establishing contact with the girl through their common love of music, but Sybilla did not dare to oppose her elder sister. She could not bring herself to copy Barbary's veiled insolence, but she repulsed every friendly overture and retreated behind a barrier of sullen silence.

With the younger children Hebe fared a little better, although James remained to her an unknown quantity, faintly alarming. He was a sturdy lad, fairer than his sisters but with the same grey eyes, and of a merry, mischievous disposition, but he was self-conscious in Hebe's presence and always escaped from it as soon as possible. Hebe, lacking any experience of schoolboys, especially those with a cheerful disregard for learning and a preoccupation with sporting pasttimes, was as uncomfortable with him as he with her, and they never progressed beyond a kind of wary politeness.

The twins were lovable but completely out of hand, perhaps because James was their only playmate. They were tomboys who, as Hebe had seen at their first encounter, were sadly apt to resort to physical combat to settle an argument, but they were friendly and confiding children, and since Hebe was prepared to give them her time and attention, to answer their questions and enter into their interests, it was not very long before they discovered that, far from disrupting their life, her coming had added a new and pleasurable dimension to it. Barbary, discovering her little sisters' treachery, dismissed them as stupid children, and devoted herself instead to preventing any similar backsliding on Sybilla's part.

In addition to trying to become acquainted with the young people, Hebe spent her first week at Astington familiarizing herself with the house and the servants, and here she found her most ardent supporter. Her knowledge of every aspect of housekeeping won Mrs Danforth's immediate respect, and her appreciation of the standard to which the house had been maintained during its owner's long absence warmed the good woman's heart. It was a joy, she told Danforth later, to talk over household matters with her ladyship. The Lord knew she had done her best all these years, but when the place had no mistress, it made a body lose heart. Things were going to be very different now.

It was while Mrs Danforth was conducting her over the house on the day after her arrival that Hebe fell in love with a small, irregularly shaped sitting room tucked away in a corner of the ground floor. Its walls were darkly panelled, most of its furniture was contemporary with the house—there was even a spinning-wheel in one corner—and its window looked out on to an old-fashioned herb garden with stone-flagged paths and a sundial. Like the rest of the house, it was beautifully kept, but it had an indefinable air of long disuse.

'It *is* a comfortable little room, ma'am,' the housekeeper agreed in response to Hebe's exclamation of delight. 'It faces south, you see, so it catches the sun even in winter, and at this time of year, if the casement's open, the scent of the lavender and such-like in the garden is so sweet you'd never believe. I've always thought it's a mortal pity the room's never used.'

'It will be used now, Mrs Danforth,' Hebe said firmly. 'I shall have it for my own sitting room, for I can think of no more pleasant place in which to pass the time.'

'Well, now!' Mrs Danforth looked pleased. 'Fancy your ladyship saying that! Ever since *I* came to Astington forty-odd years ago, and I dare say long before that, this has been called "my lady's parlour," even though her late ladyship never sat here. It wasn't the sort of room she cared for, if you take my meaning.'

Hebe took it very clearly. Sir Hugo, she thought, must

have learned the ceremonious style in which he liked to live
in his boyhood home, and a portrait of his mother, which Mrs
Danforth had pointed out in another part of the house, had
depicted a haughty dame with powdered hair and a frosty
expression, whom one could not imagine condescending to sit
in this charming, old-fashioned room. Hebe could only feel
thankful that she had never known 'her late ladyship', who
would, she felt sure, have heartily disapproved of her.

It was in 'my lady's parlour' that Hebe sat some days later
and waited for Miss Piltbury to join her. She had resolved at
the outset not to interfere, to do nothing to usurp the governess's
authority, but she had just discovered that when Barbary rode
out—and she spent hours each day in the saddle—she never
took a groom with her, no matter how far she went beyond
the confines of the estate. Shocked and alarmed, picturing the
various accidents which might result from such recklessness
and astonished that Miss Piltbury seemed blind to them, Hebe
felt that she could remain silent no longer. She sent a message
to the schoolroom, requesting the governess to spare her some
minutes of her time to discuss a matter of importance.

Presently Miss Piltbury hobbled in, leaning heavily on her
stick and looking frightened, and assured Hebe, somewhat
unconvincingly, that her rheumatism was not particularly
troublesome. She then took the chair offered to her and
perched uneasily on its edge, fixing a faded, anxious gaze on
the younger woman's face. Hebe, trying to be as tactful as
possible, smilingly expressed the hope that her summons had
not interrupted lessons.

'Oh, no, my lady! Not at all!' Miss Piltbury assured her
nervously. 'I have set the twins a task—I fear they were very
naughty this morning, and I do beg your ladyship's pardon—
and Sybilla is practising her water-colour painting in the
schoolroom, and will see that they complete it. Though in
justice to them, I must inform your ladyship that James was
the instigator of this morning's prank. He will make his
apologies to you when he returns from the rectory. He is not
really a bad boy, you know, but he does find it tedious with
only his little sisters for company.'

'I am sure he does, and will be much happier when he can
join his brothers at school,' Hebe agreed sympathetically. 'I

have never before encountered such boundless energy, for my own brother, you must know, was very studious, as well as being of a delicate constitution. But it is not of James or the twins that I wish to speak to you. It is of Miss Roxwell.'

This intelligence, far from allaying Miss Piltbury's qualms, appeared merely to increase them. Her face puckered with dismay.

'Oh, dear!' she exclaimed apprehensively. 'I *knew* your ladyship could not for long allow her conduct to pass unnoticed! I *told* her it was quite ineligible, and most discourteous, to behave as she does towards you.'

'I do not think,' Hebe said dryly, 'that that argument is likely to carry much weight with her. Why does she dislike me so? She cannot feel I have supplanted her, for I gather she has made no attempt to take charge of the household, which, at her age, I would have expected her to do. I must confess she has me in a puzzle. Most girls are only too anxious to leave the schoolroom.'

The governess nodded unhappily, but offered timid justification for her charge: 'That is very true, but your ladyship must remember that she has no mother to guide her. As you will have realized, we are very isolated here. Lady Hendreth, unfortunately, resides permanently at Bath, and most of the other ladies in the neighbourhood are too elderly to have any reason to hold the sort of entertainments at which a young girl may enter society.'

Hebe frowned. 'Are there *no* younger matrons at all?'

Miss Piltbury shook her head. 'Only the squire's wife, Mrs Lorde, but the Lordes are a young couple whose children are still in the nursery. Your ladyship will recollect that the Rector presented them to you after church last Sunday.'

Hebe nodded. It had been a considerable ordeal, two days after her arrival at Astington Park, to walk into the village church and take her place in the Roxwell pew, knowing she was the cynosure of all eyes. She had been heavily veiled, but well aware that, unable to distinguish her features, the congregation was noting every other detail of her appearance, and the mourning clothes which had seemed eminently suitable in Rome suddenly felt far too rich and fashionable for an English village. When she left the church, the Rector, who had called at the Park the previous day to pay his respects, had begged leave to present Mr and Mrs Lorde to her. Hebe had been too self-conscious to retain more than a hazy memory of the couple, but she did recall that the squire's wife was a stolid young woman, heavily pregnant, who would obviously have nothing in common with Barbary Roxwell.

'Very well,' she said after a moment, 'that may explain why Miss Roxwell seems still a schoolgirl, but it does not account for her attitude towards me—for she was determined to dislike me, was she not, from the moment she heard that I was coming here?'

'I know, my lady! Oh, I know!' Miss Piltbury twisted her hands together in distress. 'I tried to persuade her that it is wrong to prejudge *anyone*, but she would pay no heed. I cannot describe to you the mortification I feel when I reflect upon her behaviour.' She hesitated, and then added in a sudden burst of candour, 'She has always been wilful and high-spirited, but since her father died and I was obliged to remove the family here from Kent, I have had the greatest difficulty in making her mind me. She was used to being greatly indulged by him, and was, I think, his favourite among the children, but she would always obey him and endeavour to deserve his good opinion. His death, which was very sudden, struck her the hardest of all, and having to leave her home made matters worse.'

'Yes, indeed!' Hebe agreed with quick sympathy. 'Tell me, Miss Piltbury, why did Sir Hugo insist upon his wards removing here? I would have supposed it preferable to leave orphaned children in the familiar surroundings of their own home.'

The governess stared. 'Your ladyship does not know? In the circumstances, that was out of the question. Mr Roxwell, I fear, was sadly improvident. The house had to be sold to settle his debts. The house and all its contents, and his beautiful horses—even the children's ponies. Had Sir Clement not been his great-uncle's heir, I do not know what would have become of them all, but Sir Hugo was generous, very generous indeed! They have all been given every advantage.'

Yes, Hebe thought bitterly, with money he was generous enough, but to him that was the beginning and end of all responsibility. As long as he was free to pursue his chosen way of life, uninterrupted and untroubled, he did not care how much it cost. Aloud she said, 'Every advantage, Miss Piltbury, except a guardian who was concerned for them. I am very conscious of it, and hoped, by coming here, to make amends in some sort for that neglect. Especially to the girls, for with the best will in the world I cannot consider myself qualified to do anything for the boys. Let us hope, however, that *they* will fare better now that Lord Hendreth is their guardian.'

'I am sure I hope so, my lady,' Miss Piltbury agreed, though in the tone of one who had little expectation of seeing her hope fulfilled. 'I feel obliged to say, however—and I trust you will forgive the impertinence—that Lord Hendreth has never yet paid any attention to the children. Nor even to Sir Clement.'

Hebe frowned. 'How is this? Sir Hugo was under the impression that Lord Hendreth was keeping a watchful eye upon the family.'

'On the rather rare occasions when his lordship is at Abbotswood,' Miss Piltbury said carefully, 'he certainly never fails to ride around this estate and to consult with Mr Dallow, the agent. On the children he has never bestowed more than a passing glance, and I doubt whether he would recognize any one of them, should he encounter them away from Astington. Perhaps—I must say it!—perhaps that is just as well. He is a strange man, not greatly liked.'

Hebe was silent for a moment, remembering Geoffrey Fernhurst's strictures upon Hendreth, now seemingly confirmed by Miss Piltbury. Not that Geoffrey had any right to sit in judgement—! She thrust the thought of him aside and said in a matter of fact tone, 'Be that as it may, he is now their legal guardian, though I suppose one cannot expect an unmarried gentleman to interest himself in schoolboys and schoolgirls. I would have thought that where Sir Clement is concerned, he would at least—! However, that is scarcely my concern. The young ladies are.'

'I am sure,' the governess said uneasily, 'that they ought to be grateful to your ladyship.'

'Good gracious! I do not want their gratitude! What I did

hope, when I set out for England, was that I might win their trust and perhaps, in time, even their affection, though this does not now seem very likely. Upon one thing, however, I am determined. As their great-uncle's widow I have a duty towards them, and I intend to do that duty, come what may.'

This declaration had the effect of making Miss Piltbury look more uneasy than ever, but Hebe, pursuing her own train of thought, did not observe it, and continued firmly, 'It was my determination, Miss Piltbury, not to interfere, but after what I have learned today of Miss Roxwell's conduct, I can be silent no longer. How *can* you have permitted her to ride for miles around the countryside entirely alone? Good God! Did you never pause to consider what might befall her?'

Miss Piltbury blenched, but offered, in a failing voice, the suggestion that dear Barbary was a very accomplished horsewoman. Hebe shook her head impatiently.

'My dear ma'am, it is not a riding accident of which I am apprehensive. You seem to forget that Miss Roxwell is no longer a child, but a young woman. A remarkably pretty young woman. Surely you do not need *me* to tell you that her recklessness is exposing her to dangers of which she may well be unaware? It is your duty to warn her of them, if you have not already done so, and to insist that when she rides beyond the boundary of the park, she *must* have a groom with her.'

A look of despair came into the governess's face, and she said faintly, 'I will speak to her, my lady, of course, but I fear she will take no heed.'

'Then what is to be done?' Hebe demanded exasperatedly. 'It is plain that no words of *mine* will influence her, but she *must* be brought to her senses, and if you cannot accomplish that, then I fear—!'

'Oh, my lady, I beg of you!' Miss Piltbury spoke in an anguished gasp, as though the words could be held back no longer. 'I know I have no right—! I have failed in my duty, and I had resolved not to plead with you, but now it has come to the point—!' Her voice failed utterly and she pressed her handkerchief to her lips, then, seeing that Hebe looked completely bewildered, drew a deep breath and added, more coherently but no less despairingly, 'Lady Roxwell, I am seventy years old and have neither family, friends nor resources. If you turn me off, I do not know what will become of me.'

'Turn you off?' Hebe repeated blankly. 'I never had the least intention—! My dear Miss Piltbury, put the notion out of your head immediately. You cannot say that you have failed, when your charges hold you in the deepest affection, and you must not even think of leaving Astington. I am sure none of the family could bear to part with you.'

The governess stared at her, her lined face working. 'Oh, my lady! So kind! They are all I have, and I was so afraid—! Yet it is true that I can no longer carry out my duties as I should, and how could I remain here, doing nothing? It would not be right!'

'Nonsense!' Hebe retorted bracingly. 'Even if another governess were engaged, I am sure that Sir Clement would wish to make provision for *you*, and indeed, it must be thought his duty to do so, when you have devoted so much of your life to the family. Make no mistake, they will still need your affection and support.' She saw that the old lady was still eyeing her doubtfully, and added in a persuasive tone. 'Besides, if I am ever to do anything for those girls, it can only be with your help, so you see I need you too.'

'Lady Roxwell, I will do *anything*!' Miss Piltbury assured her tremulously, dabbing her eyes. 'Dear me, how foolish to cry, when I have every reason to be thankful! I do beg your ladyship's pardon, but the relief is so great—!'

Her voice became wholly suspended as her efforts to hold back the tears met with no success, and with a sob she buried her face in her handkerchief, but before Hebe could make any move to comfort her, the door was flung violently open and Barbary burst into the room. She checked in the doorway, with Sybilla's frightened face peering over her shoulder, while her stormy gaze took in the scene before her and she leapt immediately to a mistaken conclusion.

'I knew it!' she exclaimed furiously. 'I *knew*, the moment Syb told me Pilty had been sent for—!' She ran to the governess's side and flung an arm round the thin shoulders. 'Pilty, don't cry! Nothing is going to change, I promise you! Come here, Syb, and take care of her while I have this out with *her ladyship*.'

Sybilla, looking apprehensive, obeyed, while Barbary, her cheeks flushed and her eyes blazing with anger, rounded on Hebe.

'I knew this would happen!' she declared. 'I knew it would not be long before you started to interfere, but you need not suppose I will let you bully Pilty and make her unhappy. No, and you need not think you can turn her out of the house and bring in some stranger of *your* choosing, because not only I, but my brother, Clement, too, will have something to say about that.'

'Miss Roxwell! Barbary!' Miss Piltbury, raising a tear-streaked face from the handkerchief, tried to intervene. 'My dear, you must not! You do not understand—!'

'I understand only too well!' Barbary brushed the quavering protest aside and rushed on, addressing herself again to Hebe. 'What right have *you* to come here, playing the great lady, condescending to Syb about her singing, bribing the children with presents, and now trying to get rid of the only person who has cared anything for us since Mama and Papa died? Just because you were clever enough to trick Great-Uncle Hugo into marrying you—!'

'How dare you!' Hebe's voice, icy with anger, cut through the torrent of furious words. She rose to her feet, tall and dignified in her black gown and veil, and looked coldly down at the little fury confronting her. 'How *dare* you address me in this fashion! There is no question of Miss Piltbury being dismissed, though, upon my soul, *your* conduct is scarcely a credit to her teaching. Now, if you are prepared to conduct yourself like a woman of breeding instead of a screaming virago, you may remain in this room, but if not, you had better return to the schoolroom, which it appears you left far too soon.'

There was a stunned silence. Barbary, Sybilla and Miss Piltbury all stared in stupefaction at Hebe, who, almost equally astonished, spared a fleeting moment to recognize the change which eighteen months of being Lady Roxwell had wrought in her. Hebe Cullingworth would never have spoken like that . . .

Barbary was not silenced for long, though when she spoke again there was a hint of uncertainty in her voice. She said, staring belligerently at Hebe, 'It's all very well to rip up at *me*, but why is Pilty crying? I won't have her upset!'

'Does it not occur to you,' Hebe replied acidly, 'that *your* shocking want of conduct is upsetting her more than anything else? Your only justification is that you are inspired, I believe, by genuine affection and concern for her, and so I will assure you once more that there is no question of Miss Piltbury being dismissed.' She saw Barbary cast an angry, questioning glance at the governess, and added exasperatedly, 'Perhaps you had better add your assurances to mine, ma'am, since it is clear that Miss Roxwell does not intend to accept *my* word.'

'No, I don't!' Barbary agreed defiantly. 'Well, Pilty? Don't be afraid to tell the truth.'

'Barbary, how can you?' Miss Piltbury said in a tone of anguished reproach. 'Have I not even succeeded in teaching you good manners? Never did I think to suffer such mortification! Lady Roxwell has been everything that is kind, so be good enough to beg her pardon for the truly shocking things you have said to her—though if she refuses to give it, that will be no more than you deserve.'

Barbary's eyes widened with shock. It was plain that she now felt betrayed by the very person she had been trying to defend, and Hebe was sufficiently sorry for her to be prepared to offer an olive branch. Before she could do so, however, the girl found her voice again.

'I see how it is!' she said bitterly, and turned towards Hebe a look of venomous contempt. 'You have found a way of bribing Pilty, too. Well, *my lady*, you may think yourself very clever, but wait until my brother comes home from Oxford. Just wait! He is the master of this house, and things will be very different then!'

She gave none of them a chance to reply, but flung out of the room as abruptly as she had entered it, slamming the door behind her with a force which made the window rattle.

Sir Clement Roxwell was expected home from Oxford the following week, at the end of his second year. Hebe awaited his coming with foreboding, for it was clear that Barbary, ominously quiet since the scene with Miss Piltbury, was depending on her eldest brother to support her in what she seemed to regard as a crusade against the newcomer. No doubt she had already written to him, painting the blackest imaginable picture of their great-uncle's widow, so that he would come prepared to dislike her. Hebe contemplated with a sinking heart the prospect of another actively hostile person in the house. Would it, she asked herself occasionally when her spirits were particularly low, be wiser to accept defeat now, and retire to Cambridge while she could still do so in good order?

Yet there were compensations. She had gained a powerful ally in Miss Piltbury; the twins, at least, had accepted her and even sought her company; the servants, and those of the tenants whom she had so far encountered, accorded her every respect, and could, she thought, be brought in time to trust her. Besides, she had fallen in love by now with the Cotswold country, with its high, bare hills and winding valleys and buildings of golden-grey stone. She would have liked to explore the lanes and tracks which could be glimpsed traversing it, and wished she could emulate Barbary's accomplished horsemanship, for those enticing byways were mostly unsuitable for carriages. Even for the smart new barouche which Hebe had desired Mr Dallow to purchase for her when she discovered that the only conveyance in the coachhouse was the enormous and antiquated travelling carriage in which Sir Hugo's mother had ridden. Unfortunately, Hebe had never been taught to ride.

She could, however, enjoy walking, having been accustomed to take long walks with her girlhood companions. It was a form of exercise she had greatly missed while she lived in Rome, and now, with the English countryside at her door, she made a point of walking every day. It was not long before the twins, finding that a walk with her ladyship was far more stimulating than the brief, dawdling stroll through the gardens which was all that their governess could manage, were begging to accompany her. She assented gladly, finding some solace for Barbary's antagonism and Sybilla's sullen reticence in the uncritical company of the two little girls.

It was the twins who gave Hebe her first glimpse of Abbotswood, leading her on a somewhat breathless climb up the hill behind their own home, and pointing out the great house on the opposite side of the valley. It looked enormous, Hebe thought, quite in keeping with the imposing entrance she had passed on the day of her arrival, and the magnificent avenue of trees which she could now see stretching straight as a ruler across the half-mile of rolling parkland between the gates and the house. It seemed strange to her that the master of such an estate should spend so much of his time abroad.

It was that afternoon that Clement arrived home. Since Astington Park was situated within twenty miles of Oxford he made the journey on horseback, leaving his servant to follow with the baggage, and, having come across country, entered the park by way of a farm gate some distance from the drive. Cantering easily along the track which led from this towards the house, he rounded a bend to see, a short way ahead of him, a tall lady in black walking in the same direction, with one of his two youngest sisters clinging to either hand. All three looked round at the sound of his approach, and then the two little girls detached themselves from their companion and ran back to meet him, shrieking delighted greetings.

Clement reined in and hurriedly dismounted, just as the twins reached him. He staggered a little beneath the exuberance of their welcome, but Hebe noted with approval that he neither thrust them away nor rebuked them for disarranging his coat. There was a quick, affectionate hug for each in turn, and then they were dragging him towards her; or rather, Jane was dragging him, clutching his arm with both hands, while Kitty led the horse.

'Aunt Hebe! Aunt Hebe!' Barbary had been furious when she heard them say that, and their brother's reaction would probably be the same. 'This is Clement, our eldest brother.'

Hoping for the best, Hebe smiled and held out her hand. 'So I surmised. How do you do, Sir Clement? Would it be presumptuous in me to say "welcome home"?'

'Not at all! Your obedient servant, ma'am.' Clement freed himself from Jane's grasp and shook hands, looking somewhat bemused. 'Delighted to make your acquaintance.'

That was a mere formality, of course, Hebe thought, but still a decided improvement on Barbary's first words to her. In looks he was very much like his eldest sister, with the same regular features, curly black hair, thick-lashed grey eyes and determined mouth and chin. A handsome boy, though it was a pity he resembled Barbary in stature, too, for he was slightly built and not quite as tall as Hebe herself. Also he seemed to lack address, for after responding to her greeting he stood tongue-tied, looking uncertainly at her.

In that latter judgement, however, Hebe was doing him less than justice, for this encounter had thrown him completely out of his stride. As she suspected, Barbary had written to him about the widowed Lady Roxwell, describing her in such terms that Clement had formed a mental picture of a sly yet domineering busybody, an ostentatious person of no breeding who had schemed her way into marriage with their great-uncle and was now plunging with vulgar relish into the role of mistress of Astington Park. Barbary had urged Clement to be ready to assert his authority in his own house, and though he had sufficient common sense to realize that he was not yet in a position to do so, he had come home prepared to dislike the interloper and to resist whatever unwelcome changes she was endeavouring to make.

Now he had met her, and instead of the low-bred, overdressed person he had been led to expect was an elegant lady, far younger than he had imagined, with a great deal of counte-nance and an unmistakable air of refinement. One, moreover, who was held in obvious affection by his little sisters. It was a shock, and he needed time to adjust to it.

The presence of the children helped, their excited chatter making it unnecessary for him to exchange more than the merest commonplaces with Lady Roxwell as they all walked on together. At the edge of the gardens they parted, Hebe and the twins going back to the house while Clement took his horse to the stables, but even that fleeting acquaintance was enough to convince him that Barbary had been guilty of gross misrepresentation.

The next few hours were sufficient to confirm him in this opinion. In the house, he looked suspiciously for signs of change and could detect none, unless it were a subtle change in the atmosphere, too nebulous to be defined, which told that Astington had a mistress again at last. Although always meticu-lously kept, it had until now, Clement realized with faint surprise, lacked that elusive quality which transformed a house into a home. Feeling guilty because he had allowed a younger sister to delude him, and knowing that he had not appeared to advantage, he determined to do his best to correct the false impression he was sure he had made upon Lady Roxwell.

In this endeavour, during that first evening, he was entirely successful, and if Hebe was a little amused by his world-weary air, only a twinkle deep down in her eyes betrayed it. Since she had grown up in a university city, she was no stranger to the sight of very young gentlemen aping a sophistication they did not really possess, but she was so thankful to find Clement Roxwell apparently devoid of antagonism towards her that she was prepared to indulge him. They conversed very amicably together, watched balefully by Barbary, wistfully by Sybilla, and contentedly by Miss Piltbury, who was deeply gratified to see that at least one of her former charges could behave towards Lady Roxwell in a manner which was a credit to his upbringing.

Clement himself was flattered to find that her ladyship, though older than he and (he was convinced) far more experienced, talked to him as she might have done to any gentleman of her acquaintance, and not, as he had feared she might, as though to a schoolboy. It was a novelty, for this was the first time that anyone at Astington had treated him as an adult. To Miss Piltbury and the Danforths he was still 'Master Clement', while his younger brothers and sisters persistently refused to respect his position as head of the family, so Hebe's attitude towards him set him up considerably in his own esteem, and by the time he went to bed he was completely reconciled to her presence. Barbary, he decided in a patronizing way which would have infuriated his sister had she known of it, was a silly child who had taken a charming woman in unreasonable dislike, but he was able to judge Lady Roxwell at her true worth, and to see that her coming to Astington was an excellent thing. He could not imagine what had persuaded her to marry an old curmudgeon like Great-Uncle Hugo, but whatever her reasons, he felt certain they were in no way discreditable.

Clement's homecoming marked a turning-point in Hebe's relationship with the Roxwell family, for Hugo and Charles, arriving home from Winchester, took their lead from him and were polite and guardedly friendly. James, of course, imitated his elder brothers. Even Sybilla finally capitulated.

Encouraged by Clement, she had been growing steadily more responsive, but her surrender came one wet afternoon when Hebe, happening to pass the door of Sybilla's bedroom, was startled to hear the sound of bitter weeping coming from beyond it. A knock on the door brought no response, and after a moment's hesitation she softly opened it a little way to look in. Sybilla, in her petticoats, was prone on the bed, sobbing into the pillow, while beside her on the floor one of her gowns lay in a crumpled heap. Diffidence forgotten, Hebe whisked into the room, closing the door behind her, and stepped quickly across to the bed.

'My dear child, what in the world is wrong?'

At the sound of her voice Sybilla heaved herself up and round, staring with mingled chagrin and dismay, then, seeing the genuine concern in Hebe's face, collapsed into her former attitude of despair, muttering something unintelligible. Hebe sat down on the edge of the bed and patted her in a soothing way.

'I did not quite catch what you said, my dear. Tell me again what has distressed you.'

Sybilla obeyed, and though between the sobs and the pillow it was difficult to understand her, the facts eventually emerged. She had been trimming a favourite dress with new ribbons, but when she tried to put it on to see the effect, she had found it was so tight she could not struggle into it.

'I wore it only a few weeks ago, and it fitted then,' she concluded hopelessly. 'I am fat, and clumsy, and ugly and I wish I were dead!'

'My poor dear, there is no need to be in such flat despair. Nearly all girls of your age are too plump.'

'Barbary wasn't!'

'Then Barbary is uncommonly fortunate. It is not often so, believe me.'

Sybilla rolled over on to her back and stared up at Hebe, her face swollen and blotched by tears. '*You* could never have been too fat.'

'No,' Hebe admitted with a smile, 'I was excessively thin

instead. A great maypole of a creature, towering over all my friends. And there is no remedy, you know, for being too tall.'

'You are *not* too tall,' wailed Sybilla. 'You are *stately*! And Barbary is dainty and beautiful, and the twins will be just like her when they grow up. I am the only fat, ugly one!'

'Now that is nonsense!' Hebe said firmly. 'Your features are good, and your hair and eyes every bit as handsome as your sisters'. You *are* too plump, but I am convinced that a great deal of that is mere puppy-fat.'

Sybilla sniffed, dabbing at her eyes with a damp ball of handkerchief.

'Barbary says I am fat because I am greedy.'

'That is unkind,' Hebe said carefully, 'though I do think, my dear, that if you try to curb your appetite a little, you will find it beneficial. You will need to persevere, though, and be patient.'

'I will! Oh, I will!' Sybilla assured her earnestly. She hesitated, kneading the handkerchief between her hands, and then looked up again at Hebe. 'Why are you so kind to me? I don't deserve it.'

Hebe smiled faintly. 'One does not have to *deserve* kindness, Sybilla.'

'One does not have to deserve *un*kindness, either,' Sybilla said shrewdly. She hauled herself into a sitting position and looked steadily at Hebe, colour rising in her cheeks. 'Lady Roxwell, I want to beg your pardon for the way I have behaved. I did not want to, especially after Pilty told us how kind you had been to her, but when I said so to Barbary, she slapped me and told me to do as I was bidden. But that is no excuse, and I *won't* go on being horrid to you, no matter how she scolds.' She added anxiously, 'Do you think you will be able to forgive me?'

'My dear, of course I forgive you,' Hebe assured her warmly. 'It has all been a foolish misunderstanding, for my only purpose in coming here was to try to make up to you all, as far as I could, for the way you have been left to fend for yourselves since your Papa died. I never wished to change things here, you know, unless it could be for the better.'

'You have done that already,' Sybilla said shyly. 'I cannot

explain it, but there is something in the *feel* of the house since you came. It—it is as I remember it at home, when I was very small, before Mama died.'

Deeply touched, Hebe impulsively embraced her, and, in the euphoria induced by Sybilla's capitulation, could almost believe that it was now only a matter of time before Barbary, too, succumbed to the pressure of her brothers' and sisters' opinion, but she had reckoned without the girl's obstinacy. Far from being influenced by the rest of the family, Barbary became even more hostile, more reckless in her behaviour.

She had paid no heed to Miss Piltbury's warnings and entreaties, still riding alone and ranging farther afield then before, and when Hebe, knowing that any intervention of hers would do more harm than good, tentatively suggested to Clement that perhaps he could prevail upon his sister to be more circumspect, he replied with a frown, 'I have already tried to reason with her, ma'am. Pilty asked me to do so, but it is not the least use. First she told me that my notions were Gothic, and then, when I tried to warn her that if she goes on in this hurly-burly way, sooner or later some loose screw will try to take advantage of her, she said that you had put *that* idea into my head and I was only playing your game for you. Though what she thinks she means by that, I'm dashed if I know!'

'Oh, dear!' Hebe said worriedly. 'I do not suppose she knows herself, except that she has been determined from the outset to cast me in the role of wicked stepmother, or something of that sort.' A thought occurred to her. 'Are you perfectly sure she understood what you meant?'

'I have wondered that myself since,' he admitted, 'but dash it all, ma'am, it's not the sort of thing *I* can explain to her! Pilty ought to have done it, or—' He paused, looking hopefully at Hebe, who shook her head decisively. Clement sighed. 'No, I suppose not.'

'I would try,' Hebe pointed out, 'but you know very well that your sister would pay no attention to anything *I* might say. Perhaps I ought not to have come here! I would never forgive myself if my presence provoked her into behaviour which brought her any real harm.'

'That's nonsense!' he said indignantly, then, flushing darkly, 'I beg your pardon, but it is, you know! It's not just your being here which has driven Barbary to these extremes, but the fact that she can't bear to be crossed. She has always been wild to a fault! She would obey Papa, but since he died—! Well, I'm as fond of Pilty as the rest of us, but there is no denying that she has never been able to curb Barbary, and never will be. You must have seen that for yourself.'

Hebe nodded slowly. 'Yes, but I supposed that was because she now considers herself too grown-up to obey a governess's commands. Do you mean that she has always behaved so wilfully?'

'Lord, yes! Oh, she would mind her lessons, for she's needle-witted and never had the least trouble learning things, but she was for ever up to some hey-go-mad prank. And she's afraid of nothing, either!' He hesitated, and then added with some difficulty, 'Papa spoiled her, you see. In character, she is more like him than any of us, so of course she was his favourite. He even used to say—just funning, you know— that she ought to have been the eldest, and a boy.'

Hebe felt a sudden rush of sympathy, remembering what it was like to long passionately to stand well in one's father's regard. Her own parent had been so proud of his son's brilliance that he had had nothing but a kindly tolerance to spare for his little daughter; and how much worse it must have been for Clement to be outshone in his father's eyes by a younger sister.

'I believe,' she said gently, 'that this is very often the case between father and daughter, and though Barbary may be very much like her Papa in character, in looks, so Miss Piltbury tells me, she greatly resembles your Mama.'

He coloured up again, and said rather gruffly, 'Yes, she does. We all favour Mama, but she more than any.' He added hesitantly, 'Pray don't think me impertinent, ma'am, but it has occurred to me just lately that Barbary has very little respect for other women, and hates to accept their authority. Perhaps if Lord Hendreth were to speak to her—?'

'Perhaps, but as far as I can see, Lord Hendreth has no immediate intention of speaking to any of us,' Hebe retorted with some asperity. 'To the best of my belief, he is still abroad.'

'You have no news, then, of when he is likely to return? Mr Benchley said, when he came to see me at Oxford just after my great-uncle died, that he hoped his lordship's absence would not be unduly prolonged.'

'He may hope it, but there seems to be no likelihood of the hope being fulfilled in the near future,' Hebe assured him. She thought he looked a little crestfallen, and added, 'Have *you* some matter to discuss with him? If it is urgent, perhaps you could write to him, and send the letter to Mr Benchley. They must surely be in touch with each other, perhaps through his lordship's own man of business.'

'I could do that, I suppose,' Clement agreed with a marked lack of enthusiasm, 'though I would prefer to become better acquainted with him first, for we have never exchanged more than a dozen words. I think I will wait a little longer. He is very unpredictable, you know, and quite likely to arrive unannounced on the doorstep while we are supposing him to be on the other side of the world.'

PART
FOUR

As MATTERS TURNED out, however, they were not to be subjected to quite such a shock as that, for the very next day Hebe received a letter from Mr Benchley informing her that Lord Hendreth had arrived in London. He would shortly be coming to Gloucestershire, and would then, of course, wait upon Lady Roxwell. Hebe passed on this information to Clement but suggested that it might be advisable to withhold it from the rest of the household until they had more certain news of his lordship's intentions. Clement agreed.

A week went by, and then another. Hebe, living in daily expectation of receiving a visit from Lord Hendreth, passed from mild apprehension to perplexity and then to impatience. His lordship, it seemed, was as indifferent to his responsibilities as guardian as Sir Hugo had been, and meanwhile Clement was showing signs of increasing uneasiness at the delay. Eventually, at the beginning of the third week, Hebe decided to write to Hendreth, and after several false starts achieved a letter which, she felt, combined civility with an acceptable degree of peremptoriness. Not knowing Hendreth's direction, she sent it to Mr Benchley, with the request that it be conveyed immediately to his London house.

There was no response. Another ten days dragged past, and Hebe began to grow angry. Hendreth might be unconventional, but one did not expect a man of breeding to be so discourteous. Should she write again, more peremptorily than before, or would it be more dignified to wait until they were face to face before favouring him with her opinion of his conduct?

She had little leisure, however, to ponder this question, for the next few days were crowded. Miss Piltbury, who in spite of the summer weather had contracted a severe cold, finally gave up the unequal struggle against it and took to her bed, where she retarded her own recovery by fretting herself into a fever about the consequent neglect of her duties. Sybilla, having transferred her allegiance from her elder sister to Hebe with a fervour which was slightly embarrassing, announced that she would take charge of the schoolroom party, but though her intentions were of the best she found it impossible to exercise any degree of control over her three younger brothers. Clement was too preoccupied with his own problems to intervene, and it was not long before Hebe received a strong complaint of the boys' behaviour from peppery old General Gaynes, whose property adjoined Astington Park on the opposite side to Abbotswood.

Summoned before her, the guilty trio expressed contrition, and though Hebe felt tolerably certain that this was mere lip-service, she felt herself totally incapable of imposing an adequate punishment. Helplessly, she sent them away, and had barely completed the difficult task of composing a suitably soothing reply to the General, when she was obliged to sustain a visit from the Misses Nidwell.

These ladies, two elderly sinsters who lived nearby with their nonagenarian tyrant of a father, had been the first of her neighbours to call upon Hebe, but any idea that this was prompted by a kindly desire to welcome her to the community was immediately dispelled. They were excessively civil, but contrived none the less to convey their total disapproval of the Roxwell establishment in general, and in particular of a widow who had the temerity to be young, personable and fashionably dressed.

Today, however, Hebe soon discovered that she was not to be the only target for their sly malice. The usual courtesies were exchanged, and then the elder Miss Nidwell remarked with an affection of concern, 'We find you alone again,

Lady Roxwell! Pray do not think me presumptuous if I tell you this will not do, for in your present sad circumstances, you know, it is all too easy to fall into a melancholy. You should permit one of the young ladies to bear you company.'

Hebe felt her hackles begin to rise. The sort of backbiting, cloaked in spurious sympathy, in which the Nidwell sisters dealt, was something she intensely disliked even if it were not directed at her, as this taunt undoubtedly was. Miss Nidwell spoke as though she were an inconsolable widow mourning a beloved husband, which she must surely realize could not be the case.

'I am in no danger, ma'am, of falling into a melancholy,' she replied. 'As for the young ladies, Sybilla has for the time being taken charge in the schoolroom, Miss Piltbury being, unfortunately, confined to her bed with a feverish cold.'

'Poor woman!' Miss Clara Nidwell remarked. 'One cannot but feel for her, obliged as she is to bear the responsibility of so many lively young people at an age when most of us would hope to be enjoying a quiet retirement. Your ladyship is very sympathetic, to allow her to cosset herself a little.'

'So Sybilla has taken her younger brothers and sisters in charge,' Miss Nidwell added before Hebe could reply. 'She must be a great comfort to you, ma'am, for as I remarked to my sister only last Sunday as we went home from church, the dear girl is growing quite womanly. Such a pity she is so stout!'

'Oh, I am sure she will soon outgrow *that*, ma'am,' Hebe said firmly. 'It is only puppy-fat, after all.'

'I do *hope* your ladyship is right,' Miss Nidwell replied, though her tone suggested that she did not share Hebe's optimism, 'for a stout habit of body does not allow a girl to appear to advantage. Her sister, Barbary, now, is quite otherwise. A veritable beauty!'

She paused, but Hebe was so astonished by the compliment that she made no response, instead waited automatically for the praise to be qualified. Inevitably, this happened.

'So dedicated a horsewoman, too,' Miss Nidwell went on with a little laugh. 'My dear ma'am, is she *never* out of the saddle? Scarcely a day passes without us catching a glimpse of her, either from the window—for our home, as you may know, commands a wide prospect—or as we go about the neighbourhood. In all weathers, too! One must suppose her impervious to wind and rain.'

'It is true she cares very little for either,' Hebe agreed warily. 'Barbary may appear fragile, but the appearance is deceptive.'

'Deceptive, indeed!' It was Miss Clara this time, sweetly malicious. 'She is positively intrepid, for not only is her mount excessively spirited, but we notice that she perceives no need for an attendant of any kind. It would not be wonderful, dear Lady Roxwell, if you were in a constant state of anxiety about her.'

'I might be, ma'am,' Hebe countered, masking growing vexation with a smile, 'if she were a less accomplished rider, but I believe there is no need for misgiving on that score.'

'Possibly not,' the elder Miss Nidwell put in, 'but your ladyship will forgive me for observing that *here* it is not at all the thing for a young girl to go about entirely alone. I mention this, you understand, only because it may not have occurred to one who has lived abroad, where different customs may perhaps obtain.'

'I lived abroad, Miss Nidwell, only during the past two years,' Hebe assured her with determined cordiality, 'and I am perfectly well aware that, in town, a young lady does not go out unaccompanied. At home in the country, however, where she is unlikely to encounter anyone with whom she is not acquainted, such strict observance of the proprieties is surely unnecessary.'

Miss Nidwell raised her eyebrows. 'Oh, I will readily admit your ladyship to be far more conversant than I with the manners obtaining in *fashionable* circles, but here we do perhaps adhere to stricter standards, and it is here, dear ma'am, that Barbary's conduct will, for the present at least, be judged. It would be such a greaty pity, if, for the want of a little discretion, she were judged too harshly.'

'I believe, ma'am, that you refine too much upon a very trivial matter.' Inwardly seething, Hebe somehow contrived to continue to speak cordially. 'Is a girl of Barbary's age to be condemned, in the district where she has lived since childhood, simply because she is heedless enough to ride unattended? I cannot believe that our neighbours are so spiteful.'

Miss Nidwell bridled, and Miss Clara flung herself with apparent ingenuousness into the breach. 'No, no, of course not! My dear Lady Roxwell, pray do not suppose that *we* are censuring dear Barbary. One *must* remember that she has lacked a mother's guidance. I remarked to my sister only this morning, when we saw her riding out of Hunter's Wood with Mr Lorde—!'

'When you saw her—*what*?' Hebe's exclamation was involuntary, and the instant it was uttered she wished it unsaid. Attemtng to make a recovery, she forced herself to laugh and to add lightly, 'Why then, that bears out what I say. There can be no harm, when she encounters only old acquaintances.'

'Exactly so!' Miss Nidwell had recovered, and was falsely sweet again. 'Though, to be sure, in *our* day—! I can well imagine—cannot you, Clara?—what dear Papa would have had to say had he discovered one of *us* riding alone with a gentleman, however well acquainted with him we happened to be.'

Both sisters laughed heartily at this, while Hebe clenched her teeth and struggled against the temptation to point out that customs were apt to change during half a century. When she was sure she could trust herself she said, with a composure she was far from feeling, 'I am sure, ma'am, you would not wish to imply that there is any harm in a child of Barbary's age being in the company of a gentleman whom she has known, I dare say, ever since she came to Astington Park when she was twelve years old. That would be a little uncharitable, would it not?'

'Oh, I would not for the world suggest such a thing,' Miss Nidwell assured her. 'As you say, a child of her age—! She is just eighteen, is she not?'

'Robert Lorde is three-and-thirty,' Miss Clara remarked with seeming irrelevance. 'Do you remember, sister, when he was born? How proud his dear Mama was! A son and heir, after four little girls!' She sighed sentimentally, then, casting off this retrospective mood, added brightly, 'In fact, Lady Roxwell, we are on our way to the manor now, to visit Robert's wife.

She is lying-in, as I am sure you know. A second son, and such a bonny little boy!'

'But his mama, we hear, is not in spirits,' Miss Nidwell informed Hebe in a mournful tone. 'Mrs Villiers called upon her yesterday and found her very low, because Robert has been just a little less attentive that she would wish. But, as I shall tell her, one cannot expect a gentleman to be in such transports over a new infant as we women are, especially when it comes to the fourth occasion.'

Hebe forced herself to smile. 'Nevertheless, I am sure that Mr Lorde is very proud, and very relieved that all is well with both his wife and son. Pray present my compliments to Mrs Lorde, and my good wishes.'

'We shall be delighted to do so.' To Hebe's relief, Miss Nidwell rose and held out her hand. 'Goodbye, Lady Roxwell. Do not allow this large family you have inherited—they are *all* home just now, are they not?—to wear you down. You look not to be in quite such high force as your friends would wish.'

With this Parthian shot, she and her sister took their leave. Hebe restrained herself until Danforth had shown them out, and then did what she could to relieve her feelings by pacing angrily up and down the room.

Horrid old tabbies! she thought. I have never before met such a pair of mischief-makers—and now, I suppose, they have gone to drip poison into poor Mrs Lorde's ears! Oh, that *wretched* girl! Not that I believe there is a mite of truth in what they implied, for she probably regards Robert Lorde as elderly, but if she possessed an ounce of proper feeling she would listen to Miss Piltbury's advice, and her brother's. And if she does set the parish by the ears, no doubt *I* shall be blamed!

At this point her furious pacing brought her to the writing-desk, where sight of the letter she had written to General Gaynes recalled more ill usage to her mind. Hugo, Charles and James were, in their way, as great a threat to her peace of mind as Barbary was, for how could she hope to curb the high spirits of three venturesome schoolboys when she did not even know how to talk to them? As for their absent guardian—!

She felt a sudden, overwhelming need to unburden herself

of all her wrongs, but there was no one at Astington in whom she could confide, so on an impulse she sat down again at the desk and in a long letter to Mrs Hallam at Cambridge described all her difficulties. She spared no one, but her hardest words were reserved for the gentleman who ought, by rights, to be solving some of those difficulties for her.

'I begin to doubt,' she wrote, 'whether he will trouble himself to visit us at all, any more than he has troubled to acknowledge my letter. He has been described to me as unpredictable, but *I* predict that he is rude and arrogant and regardless of any wishes but his own, as well as totally indifferent to the feelings of others. That, dear ma'am, is my opinion of Lord Hendreth, and my most fervent wish is to have an opportunity to inform him of it.'

Behind her, the door of the drawing room opened again, and Danforth's voice annoucned another visitor.

'Lord Hendreth, my lady,' he said dispassionately.

Hebe gasped and swung round in her chair, a guilty flush rising to her cheeks, for it was one thing to express a wish, and quite another to have it so immediately granted. One would have preferred to have time to prepare oneself; to marshal one's thoughts into order and telling phrases.

His lordship had paused just inside the door, and was regarding her in a measuring way which did nothing to soothe her feelings. He was in his middle thirties, an exceptionally tall man with powerful shoulders under a well-cut riding coat, and long, muscular limbs clad in buckskins and top-boots. His face, blunt featured and square jawed with a wide, sardonic mouth, was deeply tanned, and his hair a very dark red. He was by no means handsome, but his height and unusual colouring commanded attention, for his eyes were a curious shade of brown only a very little darker than his hair. They held a distinctly hostile expression which, as Hebe stared at him, gave place to surprise and the faintest hint of amusement, and after looking at her very hard for a few moments he said abruptly, 'Well, I'm damned! I was told that Roxwell's widow was very much his junior, but I did not expect to meet a mere girl!'

She blinked, taken aback as much by the remark itself as

by his use of language not usually employed in feminine company, but the combination of the two jerked her out of embarrassment and into anger. Rising to her graceful height, and giving him back look for look, she replied frigidly, 'And I, my lord, was informed that you are a law unto yourself. I now perceive this to be an understatement.'

Words and manner, intended to bring home to him the enormity of his conduct, failed utterly to have the desired effect. A smile which had in it a good deal of mockery deepened the sardonic curve of his lips, and he strolled forward into the room, saying ironically, 'Kind of you to say so, but you must not flatter me, you know. Your obliging informant should have told you that I am impervious to it.'

The widow's bosom heaved. 'Flattery, sir, was not intended, though your mistake does not greatly astonish me. Your lordship's experience of flattery cannot be so great as to enable you easily to recognize it.'

'Oh, very good!' he said appreciatively. 'That has put me in my place, hasn't it?'

'Has it, my lord?' She lifted her brows in exaggerated surprise. 'Who is dealing in flattery now? I doubt very much that any words of mine could achieve that very desirable object.'

'Perceptive, too!' he remarked admiringly, 'Tell me, ma'am, why are you so determined to come to cuffs with me?'

Hebe gasped, momentarily bereft of words by his effrontery. Then, recovering, she said indignantly, 'If, my lord, your abominable conduct from the instant you entered this room were not enough to give me a disgust of you, I need only recall your discourtesy and indifference ever since you returned to England.'

He stared at her from beneath suddenly frowning brows. 'How the devil can I have been discourteous to you when we met for the first time five minutes ago?'

'You do not consider it discourteous totally to ignore the letter I wrote to you, even though I indicated that the matter was of some urgency?'

He was still frowning. 'I received no letter.'

'No?' Polite disbelief sounded in Hebe's voice. 'Yet I sent

it to Mr Benchley two weeks ago with a request that it be forwarded immediately to your London residence.'

'Ah, that explains it!' His brow cleared and he nodded, pleased to have solved the mystery. 'For the past three weeks, ma'am, I have been at Bath, visiting my mother.'

'Oh!'

A trifle deflated, Hebe continued to regard him, and was briefly diverted by the necessity, an unusual one for her, of being obliged to look up to meet his eyes. Then he recalled her to a sense of her wrongs by saying, in a decidedly sceptical tone, 'Since I did *not* receive your letter, ma'am, perhaps you will explain to me now how it comes about that a matter of urgency can suddenly have arisen between us.'

'How?' She stared at him, incredulity struggling with anger. 'Can it have escaped your lordship's memory that you are now guardian to my late husband's great-nieces and nephews?'

'No, it has not!' This time the words came with a decided snap. 'And I should very much like to know why Roxwell saw fit to drop such a responsibility on to my shoulders when we had not even met face to face for some ten years.'

'Oh, had you not? Then no doubt that explains it! I have been wondering how it came about that Sir Hugo made so grave an error of judgment.'

'Vixen!' Hendreth said dispassionately, and continued before Hebe had time to recover from the insult, 'I must warn you, ma'am, that I have no experience of dealing with children—nor, I may add, any wish to acquire it.'

'They are not babes in arms, my lord,' Hebe informed him tartly. 'Sir Clement is within a year of his majority, and even the two youngest, the twins, are ten years old. Moreover, little though you may relish the responsibility, I imagine, since you did not decline it, that you are prepared to do your duty by these unfortunate orphans.

'I would have declined it very promptly, ma'am, had Roxwell done me the courtesy of informing me of his intention,' he replied trenchantly. 'Since I was not made aware of it until some three months after his death, when the letter from his man of business finally caught up with me, there was little I could do. Fortunately my guardianship need not be of long duration. As soon as their brother comes of age, he can relieve me of it.'

'Which I feel certain, my lord, he will be very happy to do,' Hebe said furiously. 'In the meantime, however, I wish to inform you why I found it necessary to write that letter.'

'I am sure you do,' he agreed sympathetically. 'Shall we sit down? I infer from your expression that the explanation will be a long one.'

Recalled thus to her duties as hostess, which his lordship's deplorable manners had caused her to forget, Hebe inclined her head with freezing dignity and moved in a very stately way to a chair on one side of the fireplace. As Hendreth took a seat facing her, she inquired politely, if rather belatedly, whether she could have the pleasure of offering him some refreshment. He declined with tongue-in-cheek formality and leaned back in his chair, watching her with a sardonic expression which did nothing to soothe her ruffled feelings.

'Well, ma'am?' he inquired after a moment. 'You see me all attention. In what desperate circumstances do you find yourself?'

Perversely, now that she was presented with the opportunity which, only a short time ago, she had so urgently desired, she found it exceedingly difficult to avail herself of it. She had experienced no trouble in cataloguing her problems in the letter to Mrs Hallam, but unfortunately could now remember not a word she had written except for the paragraph she had just completed when Hendreth was shown into the room. That was imprinted with the utmost clarity upon her memory, and though the encounter with his lordship had proved her right, she could not rid herself of an uncomfortable and quite illogical dread that he would somehow happen to read her description of him before he left the house. After a considerable pause she said carefully, 'For one thing, sir, I understand that Sir Clement is exceedingly anxious to talk to you.'

'Is he? Then no doubt your butler will inform him that I am here, and he will presently join us.'

'No doubt he would, my lord, if he were at home. Unfortunately he decided to ride to Oxford today, I believe to visit a friend there, and I do not expect him to return until late this evening. Of course,' she added pensively, 'if your lordship had apprised me of your intention to call upon us today, Sir Clement would naturally have been here to welcome you.'

Since her brief acquaintance with Lord Hendreth had given her no reason to suppose that he possessed any proper feelings, she was not disappointed when this sally provoked no response apart from an amused and comprehending look as he said bluntly, 'Why does he want to see me?'

'That, my lord, is for him to tell you.' Even if she had known, she would not have betrayed Clement's confidence, though she could not resist adding, 'I have, of course, known him for only a few weeks, but I have the impression that he is very worried about something.'

'Debts, or a lightskirt, or both,' Hendreth diagnosed cynically, and grinned unrepentantly at her outraged expression. 'Tell him he may dine with me tomorrow. There will be no one else present and he may unburden himself to his heart's content. What else?'

'The three younger boys,' Hebe found to her annoyance that his lordship's blunt way of speaking seemed to be catching. 'General Gaynes has complained of their behaviour.'

'What have the little devils been doing?'

Thinking it best to let the General's letter speak for itself, Hebe went to fetch it from the desk. She would have liked at the same time to put her own letter to Mrs Hallam out of sight, but Hendreth, who had risen when she did, was looking in her direction and she was unable to do so. She handed him the General's letter and resumed her seat, watching him as he glanced rapidly through it.

'Storm in a teacup!' he said impatiently when he came to the end. 'Mind you, the young sapskulls have lived here long enough to know better than to run riot on the General's property, and deserve a trimming for their folly. Do you want me to administer it? Send for them now and let us see what they have to say for themselves. Shall I ring your butler?'

'Pray do, my lord,' she said graciously, but added as an afterthought, 'They may not, of course, be in the house. I took them to task myself earlier, but though they assured me they were sorry and would behave better in the future, I cannot flatter myself that they set any great store by what I said.'

However, when Danforth appeared he said that he fancied the young gentlemen were in the billiard room, so Hebe requested him to tell them to come and present themselves to Lord Hendreth, and, in parenthesis, to do his best to see that they did not come to the drawing room looking like a set of ragamuffins.

'Which they always seem to do within an hour of getting up in the morning,' she said resignedly to his lordship as the butler went out. 'It is a mystery to me how they contrive it.'

He looked amused. 'Did *your* brother never get dirty or tear his clothes when he was a schoolboy?'

'No, he was always—!' She broke off, frowning. 'How did you know, sir, that I had a brother?'

'Oh, Roxwell and I did correspond with each other from time to time, and on one of those occasions, about two years ago, he spoke of a young man of exceptional brilliance who was staying at his house. A young man named Cullingworth. So when I later received the surprising intelligence that Roxwell had married a *Miss* Cullingworth, I deduced that she was that young man's sister. Your brother died, I understand. Accept my condolences.'

'Thank you.' Unexpectedly, Hebe was touched, even though his voice was completely unemotional. 'Felix *was* a brilliant scholar. Everyone said so. That is why it seemed such a *waste*—!' She paused for a moment, and then went on in a lighter tone. 'He cared only for his books, and never for any of the pastimes most boys seem to enjoy, which is why I find it almost impossible even to talk to Hugo and Charles and James, let alone tell them how they should go on. Nor do I suppose they would attend to me if I did.'

'No liking for petticoat government, eh?' he said mockingly. 'Can't say I blame them.'

He eyed her expectantly as he spoke, but Hebe, who felt that there was perhaps some truth in the remark, treated it with dignified indifference. Seeing that she did not intend to rise to the bait, Hendreth went on, 'So! Clement has some undisclosed problem he is anxious to discuss with me, and the other young rips have fallen foul of the General. If this is the sum total of your difficulties, ma'am, I tremble to think what might happen if you were confronted with a genuine crisis.'

His caustic tone, and his evident assumption that she was a foolish, incompetent female ready to make a mountain out of the most insignificant molehill, stung her. Her eyes flashed, and she said indignantly, 'It is *not* the sum total, my lord! I only wish it were! *Barbary* is the chief cause of my concern.'

'Barbary?' He looked blank for a moment, then, realizing to whom she referred, added with a flash of genuine impatience, 'Good God, ma'am! Are you incapable even of dealing with a schoolgirl? And what the devil do you expect *me* to do about it?'

'I *hope*, my lord, that you will permit me to explain, instead of ripping up at me in terms more suitable to a taproom than my drawing room,' she retorted angrily. 'And Barbary is no longer a schoolgirl. She is eighteen years old.'

'Is she, indeed!' Her anger seemed to enable him to recover from his own annoyance, and the ironic note was back in his voice. 'I admit my error, then. By the bye, how does your ladyship happen to know what terms are suitable to a taproom?' Hebe gave an outraged gasp, and he laughed suddenly. 'No, don't eat me! That was an underhand blow, and I apologize for it. Tell me why you are concerned about this confounded girl.'

Slightly mollified, but still very much upon her dignity, Hebe told him, concluding with an account of the Misses Nidwells' visit. Hendreth listened with growing exasperation, and when she had finished, said trenchantly, 'It sounds to me as though she deserves to be soundly spanked, but I suppose that at eighteen she is too old for such summary punishment. You are quite right to be concerned, if the Nidwell tabbies have their claws into her. They have destroyed more than one reputation.'

'That is what I fear,' Hebe agreed worriedly. 'Most of our neighbours, I believe, still think of Barbary as a heedless child, but once *that* sort of poison is spread abroad they will begin to regard her in a far less charitable way. It may even be said that she is *fast.*'

'It will undoubtedly be said, unless she mends her ways! What has the governess been about, to allow her such licence? The woman must be a fool!'

'I do not believe, my lord, that Miss Piltbury can be held

responsible, for it seems that Barbary was her father's favourite, and greatly indulged by him. Sir Clement is of the opinion that she has little respect for other women, and resents being obliged to accept their authority. I am inclined to agree. She has certainly resented *me*, from the moment she heard I was coming here.'

'The chit is jealous of you.'

Hebe shook her head. 'No, though I admit that was what I thought at first, but as she has never regarded herself as mistress of the house, she cannot feel that I have usurped her position here.'

'Has it never occurred to you that she might be jealous of you for a quite different reason?'

She looked perplexed, but then his meaning dawned upon her and she burst out laughing. 'Indeed it has not! Barbary, my lord, is exceedingly pretty, and could in fact be a beauty, if she could be persuaded to pay more heed to her appearance. She has no need to be jealous of a widow, with no pretension to good looks, who is already well past the first blush of youth.'

He cast her a hard, penetrating look, as though trying to decide whether or not to take her words at face value, but was prevented from pursuing the matter by the entry into the room of Hugo, Charles and James, looking unwontedly subdued, more than a little apprehensive and, as Hebe observed with relief, reasonably clean and tidy. She presented them, and each in turn made his bow to his unresponsive guardian, receiving only the acknowledgement of a curt nod.

'Lady Roxwell informs me,' Hendreth said abruptly when these civilities had been concluded, 'that she has today received a complaint of your conduct from General Gaynes. Conduct for which you will all, of course, immediately beg his pardon, and of which there will be no repetition. Is that understood?'

A ragged chorus of affirmatives assured him that it was, but his lordship had not yet done with them. There were, he continued, several other matters which must be understood, and he then proceeded to administer a trimming so masterly that Hebe could only listen in silent admiration. He might have no experience of children, but, she thought with surprise, he appeared to find no difficulty in dealing with these three.

He was to surprise her yet again. When he had finished, he stood for a few moments, silently regarding the hangdog trio before him, and she saw a hint of amusement come into his face. Then he said, as abruptly as before, 'Present yourselves at Abbotswood tomorrow morning. I will have a word with my head keeper, and no doubt he will find occupations for you more entertaining, and less conducive of ill-feeling with our neighbours, than your present exploits.'

Three incredulous faces were lifted towards him; three pairs of eyes, round with astonishment and dawning delight, stared wonderingly at him. Then Hugo, seconded by vigorous nods from his juniors, began to stammer thanks, but his lordship cut these short by jerking his head in a dismissive gesture in the direction of the door. The boys hesitated, looking doubtfully at Hebe, but when she smiled and nodded, they hurried thankfully from the room.

Hebe looked at Hendreth. 'Thank you,' she said with real gratitude. 'That was kind.'

He shrugged. 'They need some congenial occupation to keep them out of mischief. Bridge, my head keeper, taught *me* to fish and to shoot when I was about their age, and it is time those three had similar instruction. There is no one here to give it. Roxwell, even when he lived at Astington, indulged in no sporting pastimes.'

Hebe found no difficulty in believing this. The thought of Sir Hugo fishing, shooting or following the hounds was so incongruous that it was absurd. Lord Hendreth, on the other hand, looked as though he might be thoroughly at home with every kind of sport, and no doubt for that reason would prove far more congenial a guardian for the Roxwell boys than their great-uncle could ever have been, even if he had taken any interest in his wards. Whether Hendreth would be equally acceptable to the girls, and especially to Barbary, seemed less certain.

'I am very grateful to you, sir, for dealing with the boys,' she said with determined civility, 'and I feel sure they will mind you very well in future.'

'It will be more to the point, ma'am, if they mind *you* very well,' he replied caustically. 'Should they transgress again, you are at liberty to threaten them with retribution from me, but don't expect me to come dashing to your rescue every time one of them goes a little beyond the line.'

She eyed him with dislike, the kindlier feelings with which she had begun to regard him perishing abruptly.

'I will endeavour to refrain from troubling you, my lord,' she said frostily, 'though it will be helpful if your lordship will indicate to me just where that line should be drawn.'

'Oh, for God's sake, woman, use some common sense!' he retorted irritably. 'Surely you can judge the difference between ordinary devilment and serious misbehaviour? You don't need me to point it out to you.'

'Oh, this is too much!' Hebe sprang to her feet and confronted him with heaving breast and flashing eyes. 'I would not expect *you*, Lord Hendreth, to be able to point out the difference between good manners and bad, for it is plain that you are not aware of it. You are the rudest person it has ever been my misfortune to meet. Pray go!'

He grinned, his eyes mocking her. 'What, without encountering the hard-riding termagant who is about to set the county by the ears? I thought you wanted me to rake *her* down, too.'

'I have changed my mind,' she informed him furiously. 'I do not consider your lordship to be a fitting guardian, or, indeed, fit company for a young girl. Or, for that matter, for any person with the least pretension to sensibility and refinement. I don't believe you have ever had a proper feeling in your life!'

'Wrong, Lady Roxwell!' he said shamelessly. 'In my youth I was as greatly burdened with them as any man, but I managed to rid myself of them. That is why a well-bred person such as yourself will never get the better of me in an argument. You are too much at a disadvantage.'

Hebe became aware of the fact that her fingers were itching to box his ears. Dismayed by so unladylike an impulse, she clenched the offending hand hard on a fold of her skirt while she tried in vain to think of a sufficiently crushing retort.

It was at this interesting point in the conversation that the door opened again and Barbary walked into the room.

* * *

She had apparently just returned to the house. She was dressed in her riding-habit, and though there was nothing unusual about this, Hebe felt that she had never before noticed how worn and shabby the garment was. It was positively threadbare, she thought with vexation, as well as being so outgrown that it was unbecomingly tight. Beneath the plain, childish hat Barbary's black curls were wildly untidy, for she had not troubled to put her hair up, but merely tied it at the nape of her neck with a frayed ribbon.

Barbary herself, having learned at the stables that Lord Hendreth was in the house, had come impetuously to enlist his support against Hebe, and the fact that when she entered the room its occupants were very obviously at odds with each other encouraged her to think that such support would be forthcoming. She was speedily undeceived. His lordship looked round as the door opened, studied her dispassionately as she came towards him, and then said, without waiting for her to speak or Hebe to introduce them, 'So you are the hoyden whose bad behaviour is setting everyone in an uproar! By God, you look it!'

Barbary's eyes widened with shock and she halted as abruptly as though she had walked into an invisible wall. Colour flamed across her face, and she said, stammering a little, 'Wh-what do you mean?'

'I mean,' he replied ruthlessly, 'that you look heated, untidy and thoroughly blowsy, more like a scullery-maid than a lady of quality. Do you usually come into Lady Roxwell's drawing room in this disreputable state? I am amazed that she tolerates it.'

Hebe cringed inwardly, thinking how thoroughly demoralized she would have been at Barbary's age by so blistering a reproof, but Miss Roxwell was made of sterner stuff. Scarlet with mortification, she darted a venomous look at the older woman and said furiously, 'I suppose *her ladyship* has been pouring out complaints about me. I might have known that *she* would lose no time in making mischief!'

'Don't talk fustian to me!' he said impatiently. 'Anything Lady Roxwell has told me is for your own good. The mischief-making *you* need to worry about, my girl, is that of the Nidwell sisters and their like.'

Barbary tossed her head. 'Spiteful old cats! I don't care for *them*!'

'Then you are a fool!' her guardian informed her bluntly. 'A girl should always care what spiteful old cats say about her, for their tongues do damage which can't be repaired. Now attend to what I say! I am told that you have repeatedly been advised of the recklessness and folly of ranging the countryside alone and unattended, but that you take no heed. I do not intend to repeat that advice.' Both ladies looked startled, but after only the briefest of pauses he continued calmly, 'I have no intention of offering *advice* to any self-willed, self-opinionated young person who is under my authority. I will simply tell you that in future you are forbidden to ride outside the gates of this house unless you are accompanied by a responsible servant. Is that understood?'

Barbary glared at him, still flushed with anger and mortification, her lower lip mutinously out-thrust. Hebe could see that she was actually trembling with temper.

'Is that understood?' Hendreth repeated remorselessly, and after another pause, while it seemed to Hebe that she could feel the clash of wills between them, Barbary said sullenly, and almost inaudibly, 'Yes.'

'Good. Now go and make yourself presentable. I don't want to see you looking like a gipsy again.' He nodded dismissal, and turned back to Hebe. 'For God's sake, ma'am, see that she gets a new habit. That one would disgrace a scarecrow.'

Hebe scarcely heard him. She was watching Barbary, waiting for the explosion which seemed inevitable, but which to her amazement did not come. After glaring at Hendreth's back for a few moments of fuming, frustrated silence, Barbary stamped her foot and ran out of the room, expressing her feelings in her usual manner by slamming the door as hard as she could. Hebe winced, and Hendreth said bluntly, 'You have my sympathy. It's a miracle there is any glass left in the windows. That little wildcat must certainly be tamed.'

'Indeed she must, though I fancy the task will be less

simple than your lordship imagines,' Hebe replied sharply. 'Do you really expect her to obey you?'

'Lord, no!' he replied cheerfully. 'This was merely an opening skirmish. Battle has yet to be joined in earnest. I intend to remain at Abbotswood for a few days, however, and will lay odds I have a complete capitulation before I leave.'

She thought him odiously cocksure, and was almost (though not quite) prepared to hope that Barbary would get the better of him. One thing at least was certain. She would put up a spirited resistance, and a battle royal would have to take place before she surrendered. Hebe viewed the prospect with a sinking heart.

'Don't look so downcast,' Hendreth remarked with some amusement, reading her thoughts with disquieting accuracy. 'It has to be done, you know! You cannot continue to live with that sort of childish spite. Does she always refer to your ladyship in capital letters?'

Hebe was betrayed into a chuckle, for this was exactly how Barbary's insolent emphasis on the title had always sounded to her, though she had never before found it amusing.

'Always,' she said ruefully, 'and though you may think it absurd, that vexes me more than all the rest. It sets my teeth on edge to such an extent that I frequently feel like slapping her.'

'Yield to the impulse,' he advised her dryly. 'It will relieve *your* feelings, and may even teach *her* a trifle of respect.'

'Oh, no, I could not!' Hebe was shocked. 'That would quite ruin any chance I may have of coming to a better understanding with her.' She paused, then, casting him a sidelong glance, added sweetly, 'I am sure that *you*, dear sir, are much more capable than I of instilling respect—since you are not burdened with any proper feelings!'

'Precisely,' he agreed promptly. 'I am delighted to discover such ready understanding in you, ma'am.'

She cast him a very speaking look, which he met with unrepentant mockery, and said with dignity, 'I will send for Sybilla and the twins. I take it, my lord, that you wish to meet them?'

'Not in the least,' he replied indifferently, 'but I suppose I may as well run my eye over the whole pack while I am here. What trouble have they been causing?'

'None whatsoever,' she replied indignantly. 'The twins are delightful children, and though Sybilla was at first very much under her sister's influence, we have since become good friends.'

He looked thoughtfully at her. 'Are you on terms of cordiality with young Clement, too?'

'Most certainly! He is an excellent young man.'

'And the servants? Danforth and his wife, and the governess?'

'There has been no difficulty. Lord Hendreth, what is the purpose of this interrogation?'

He laughed. 'Don't fly up into the boughs! I was merely trying to discover whether or not Miss Barbary can reckon on any support against me. It seems she cannot. You have her outflanked and surrounded.'

'What a hateful thing to say!' she flared at him. 'You make it sound as though I had some underhand reason for coming here.'

'And had you?'

'No, my lord, I had not! I came because I had been concerned about these children from the moment I learned of their existence. It seemed to me that nobody cared what became of them. To Sir Hugo they were simply an unwanted responsibility, and what I had heard of *you*, my lord, inspired no confidence at all.'

'How gratifying for you to find your worst suspicions confirmed,' he said sardonically, although he did not seem to be put out. 'Now, are you going to parade the rest of your flock before me, or are you not?'

Hebe gave him a dagger-look, and moved away to ring for Danforth. Hendreth grinned, then, seeing that General Gaynes's letter, which he had laid on a table, had been wafted to the floor by the draught of Barbary's violent exit, stooped to retrieve it. Hebe turned towards him again as he straightened up with the letter in his hand, and watched in frozen horror as he went to replace it on the writing-desk. He was about to put it down when his glance fell on the other letter, the one to Mrs Hallam, which lay there; he checked, his glance passing swiftly across the page, then he dropped the General's letter on top of it and looked across at Hebe, the sardonic curve of his lips very pronounced.

'Masterly!' he remarked. 'How fortunate I afforded you the opportunity you desired. It's not often I have the privilege of granting a lady's most fervent wish within a few minutes of meeting her for the first time.'

Hebe blushed, a blush which seemed to start at her toes and engulf her whole body in a hot tide of mortification before it finally flamed up across her face to the roots of her hair. She had never been so embarrassed in her life, but she said in a goaded voice, 'I *knew* you would somehow contrive to see that! I suppose it is your custom to read letters not intended for your eyes!'

'Only when I happen to notice my own name in them,' he assured her, adding with a laugh, 'Don't look so contemptuous! You know damned well you would have done the same. I defy anyone to see himself mentioned and not be curious to find out what has been said.'

'Then I trust, my lord, that you are not disappointed.'

'Ah, but I am! You have already said much the same thing to my face, which shows a sad lack of originality. Never mind! You will now be able to add another paragraph, assuring your friend that all your worst suspicions were justified.'

'I doubt very much, sir, whether she would believe me. She is accustomed to society in which the normal civilities are observed. As, indeed, I was, until I had the extraordinary experience of making your lordship's acquaintance.'

'New experiences are invaluable.' He strolled back and stood looking down at her, and she saw that the brown eyes were alight with laughter. 'Besides, you will soon grow accustomed to it. We shall be seeing a good deal of each other.'

'I cannot imagine,' she retorted between her teeth, 'why you should suppose that.'

'Now don't be hen-witted,' he begged her. 'Your concern for these wards of mine makes it inevitable, for you know you will never bring yourself to abandon them to my evil influence.'

There was so much truth in this, for though it might be going a little too far to describe Hendreth's influence as evil, it was certainly undesirable, that Hebe could find no answer. She found herself driven into a corner, and was furious with him for putting her there.

Fortunately, before she was obliged to admit defeat, Danforth arrived, and by the time she had instructed him to ask Miss Sybilla to bring her little sisters to the drawing room Hebe had recovered a degree of composure. While they waited, she ignored her unpredictable guest and went to stand by the open window, hoping that the air would cool her heated countenance. She had her back to her companion, but was uncomfortably conscious that he was studying her.

Only a very short time elasped before Sybilla came in, shepherding the twins before her, and Hebe, turning as the door opened, saw with relief that the girl had obviously anticipated this summons. Kitty and Jane wore fresh gowns of sprig muslin with satin sashes, one pink and one blue, while Sybilla herself had changed her dress and combed her hair. Hebe gave her a look of warm approval, and went forward to perform introductions.

Now at last she had the satisfaction of seeing Hendreth at a disadvantage, for it was plain that as far as he was concerned, small girls were an unknown quantity. The twins made their curtsies and then stood looking curiously up at him, and Hebe could see that he found the intent, inquiring gaze of two identical pairs of eyes unnerving. She would have been maliciously pleased to prolong the interview, but cut it as short as possible for Sybilla's sake. Always self-conscious, the girl was reduced by her guardian's presence to a state of blushing inadequacy, and could offer only stammered monosyllables in response to the few brief remarks addressed to her. Hebe read growing impatience in Hendreth's face, and sent the three back to the schoolroom.

'So now, my lord,' she remarked when the door had closed behind them, 'you will admit, I hope, that not all the girls are gipsy hoydens.'

'Yes, that pair will cause a stir in town in seven or eight years' time,' he agreed, 'though I can't say the same for the elder one. Seemed idiotish to me!'

'Sybilla is shy,' Hebe said indignantly, 'and I, at least, do not consider that a fault in a girl of her age.'

'No countenance,' he said dismissively, 'and though you may contrive in time to do something about her size and her complexion, I doubt very much whether you will be able to remedy that.'

Hebe was so vexed by this that she said no more in Sybilla's defence, merely resolving to prove him wrong. He then took his leave, reminding her that he would expect to see Clement at Abbotswood the following evening, and advising her not to trouble her head any further over Barbary, but to leave the little shrew to him. Hebe assured him repressively that she would be very happy to do so, and with a careless nod he left her, not waiting for the formality of Danforth being summoned to show him out.

'Odious man!' Hebe said aloud, and marched across to the writing-desk to finish her letter, only to find that for some reason the desire to confide her woes to Mrs Hallam had evaporated. For several minutes she sat staring thoughtfully before her, brushing the feather of the pen to and fro against her chin, and then, casting it aside, picked up the letter and tore it across and across until it was in fragments.

Lord Hendreth was quite right. Barbary did not obey him, any slight inclination to do so which she might have felt being banished by the attitude of her brothers. The three younger ones, coming home tired and dirty after a blissful day spent with his lordship's head keeper, and with the prospect of similar days to look forward to, were loud in praise of their new guardian, while Clement, who had gone to dine at Abbotswood in a state of considerable trepidation, returned wearing the aspect of one who had had a great weight lifted from his shoulders. He later confided to Hebe that he had come home from Oxford deeply in debt, and with no prospect of being able to satisfy his creditors.

'You see, ma'am,' he explained diffidently, 'when I went up to University, my allowance—the amount of it, that is— was decided by Great-Uncle Hugo. I dare say he thought it adequate, but things have changed a great deal since his day, and try as I would I could not manage on it. He would not consent to increase it, so I was obliged to live on credit and just got in deeper and deeper until I was at a stand. That is why I was so anxious to talk to Lord Hendreth, for I realized the only thing to do was to make a clean breast of it and take whatever trimming he saw fit to give me, in the hope that he might agree to set matters to rights.'

Hebe looked curiously at him. 'And did he?'

Clement nodded. 'Yes, for as soon as I told him what my allowance was he said it was no wonder I was in such a fix, and it should be increased immediately. *And* he agreed that all my debts should be settled straight away.'

She stared at him. 'Do you mean to tell me,' she asked incredulously, 'that Lord Hendreth had *no* criticism to offer?'

Clement laughed. 'Well, he did say that he would give me only one chance, and that if I got into difficulties again he would ring such a peal over me that I would wish I had never been born. But I won't, you know! Get into difficulties, I mean. I made up my mind, when Papa died, that since I was fortunate enough to be Great-Uncle Hugo's heir, we must never find ourselves in such a situation again. I have all the younger ones to think of, you see.' He broke off, colouring and giving a little, embarrassed laugh. 'I suppose that makes me sound abominably pompous and priggish.'

'I think it does you great credit.' Hebe said gently. 'Tell me, did Lord Hendreth say anything to you about assuming the guardianship of your brothers and sisters as soon as you come of age?'

'He told me I had the right to do so, but that in his opinion I should wait until I am twenty-five. I must say I was relieved to hear it. I am exceedingly fond of them all, but there's no doubt they don't mind me as they should.'

Hebe digested this information in silence, wondering what had made Hendreth change his mind, or whether, the previous day, he had spoken out of a momentary irritation, with no intention of handing over his responsibilities. It would certainly be better if he did not, though if it were his custom to spend most of his time abroad it was difficult to see how he could properly discharge the duties of guardian.

For the next two days no more was heard of his lordship at Astington Park, but Hebe reflected apprehensively that this was probably the lull before the storm. Barbary, ignoring all representations made to her, continued to spend the greater part of the day riding about the countryside totally unattended, until Clement said he washed his hands of her; Miss Piltbury, now up and about again, gave up in despair; and Hebe, having had her well-intentioned advice flung back in her face with even greater rudeness than usual, was dismayed to find herself vindictive enough to hope that Barbary would receive short shrift from her guardian.

The hope was to be fulfilled. On the third morning Hebe was in her parlour, going through some household accounts, when the door was thrown open and Hendreth stalked without ceremony into the room, propelling Barbary before him by a firm grip on her shoulder. An amazingly subdued and chastened Barbary, her head drooping, her face pale and streaked with tears. As Hebe stared, his lordship marched his captive to a chair and thrust her none too gently down on to it, curtly commanding her to sit there and not move until he gave her leave. Then he turned to Hebe, saying without any preamble, 'I dare say you arranged for my ward to have a new riding-habit. Don't put yourself to that trouble! She will have no immediate need of such a garment.'

Hebe blinked at him. 'She will not?'

'She will not!' he agreed with finality. 'In fact, when she presently takes off the one she is now wearing, you will oblige me by instructing the servants to burn it. Miss Barbary will not ride again until I give her permission to do so, and that permission will have to be earned. She'll not find that easy.'

Barbary gave a gasp and burst into tears, covering her face with her hands. Hendreth cast an indifferent glance in her direction and then looked again at Hebe.

'I don't brook defiance,' he said conversationally. 'She had a chance to mend her ways, and didn't avail herself of it, so now she must take the consequences. She refuses to ride with a groom in attendance, therefore she will not ride at all.'

A fresh burst of sobbing greeted this pronouncement. Hebe looked at the woebegone figure and shook her head.

'Oh, Barbary,' she said resignedly, 'why would you not listen to us? We all warned you! What a foolish girl you are!'

'Not foolish, ma'am. Stubborn and stupid,' Hendreth corrected heartlessly. 'People of that sort never listen to warnings or advice. They need to have the error of their ways demonstrated to them in a practical fashion. Something simple which even they can understand.'

'Lord Hendreth!' Hebe felt that this was going a little too far. 'It is unjust to call Barbary stupid.'

His brows lifted. 'Is it? I find it damnably stupid wilfully to disobey an order without pausing to consider why it was given. A young woman takes a servant with her for her own protection, not just to safeguard her reputation but against more tangible dangers. I suppose it's possible that misplaced delicacy prevented you and the governess from explaining exactly what those dangers are, but that omission has now been repaired.'

Hebe cast him a startled glance, but before she could inquire further, Barbary lifted a tear-stained face and said desperately, 'I did not think! If you will let me go on riding I will *always* take a groom with me. I promise!'

'Too late!' he replied shortly. 'I am by no means convinced that your word is to be depended upon. Show me you are capable of behaving like a sensible woman instead of a spoiled and disobedient child, and we'll discuss the matter again. Until then, you will stay out of the saddle.'

'But what shall I *do*?' she wailed. 'If I am forbidden to go riding, how can I pass the time?'

'You will have plenty to do,' he informed her curtly. 'Next season you will be entering society, and by then you will have had to learn how to conduct yourself in polite company. From what I have seen, I imagine you will need all the practice you can get.'

A hint of the former rebelliousness crept into her face. 'I don't want to go to London.'

'What *you* want,' Hendreth replied crushingly, 'is of very little interest to me. You will do what your parents would undoubtedly have wished. You will spend the season in London, and perhaps, if you have learned some manners by then, and can successfully disguise your temper, you may be fortunate enough to catch a husband.' He saw Hebe's disapproving look, and added mockingly, 'Her ladyship thinks I should have said "form an eligible connection". It amounts to the same thing.'

'I don't want—!' Barbary encountered his lordship's sardonic glance and hastily revised what she had been about to say. 'Why should I try to catch a husband?'

'Oh, good God! Has that governess of yours taught you nothing?' he exclaimed exasperatedly, and swung round to Hebe. 'Tell her, ma'am! Explain to her why marriage, which in my ignorance I supposed to be every girl's ambition, is also a female's duty.'

Hebe was not altogether sure that she agreed with this, but, disdaining to enter into an argument with him, said kindly to Barbary, 'You wish, do you not, one day to have a home of your own, and perhaps a family?'

Barbary shrugged. 'I prefer horses to children, and I have a very good home here. Or I did have, until *you* thrust yourself into it.'

'That's enough of your damned impertinence!' Even Hebe jumped at the harshness of Hendreth's voice. 'Lady Roxwell is the mistress of her late husband's household, and will remain so until your brother Clement marries. As for you, my girl, I advise you not to assume that you will be welcome to live here after *that* event.'

She looked disconcerted, but said defiantly, 'Clement will let me stay as long as I like.'

'Don't depend on it,' his lordship advised her sardonically. 'I cannot imagine his bride, whoever she may prove to be, taking kindly to the notion of sharing her home with a shrewish spinster sister. And since Clement may not marry for another ten years, you will be past the age then for picking and choosing, and will be obliged to settle for what you can get.'

He paused, but Hebe, in a calm voice though with slightly heightened colour, completed the argument for him, ' "As Lady Roxwell did". I am sure, Barbary, that that is what Lord Hendreth is implying, and since it cannot possibly be delicacy or consideration which sets a curb on his tongue, I cannot imagine why he does not say so.'

She had the satisfaction of knowing that she had startled him. He bestowed on her a hard, penetrating look from beneath frowning brows, and then gave a sudden crack of laughter.

'Believe it or not, ma'am, that thought never entered my head. In any event, remaining unmarried in order to keep house for an ailing brother is a very different matter. No such selfless reason presents itself in my ward's case, and for your sake I most devoutly hope that we may get her off our hands with the least possible delay.'

Barbary cast him a look of dark suspicion. 'What do you mean—for *her* sake?'

'You know, you are even more stupid than I thought,' he remarked dispassionately. 'You do not imagine, do you, that if you remain unmarried, and are not welcome here, you will be allowed to set up house on your own? You will still need a chaperone, and as you have no older female relatives of your own, you may be grateful if Lady Roxwell's sense of duty, which I suspect to be very strong, prevails upon her to let you go on living under her roof.'

It was plain from Barbary's expression that this picture of her future appalled her. Her guardian waited a moment for the full implication of what he had said to sink in, and then curtly commanded her to go and change her clothes, and present herself again for his inspection.

'And it's to be hoped you look less of a hoyden in a gown than you do in that habit,' he concluded bluntly. 'Make haste about it! I have no intention of waiting all day.'

Without a word Barbary obeyed him, going with dragging steps out of the room. Hebe watched, fascinated, until the door closed behind her, and then transferred her astonished gaze to his lordship.

'I can scarcely believe it!' she said frankly. 'My dear sir, how in the world did you work this miracle?'

He eyed her consideringly and then shook his head. 'I don't think I'll tell you,' he said with a grin, 'for I fancy you would not approve of my methods. And as I'm damned certain Barbary won't confide in you, I advise you not to lay yourself open to a snub by asking her.' He met the widow's wrathful gaze with a look of unholy amusement, and added cheerfully, 'Content yourself with the fact that Miss Barbary now knows beyond all doubt that I am not to be trifled with, and do your best to cultivate the seeds I have sown. Between us, we should be able to convince her that to escape from our tyranny by finding a husband is a matter of the most urgent necessity.'

Hebe looked troubled. 'We cannot conspire to force that child unwillingly into marriage.'

'Oh, ye gods!' he said impatiently. 'What makes you suppose she will be unwilling? Though I would not tell her so for the world, she is a devilish pretty girl, and her brother can afford to give her a respectable marriage portion, so she will have suitors enough to choose from.' Then, with an abrupt and totally unexpected change of subject, he added bluntly, 'What persuaded *you* to marry Roxwell?'

Hebe gasped, stared at him in astonished disbelief, saw that he clearly expected an answer, and finally said feebly, 'You have no right to ask me such an impertinent question. It—is quite outrageous!'

'I know,' he admitted calmly, 'but since we agreed at our first meeting that I am a stranger to all proper feelings, you cannot be surprised that I have asked it.' Seeing her at a loss for words, he strolled forward and leaned his hands lightly on the opposite edge of the table at which she was still seated, looking consideringly down at her. 'When I first heard of the marriage,' he went on in a conversational way, 'I naturally assumed your motives to be entirely mercenary. The advantages to a young woman alone in the world of a rich, elderly husband totally indifferent to the female sex are too obvious to need enumerating. Having now made your acquaintance, I realize that I misjudged you.'

Hebe pushed back her chair and got up, for there was something oddly disturbing in having Hendreth looming over her in that fashion. He was too big, too masculine, altogether overpowering. She moved away from him to the window, where the casement stood open to a gentle breeze, and when she had recovered a little, said sweetly, 'I am overwhelmed to learn that I have made so favourable an impression upon your lordship. You cannot imagine what a relief to me it is.'

Appreciative laughter leapt into his eyes. 'You are nothing of the sort,' he said affably, 'and wish only to put me in my place, but you won't do it, you know. I am abominably persistent. Why *did* you marry the old man? You were not left destitute by your brother's death?'

Hebe sighed. She saw no reason to doubt Hendreth's reading of his own character, and it would be easier, and more dignified, to answer his impertinent question now than to enter into an argument. She had nothing of which to be ashamed.

'No,' she said resignedly, 'I was not destitute. My brother left me our house at Cambridge, and a small independence. I suppose my reasons for marrying Sir Hugo were very similar to those you have just been trying to impress upon Barbary. It would not have been thought proper for me, as a spinster, to live alone, and since, unlike Barbary, I had for years been accustomed to being the mistress of a household, the prospect of being obliged to live under another woman's roof appalled me.'

'Weren't you appalled by the prospect of tying yourself to a man old enough, I imagine, to be your grandfather?'

'Not in the least.' Hebe spoke lightly, trying to ignore the familiar stab of pain, and the bitter thought that regret had come later, much too late. 'I was not a romantic young girl, you know! Sir Hugo offered an arrangement of mutual benefit, for I had long been accustomed to ordering a scholar's household, and had, in fact, taken charge of his, which was in sad disarray, soon after my brother and I became his guests. He wished the arrangement to continue, and I was more than happy for it to do so. I like to feel that I am of use to *somebody*.'

Hendreth had followed her to the window, and now leaned his shoulders against the wall beside it, watching her while he took out his snuff-box and thoughtfully inhaled a pinch. At length he said, 'It sounds a practical, unsentimental, cold-blooded arrangement.'

She shrugged slightly, wishing he had stayed where he was, but reluctant to give the impression of flight by moving away from him again.

'No doubt I am a practical, unsentimental, cold-blooded person.'

He did not reply at once, but continued to study her, his gaze moving deliberately across her features, lingering for a long, disquieting moment on her lips and then lifting again to meet her eyes. Flustered, and furious to feel the colour rising to her cheeks, she looked quickly away from him into the garden, waiting apprehensively for whatever outrageous comment he might choose to make. He surprised her yet again.

'It must have come as a shock to discover that your bargain had burdened you with a ready-made family.'

'It came, sir, as an agreeable surprise!' she replied sharply, glad to take refuge in vexation from the agitating sensations of the past few minutes. 'May I remind your lordship that the choice to come here was my own? I could just as easily have returned to Cambridge, since now that I am a widow, it would have been perfectly proper for me to live alone.'

'Ridiculous, isn't it?' he agreed cordially. 'I'll lay odds, though, that there have been times when you wished you *had* gone back to Cambridge.'

She thought of all the occasions when Barbary's hostility had prompted her to wish precisely that, but she would not give him any satisfaction by admitting it. Instead she said loftily, 'I hope I have a sense of duty strong enough to preclude my doing so.'

'Oh, so high!' he said mockingly. 'Come down out of the boughs, my girl, and confess there have been occasions since you arrived here when to be living alone in your own house has seemed the most desirable thing in the world. Or is there no grain of truth in you?'

She eyed him with hostility. 'Tell me, my lord, do you talk to everybody in this uncivil fashion, or am I especially favoured?'

'No, no!' he assured her hastily, though with a satirical gleam in his eyes. 'Don't, I beg of you, imagine that my conduct towards your ladyship is in any way particular. I am uncivil to everybody.'

'That, my lord, is nothing to be proud of,' she said severely. 'Permit me to tell you that had I been fully conversant with your extraordinary manners, nothing in the world would have persuaded me to establish myself where I would be obliged to enter into an acquaintance with you.'

He shook his head reproachfully. 'Completely untruthful!' he said sadly. 'You know damned well you would have come here all the faster to protect Roxwell's young relatives from my pernicious influence. Don't worry! Clement seems set in the habit of excellent manners, and I am not likely to see enough of the others to undermine their characters.'

Mention of Clement reminded Hebe of an earlier conversation with Hendreth, and she said curiously, 'I understand from Sir Clement that you do not, after all, insist upon him assuming guardianship of his brothers and sisters as soon as he comes of age.'

His lordship frowned. 'It wouldn't serve,' he said shortly. 'We'll defer any change until he is twenty-five. The two elder girls should be established by then, and the younger boys have made up their minds what they want to do with their lives. As for the twins, if Clement has not married by the time they make their come-out, their eldest sister can chaperone them.'

Hebe looked challengingly at him. 'I would like,' she stated firmly, 'to keep the twins with me. By the time they are old enough to enter society, it is highly probable that Barbary and Sybilla will be preoccupied with young families of their own.'

He raised a quizzical eyebrow at her. 'Surely it is not totally *im*probable that you may find yourself in a similar situation. Or have you set your mind irrevocably against marrying again?'

She flushed, as much with anger as embarrassment. 'That remark, sir, is in the worst possible taste. You are not speaking to a young girl, you know!'

He grinned at her. 'Pardon me, I had not realized you are so stricken in years. You carry your age remarkably well!'

For the second time in their brief acquaintance, Hebe's fingers itched to box his lordship's ears. He observed the involuntary clenching of her hand, and laughed softly.

'Don't attempt it!' he advised her wickedly. 'You will come off very much the worse.'

It was perhaps fortunate that at that moment, as on a previous occasion, they were interrupted by Barbary coming into the room. She had been sufficiently impressed by the advisability of obeying her guardian to make all the haste she could in changing her dress, but the result left a good deal to be desired. Her white muslin gown looked crumpled, the sash was tied anyhow, and she could not, Hebe thought despairingly, have done so much as drag a comb through her hair. She was not surprised to see that Hendreth looked disgusted.

'Good God! is that the best you can do?' he demanded. 'Where the devil did you get that garment you are wearing?'

Barbary glanced down at herself and tugged ineffectually at the sash. 'It's my newest dress,' she said defensively. 'Miss Medgate made it. She makes all our dresses.'

'The village dressmaker! I can well believe it!' he said disparagingly. 'Though even that does not explain why you look as though you have been dragged backwards through a bramble bush. Have you no maid?'

'Jessie waits on us, but I didn't bother to ring for her,' Barbary explained, and added in exculpation, 'You told me to make haste.'

Hendreth turned to Hebe. 'If you enjoy a challenge, ma'am, this one should delight you,' he said dryly. 'For God's sake buy her some new clothes! Clothes suitable for a young lady and not a hurly-burly schoolgirl. I suggest you take her to spend a few days at Cheltenham. It is a spa town, and so you will find there some excellent shops. And hire a good abigail for her. You are going to need all the help you can get.'

Hebe was inclined to agree with him, though she felt uneasily that the help she would need most of all was not of a kind which even the most experienced abigail could offer, since the greatest difficulty would be to persuade Barbary to pay any heed to her. Hendreth, however, had already thought of that.

'You,' he continued, addressing himself again to his ward, 'will do exactly as Lady Roxwell bids you, or you will answer to me, and I think you have learned today that answering to me can be a very unpleasant experience. I wish to hear of no more defiance or disobedience, and by the time you return from Cheltenham I expect your appearance to bear some faint resemblance to that of a young lady of fashion, even if, as yet, your manners do not. Do you understand me?'

Barbary said meekly that she did, but added, with just the

faintest echo of defiance, that she knew nothing at all about fashion. Hendreth looked her up and down.

'That,' he said blightingly, 'is painfully obvious, so it is fortunate that you will have the advice and guidance of someone who does.' He cast a glance of glinting mockery in Hebe's direction. 'In spite of her advanced years, your great-aunt has excellent style!'

PART
FIVE

HEBE HAD FOUND a patch of snowdrops in bloom in a sheltered corner of the garden, a welcome hint that an exceptionally long, hard winter would soon be over. She stood looking down at the delicate, green-flecked blossoms dancing in the cold March wind, and could not decide whether she was glad or sorry that spring would soon be upon her. During the past six months, life had settled into a pleasant if unexciting rhythm, but now change was in the air again and she was not sure that she was ready to face it.

Only occasionally, and very briefly, did she now regret her decision to come to Astington Park, when Barbary was difficult or Lord Hendreth more than usually aggravating. There were compensations which far outweighed the disadvantages. The affection of Sybilla and the twins, and the fact that the three younger boys, too, had come to accept her; the pleasure of having in her hands the reins of a large household; above all, the sense of belonging and the knowledge that she was needed. Her ready-made family, as Hendreth called it, had filled the empty reaches of her life, and their regard for her laid healing hands upon the wound which Geoffrey Fernhurst had dealt. Her brief, disastrous love affair was now but a bitter-sweet memory, and if the doubts and questions which had plagued her were not entirely forgotten, they had retreated to the back of her mind, thrust out of conscious thought by an established day-to-day routine, and the small triumphs and failures which now made up her life.

Hebe had been a widow for a year, and her twenty-sixth birthday was four months past. There were times when she felt positively middle-aged, especially when she looked at Barbary poised expectantly on the brink of a young womanhood which would be very different from the one Hebe herself had known. At the time she had been happy enough, caring for her father and brother and feeling no sense of deprivation, but it was now, looking back, that she realized how little real girlhood she had known. Barbary held up a mirror into which it was hurtful to look, for it made one think wistfully that it must be pleasant to be eighteen years old, blessed with beauty and self-confidence and ready to rush forward to meet life with open arms.

For Barbary, on the surface at least, was one of Hebe's greater triumphs. There had been a short, difficult period of rebellion and upheaval following Hendreth's ultimatum, but then she had pulled herself together and with single-minded determination set out to prepare for her approaching debut. No longer actively hostile to her great-uncle's widow—though she did, thanks to his lordship's misguided humour, take mocking satisfaction in always addressing her as 'Aunt Hebe' —her attitude had become one of guarded tolerance, and she meekly accepted the elder woman's guidance in all matters of dress and deportment. With this advice, and the help of a well-trained abigail, Barbary had achieved a startling transformation, emerging, like a butterfly from its chrysalis, as the beauty Hebe had always known she could be. Nor was it only her looks which had been improved; she had mended her manners, too, and learned to make herself agreeable in any company, cultivating a demurely mischievous demeanour which was very appealing. Miss Piltbury had been overjoyed, but Hebe was conscious of a little, nagging disquiet underlying her own gratification. There was nothing spontaneous about Barbary's metamorphosis. It came from her head and not her heart, for she was deliberately acquiring beauty and charm like a general mustering his forces for a campaign, and there was little doubt in Hebe's mind what the objective of the campaign was to be. Barbary had no intention of spending another winter as an unmarried daughter of the house.

I suppose there is nothing wrong in that, Hebe thought, gazing at the snowdrops and thinking that they were rather like Barbary herself; deceptively fragile and dainty in appearance, yet hardy enough to survive the harshest weather. Every girl wants to be married, but Barbary's desire springs from the wrong reasons. She wants only to be free of Hendreth and of me.

Thought of Hendreth brought a familiar spurt of mingled exasperation and apprehension. One never knew what his lordship would do or say next, and his visits were always unsettling, though for nearly three months now they had not seen him. During the latter part of the summer and a long, golden autumn he had been quite often at Abbotswood, and a frequent visitor to Astington Park, but Christmas he had spent at his mother's house at Bath, and since then the weather had been severe enough to discourage all but the most essential journeys. The first snow had fallen on New Year's Eve, and thereafter Hebe saw the Cotswolds in a different and less friendly guise, with gales roaring across the hills and piling up great drifts which rendered roads impassable and cut off isolated houses and even whole villages for weeks at a time. Even now, in the first week of March, the highest crests were still white with snow.

The sound of the twins' voices roused Hebe from her thoughts, and she looked round to see them running along the path towards her, followed more decorously by Sybilla. They had been playing ball and their faces were flushed and glowing, and as Hebe held out both her hands to them, she was conscious of a surge of affection for them. Whatever conflicting emotions might trouble her, the uncomplicated love of these two little girls was a constant source of delight.

'We have been looking everywhere for you, Aunt Hebe,' Jane told her reproachfully, clutching one of the outstretched hands. 'Were you hiding from us?'

'No, I came into the shrubbery because it is sheltered from the wind, and see what I have found. The first snowdrops.'

They exclaimed with pleasure, crouching down to admire the flowers, and Kitty was stretching out her hand to pick one when Sybilla, coming up to them at that moment, said quickly, 'Oh, don't, Kit! Leave them where they are.' She glanced shyly at Hebe. 'It seems such a shame to pick them. They fade so quickly when they are brought indoors.'

'I wasn't going to take them indoors,' Kitty said with dignity. 'I was going to pick them for Pilty.'

There was a little silence. In the coldest, darkest days of January, Miss Piltbury had contracted a chill which developed with frightening speed into an inflammation of the lung, and carried her off within a week. Her death had come as a severe shock to the whole family, but most of all to the twins. Hebe said gently, 'Pick them in the morning, my love, if it is fine, and I will take you to the village so that you may put them on her grave. Come, let us go indoors.'

Subdued now, Kitty and Jane began walking towards the house. Hebe, following with Sybilla, said with a sigh, 'Now that the worst of the winter is over, I must see about engaging another governess.' Sybilla made a little gesture of protest, and she added kindly, 'I know, my dear, but we cannot go on as we are. It was well enough, while the roads were impassable, for me to give the twins their lessons and to speak French and Italian with you and Barbary, but it will not do now. Don't be alarmed! I know I can never give you another Pilty, but I assure you I will find someone congenial.'

'Yes, ma'am, I know you will,' Sybilla admitted, trying to smile. 'It is just that Pilty had always been there, ever since I can remember, and to be without her—! But it could have been so much worse! We might not have had *you*.'

Hebe looked affectionately at her. Sybilla, she thought, had improved out of all knowledge during the past six months. She was beginning to conquer her shyness a little, and to display the sweetness of nature and maturity of outlook which her beautiful, self-willed elder sister so signally lacked. Her looks were improving, too. She had started to lose her puppy-fat, and, encouraged by this, made conscientious attempts to curb her appetite, so that she was not only slimmer, but had a better complexion. She would never be able to compete with Barbary, but Hebe thought that in another year or so she would be able to enter society with reasonable confidence.

They reached the house to find that letters had just been

fetched from the post office, including one for Hebe addressed in a hand she did not recognize, and a little later, settled comfortably by the fire in her sitting room, she yielded to curiosity and opened that one first. Its contents astonished her. It was from Lady Hendreth, inviting Lady Roxwell and Miss Barbary Roxwell to stay with her at Bath.

Hebe did not know what to make of this. Hendreth rarely spoke of his mother, but since she never came to Abbotswood it was generally assumed that her health did not permit her to travel, and it seemed in the highest degree unlikely that a middle-aged invalid would choose to invite two strangers, one of them little more than a schoolgirl, to stay in her house. Hendreth himself must have prevailed upon her to write that letter, for some purpose of his own. How like him, how *very* like him, Hebe reflected bitterly, to do such a thing without a word to her.

It placed her in an exceedingly difficult situation. She had no desire to visit Bath, much less to take Barbary there, but if she made some civil excuse, his lordship would hear of it and probably come to see for himself if there were any truth in it. Polite subterfuges would carry no weight with him; he would not, out of courtesy, pretend to believe them, but would brush them aside and insist upon knowing the truth. Would, in fact, behave in his usual uncivil and overbearing manner.

Hebe felt that she needed time to consider, so she decided that for the time being she would say nothing to Barbary about the letter. She was exceedingly reluctant herself to leave Astington Park and go out again into society, even the sedate and elderly society of Bath. The town was no longer a resort of high fashion, having been supplanted in that position by Brighton, but the few days spent at Cheltenham the previous summer had shown Hebe that a spa town had its own social round; the visits to the Pump Room, the fashionable promenades, the select assemblies and concerts. She was far happier at Astington, and if Hendreth wanted his ward to sample the social life of Bath before launching her into a London season, let him persuade whichever fashionable matron he had found to sponsor Barbary's London debut to take charge also of the visit to Bath. Not even to herself would Hebe admit that some part at least of her own reluctance to visit the spa was due to the fact that it was Lady Hendreth who had been responsible for Geoffrey's visit to the Roxwell establishment in Rome.

Next afternoon she was still trying to make up her mind whether to decline her ladyship's invitation without delay, or to wait a little while in the hope that some indication of Hendreth's purpose might be forthcoming, when this hope was fulfilled in a way she had not bargained for. She was in the schoolroom, guiding a reluctant Kitty and Jane through an arithmetic lesson, when Danforth came to tell her that his lordship had arrived, and was awaiting her in the drawing room.

The twins looked pleased, for Barbary and Sybilla were out walking and they foresaw an end to the lesson, but Hebe could not share their satisfaction. She had no doubt that Hendreth's arrival was directly connected with his mother's invitation and that he would ruthlessly brush aside all her arguments against accepting it.

She was quite right. When they had exchanged greetings, and she expressed polite surprise at his lordship's unlooked-for arrival, he regarded her with an amused and sapient eye and said frankly, 'You are no more surprised than I am! I've come to escort you and Barbary to Bath.' Hebe gasped, and he raised his eyebrows in apparent surprise. 'Don't tell me you've not yet received my mother's letter!'

'Lady Hendreth's invitation reached me only yesterday,' Hebe informed him coldly. 'I have barely had time to consider it, much less to reply.'

'No need,' he replied carelessly. 'She knows I intend to bring you to her.'

Hebe glared at him. 'I said, my lord, that I had barely had time to consider it.'

'I know you did. What is there to consider?'

'A great deal,' she replied with careful restraint. 'For one thing, though it may be your lordship's custom to set out on a visit at a moment's notice, it is not mine. There would be any number of things to attend to before I could leave this house.'

'Make yourself easy on that score. I have some business to attend to at Abbotswood which will keep me occupied for several days.'

'A gentleman,' Hebe remarked tartly, unwisely allowing herself to be diverted, 'would have said that he would wait upon my convenience.'

'Very likely, but you would be astonished if *I* started telling you polite lies. We'll set out on Thursday morning. That should give you time to get all your fripperies packed.'

'We shall do nothing of the kind,' she retorted furiously. 'It is out of the question!'

'You need longer than that? Good God, ma'am, you are only going to Bath, not Windsor Castle!'

'I am not going anywhere! It is out of the question for me to leave Astington at present.' She saw that he was about to demand why, and triumphantly forestalled him. 'You are not aware of it, but poor Miss Piltbury died six weeks ago, and there is no one to look after the twins.'

'That won't fadge! There is their sister, Sybilla, Mrs Danforth and I know not how many female servants. Try again!'

'I have to see about engaging a new governess.'

'It will be far easier to find one in Bath. In fact, I believe my mother already has a very good woman in her eye.' He grinned at Hebe's stare of disbelief. 'Oh yes, I was aware that the old governess had died. You informed Benchley, and he mentioned it to me.'

Hebe thought it prudent to ignore this, and tried another approach. 'I am obliged to Lady Hendreth for her kind invitation, but cannot possibly impose upon her by accepting it. I am astonished that you should wish it! It shows a sad lack of consideration for her.'

'Oh, I don't know!' he said consideringly. 'I've tamed young Barbary, and I wouldn't have supposed *you* to be a very trying guest.'

Hebe drew a sharp breath, and fought a silent battle with herself for a few moments, while he watched her expectantly. She was gratified, finally, to be able to disappoint him by saying frigidly, 'I was referring, sir, to her ladyship's health. She is, I have been given to understand, an invalid.'

'Oh, I see! Set your mind at rest on that score. It is certainly many years since my mother enjoyed really robust health, but there's nothing she likes better than entertaining her friends, and compared with your life here, hers is gay to dissipation. The truth is, she detests Abbotswood! Always has, ever since she came there as a bride. She only enjoys town life, but the London air does not agree with her constitution, so she has chosen to live at Bath.'

'Lady Hendreth may like entertaining her *friends,* sir, but that does not mean she would enjoy having two strangers foisted upon her. And do not deny that the invitation was offered at your instigation, for I shall not believe you.'

'Unjust, my lady! I don't say I would *not* have urged my mother to invite you, but there was no need. She has the liveliest desire to make your acquaintance.'

Hebe was about to retort that she could not imagine why, when she remembered, not only that Lady Hendreth had been responsible for Geoffrey Fernhurst's visit to the villa, but also that Geoffrey himself had said that her ladyship was a close friend of one of his aunts, who also lived at Bath. A sense of panic took possession of her. It was one thing to muse sadly upon what might have been, but it was quite another to be forced into a situation where she might be obliged to put her doubts and questions to the test. If she went to Bath she would not only meet Lady Hendreth, but almost certainly the unknown aunt as well; it was not entirely beyond the bounds of possibility that she might even encounter Geoffrey himself.

She could not face it. She had found sanctuary, and a precarious measure of contentment, and she would not risk that hard-won peace of mind at Hendreth's bidding. She had found a new role for herself as the widowed chatelaine of Astington Park, and a sense of purpose in creating a real home for the orphaned Roxwell family. They needed her, she was already deeply attached to them, and all more passionate emotions were a thing of the past. The issue was crystal-clear in her own mind, and all that remained was to convince her odiously interfering companion (without, of course, allowing him to suspect the truth) that her decision was irrevocable.

'Lady Hendreth is very kind,' she said carefully, 'and I shall, of course, write to her to express my sense of obligation, but I cannot feel it would be right to go away from Astington at the present. Had Miss Piltbury still been with us, then perhaps—!'

'Don't talk polite flummery to me, ma'am,' he interrupted

impatiently. 'Tell me the truth! Is that little minx throwing one of her tantrums at the prospect of visiting my mother?'

'No! Oh, no, indeed!' In her anxiety to save Barbary from undeserved blame, Hebe spoke without sufficient thought. 'I have not yet mentioned the matter to her, but I can think of no reason why she should dislike it.'

'Then it is you, Lady Roxwell, who find the notion disagreeable? Strange! I thought you would welcome a little mild diversion.'

Hebe bestowed a quelling glance upon him. 'Whether I would welcome it, my lord, or not, it would scarcely be thought proper—!' A little gesture indicating her widow's weeds completed the sentence.

'Rubbish!' he said shortly. 'Roxwell has been dead for a year, your period of strict mourning is over, and not even the most censorious will blame you for putting off your weeds, especially since you find yourself obliged to act as Barbary's duenna. Or do you propose to accompany her to balls and parties swathed from head to foot in black?'

'Accompany her to balls and parties?' she repeated blankly.

'That *is* one of the duties of a chaperone, you know,' he informed her sarcastically. 'Even at Bath you will be going into company, and when you take her to London—!'

'When *I* take her to London—?'

Hebe was so taken aback that the words came out in an undignified squeak, but she was too perturbed to care. His lordship grinned unsympathetically.'

'Don't keep repeating everything I say, there's a good girl! I thought we had agreed that Barbary should make her come-out this season?'

'Yes, but—but not in *my* care!'

'Who the devil do you expect to take charge of her if you do not? Why, I have already had Benchley find a suitable house in town for you to hire!'

'A suit—!' Hebe encountered Hendreth's satirical glance and choked back her involuntary repetition of his words. 'I don't need a house in town.'

'Well, you can't stay in mine, you know,' he pointed out reasonably. 'You would be more than welcome, but it would set all the tongues wagging.'

'Oh, you are abominable!' Hebe sprang up from her chair and began to pace agitatedly about the room. '*I* cannot take Barbary to London! I have not one single acquaintance there.'

'Don't let that disturb you! My aunt, Lady Felchester, my father's elder sister, will be in town then and will perform all the necessary introductions. She's willing to do that, and to present Barbary at one of the Royal Drawing rooms, but won't consider taking charge of her. Wouldn't answer if she did! She's damnably outspoken, and would drive the chit into some prank or other within the week. But she *will* see you are invited to all the *ton* parties, and is confident that she can obtain vouchers for you for Almack's. They call that the Marriage Mart, you know,' he added in a tone of kindly explanation.

'Thank you, my lord,' Hebe replied cuttingly. 'I may be an ignorant provincial, but I *have* heard of the most exclusive club in London. And what I have heard,' she continued with increasing agitation, 'makes me more than ever convinced that you must find someone else to be Barbary's duenna. *I* have no place in that world.'

'Damn it, woman! Stop talking as though you had been reared in a shop or a farmyard,' Hendreth said violently. 'You are a gentlewoman, you are Hugo Roxwell's widow— what the *devil* makes you imagine that you do not belong in polite society? I've never heard such confounded nonsense in my life!'

'And I, my lord, have never before in my life been sworn at and abused,' she retorted, agitation and resentment bringing her to the verge of tears. 'One would never suppose, from your conduct, that *your lordship* belongs in polite society.'

He gave one of his sudden cracks of laughter. 'I don't! In my case, only my birth makes me acceptable.'

Hebe paid very little heed to this. A prey to the most agitating reflections, she was still walking about the room, twisting her hands together and biting her lip. Hendreth watched her for a moment or two with a slight frown, then, as she came within reach, stretched out a long arm and grasped her by the wrist. Startled, she halted and looked up at him, trying to pull away, but his grip only tightened a little.

'Compose yourself, ma'am!' He spoke in a tone of some

amusement, but she saw with surprise that his expression was not unsympathetic. 'If the violence of my language has reduced you to this state, I apologize for it.' He paused, looking so searchingly at her that she felt her colour rise, and was obliged to turn her head away. 'It is more than that, isn't it? Why does the prospect of going into society cast you into such a fret?'

Again Hebe tried to free herself, and this time he let her go. She moved away from him and sat down, trying to be calm. She could not tell him that dread of meeting Geoffrey Fernhurst, of rekindling emotions which had brought her nothing but pain, lay at the root of her distress, and indeed, this was not its only cause. After a pause, she said in a low voice, 'I think you do not realize how restricted my life has been. My home was a very simple and scholarly one, my circle of friends very small and drawn from a similar scholastic background, and though I travelled with my brother, our journey never took us into the haunts of fashion. Sir Hugo's household was in many ways similar to my father's, and in any event, for most of my married life I was in mourning for Felix, and so did not go into company. I am almost totally without experience of polite society, and though in a girl of Barbary's age that may appear charming, in a woman of mine it can only seem ridiculous.'

'I thought it wouldn't be long before the question of your advanced years raised its head,' he remarked lightly, and, somewhat to her discomfiture, came to sit beside her on the sofa where she had unthinkingly sunk down. 'Let me tell you, Lady Roxwell, with the utmost sincerity, that I believe, whatever your inward misgivings, you will always appear at ease in any company. You have a great deal of countenance, and a natural dignity.'

Hebe was so astonished that she could only stare wordlessly at him. A smile touched his lips, and he added, with a return to his usual mockery, 'Except, of course, when *my* appalling manners leave you totally at a loss, but take comfort in the thought that you are unlikely to encounter anything of that sort from anyone else.'

'That is reassuring, of course,' Hebe replied, doing her best to make a recovery, 'but even so—!'

'Let me explain to you,' he interrupted, 'why my mother believes it essential for Barbary to spend two or three weeks at Bath. The girl has lived all her life in the country—was not her visit with you to Cheltenham last year the first time she had ever stayed in a town?—and for obvious reasons has never experienced even the very limited social life one usually finds in a village community. My mother considers that rather than thrust her headlong into fashionable London society, we should first encourage her to spread her wings a little in a more limited sphere. That sounds to me like common sense.'

'Yes, indeed!' Hebe agreed earnestly. 'I will not conceal from you, sir, that it has had me in quite a worry, fearing that London life might turn Barbary's head, and encourage her to go beyond the line of what is proper. I am entirely in agreement with Lady Hendreth and very grateful to her, but as far as *I* am concerned—!'

'You don't feel that what applies to Barbary applies also to you? That a few weeks at Bath might enable you to face London with greater equanimity?'

'No, I do not,' she said crossly. 'I wish you would abandon this absurd notion, and turn your mind instead to the question of finding someone else to act as her chaperone.'

'Now don't be bird-witted!' he begged. 'How many women do you suppose I could approach with such a request? I've no sisters or sisters-in-law, my aunt won't do it, and *her* son's wife is bringing out one of her own girls this year. The chit can't hold a candle to Barbary, so the mother is not likely to be ready to oblige me. You will have to do it.' He saw that she was about to protest again, and went on before she could speak, 'What's become of your strong sense of duty? I thought you liked to be needed?'

'Sybilla and the twins,' Hebe replied with dignity, 'need me more than Barbary does. I could not go to London and leave them with a strange governess.'

'No need! They can all go with you. It will do the children good to see something of London, and Sybilla can have the kind of singing lessons you have so often told me her voice deserves.' He paused, regarding her with a satirical eye. 'And before you cast the boys in my face, allow me to point out that if you come to Bath this week, you may return in time to spend Easter with them here, and then remove to London as soon as they go back to Winchester.'

'I might have known,' Hebe said bitterly, 'that you would not listen to any objections I might make.'

'But I *have* listened,' he replied in an injured tone, 'I have listened, and I have smoothed all the obstacles from your path, but are you grateful to me? Not in the least!'

'*You* may call it smoothing the obstacles from my path. *I* call it brushing my wishes aside without one hint of compunction! And the reason you have done that, my lord, is so that you can bully me into doing what *you* wish to be done. Well, you will not succeed! I do not want to go to London, nor, with the greatest respect to Lady Hendreth, to Bath!'

'I know you don't,' he agreed cordially. 'You want to shut yourself away here and never face anything more demanding than a dinner party with the Lordes or old Gaynes and his wife, or a morning call at the rectory. You know, if you were so determined to renounce the world, you should have stayed in Italy, turned papist and immured yourself in a convent.'

Hebe eyed him with hostility. 'When I reflect, my lord, that I would then have been placed beyond the most remote possibility of ever being obliged to meet *you*, I can almost wish that I had done so. And I am not determined to renounce the world! As I have tried to explain to you, I have always been accustomed to live very quietly, just as I am doing here. It suits me admirably.'

'Does it?' he said sardonically. 'Have you paused to consider the future? You will stay here, devoting yourself to the children, mistress of the house only until Clement brings home a bride to supplant you, and then, when the twins have left the nest, you will either go back to Cambridge and devote yourself to good works, or take a house in this neighbourhood and allow yourself to be at the beck and call of all the young Roxwells and their families. Had you thought of that?'

She had, in a nebulous way, and had almost succeeded in convincing herself that, lacking a family of her own, she could count herself fortunate in having acquired one, but this comforting conviction was not proof against Hendreth's ruthless word-picture. She knew suddenly that she had been deluding herself, and, being unable to think of an acceptable alternative, was furious with him for forcing her to acknowledge it.

'Whether I have, sir, or have not,' she said angrily, 'I cannot conceive what it has to do with you.'

'I abhor waste,' he said frankly, 'and I could not reconcile it with my conscience to stand by and watch you dwindle into solitary middle-age without making some push to point out the error of your ways.'

'Oh, you are insufferable!' she exclaimed, springing to her feet and confronting him as he rose lazily from the sofa. 'If you have a conscience, which I very much doubt, I wonder that it does not reproach you for trying to order other people's lives just to suit your own convenience. For the last time, I will not go to Bath, and I will not go to London!'

There was a pause. They stood facing each other, she flushed and angry, he looking down at her with the sardonic curve of his lips very pronounced and a faint expression of scorn in his eyes. Then he said pityingly, 'I know you won't! You have many admirable qualities, Lady Roxwell, but one fault which outweighs them all. You are a coward!'

'A—a coward?' Hebe was stammering with fury, and could scarcely get the words out. 'How dare you say such a thing to me!'

'A coward,' he repeated ruthlessly. 'It takes courage to leave a snug little harbour and venture out upon seas which may prove stormy. Never mind! We cannot help our natures, and no blame attaches to you because you lack that courage. I will consult my mother, and see if *she* can think of someone who will be willing to make herself responsible for Barbary.'

Hebe's temper, in spite of her coppery hair, was not generally ungovernable, and though Hendreth had frequently vexed her in the past, she had hitherto been able to relieve her feelings by paying him back in his own coin with some barbed retort. This time, however, possibly because there was a grain of truth in what he said, he had made her so angry that she was incapable of coherent thought, and plunged headlong into the trap he had quite deliberately set for her.

'You will do no such thing! I intend to make you eat those words, my lord! You will oblige me by telling Mr Benchley that I will take the house he has found, and by being ready to escort Barbary and me to Bath on Thursday.'

By the time they reached Bath, Hebe was in a quivering state of nerves, and bitterly regretting that she had allowed Hendreth to taunt her into agreeing to the visit. She had begun to regret it as soon as her temper cooled, and only pride, and a determination not to let him get the better of her, had prevented her from retracting, but in the bustle of preparation, and all the arrangements to be made for her absence from Astington Park, she had had no leisure to indulge it. Once they were on their way, however, and she had little to engage her attention but the passing scenery, all her doubts returned with redoubled force.

She had nothing to distract her from them. Hendreth had lent his own luxurious chaise for the journey, but since he preceded it, driving the curricle in which he had come from Bath, and had yielded to Barbary's entreaties to be allowed to accompany him—he had taken her driving once or twice the previous autumn—Hebe found herself with only the servants, Lucia and Miss Roxwell's abigail, for company. Hendreth, having told his ward she could go with him as long as she behaved herself, and Lady Roxwell had no objection, informed Hebe, as he handed her up into the chaise, that she would probably be more comfortable alone, Barbary having remarked that to sit still in a closed carriage for hours on end drove her to distraction. This was undoubtedly true, but even Barbary's fidgets would, Hebe thought regretfully, have done something to distract her from her own thoughts.

Her emotions were once again in turmoil, showing her how superficial the seeming contentment of the past few months had been. Apart from her misgivings about being thrust into fashionable society, she was longing for news of Geoffrey, and yet at the same time dreading it, convinced at one moment that he had deceived her, and the next that they had been parted by malice or misfortune. She found herself alternately on the heights and in the depths, and despised herself for feelings more appropriate to Barbary's age than to her own. It was all Hendreth's fault, she thought resentfully. He who had cut up her comfort with his ruthless interference, his

complete lack of courtesy or conscience, his heartless indifference to anyone's convenience but his own. She concentrated
her thoughts resolutely on his lordship's shortcomings, doing
her best to ignore the voice of common sense which reminded
her that Hendreth was in no way to blame for what had
happened in Rome.

Lady Hendreth's house was in Laura Place, and Hebe
alighted at its door feeling quite sick with apprehension and
excitement. The groom was just driving the curricle away,
and Hendreth, having taken his ward into the house, came out
again to escort Hebe indoors. Critically studying her, he said
with his usual lack of ceremony, 'My mother will be resting
before dressing for dinner, and I advise you to do the same.
You look tired.'

'Thank you,' Hebe replied bitterly. 'Your lordship knows
precisely how to inspire confidence. Why not tell me I look a
complete fright, and have done with it?'

'Because my insults are never gratuitous, and that is an
accusation unlikely ever to be levelled against you.' They
were bowed into the house by the butler, and found a pleasant-
faced housekeeper awaiting them. 'Ah, Mrs Balham! Be good
enough to take Lady Roxwell and Miss Roxwell to their
rooms. Her ladyship is tired after the journey and just a trifle
naggy, but you will know how to make her comfortable.'

Hebe cast him a dagger-look, which made him laugh, and
followed the housekeeper up the stairs. The house was large
and handsome and furnished with great elegance, not in the
least like Hebe's mental picture of the retreat of a middle-
aged widow in delicate health, but Mrs Balham spared no
effort to make sure that the guests were comfortable, and
Barbary, a trifle subdued by her surroundings, was on her
best behaviour. Everything should have combined to set Hebe
at her ease, but the knot of tension within her continued to
tighten, and though she dreaded the first meeting with her
hostess, it was almost a relief when the time came to join
Lady Hendreth in the drawing room.

Before leaving her own room, she sent Lucia to fetch
Barbary, and looked first critically and then with approval at
the girl's simple but elegant dress of white muslin with its tiny
puffed sleeves and triple flounce at the hem. It was trimmed

with lace and rose-coloured ribbon, a matching ribbon was threaded through Barbary's black curls, and a shawl of Norwich silk draped round her shoulders. She looked beautiful, youthful and charming, and Hebe, catching a glimpse of her own reflection in the mirror close by, suffered a pang of envy as sharp as it was unexpected. Her evening gown of black satin was extremely fashionable, and so was the black silk turban ornamented with jet, but they looked sombre and— Hendreth's words echoed in her memory—middle-aged. How foolish, then, was the tremulous hope which she could no longer deny; the hope that somehow, now that she was emerging into society again, the misery and humiliation of her parting from Geoffrey might be explained away.

They found Hendreth already in the drawing room, and Hebe's immediate impression was that mother and son were strikingly alike, but a moment later she realized that the resemblance existed only in colouring and expression. Lady Hendreth's hair was liberally streaked with grey, but it was easy to see that it had once been the same dark red as his, while the warm brown of the eyes was identical. The likeness ended there. Her features were finely chiselled, lined more, it seemed, by ill health than by age; she was slightly built, and very thin; and the hand she extended in greeting looked too fragile for the heavy rings upon it; yet she was clearly no house-bound invalid. Her clothes were as modish as Hebe's own. She welcomed her guests warmly, and Hebe reflected that wherever his lordship had acquired his eccentric manners, it was not from his parent.

She had not expected to like Lady Hendreth, but from the very first found herself drawn to the older woman almost against her will. She had the impression that her ladyship was a tolerant observer of life, her judgements kindly, and leavened with humour, and it was plain that a very strong bond of affection and understanding did indeed exist between her and her son. He made no attempt to abate his abrupt outspokenness in her presence, but there was a subtle difference between his attitude towards her and towards the rest of the world.

Barbary was a little shy of her hostess at first, but soon recovered sufficiently to confide to her how much she had enjoyed the journey to Bath, and how Lord Hendreth had promised to teach her to drive. Hebe, to whom the sporting curricles and high-perch phaetons which were Hendreth's favourite mode of transport seemed appallingly dangerous, looked alarmed at this, a fact not lost upon his lordship, who said mockingly, 'Lady Roxwell does not approve. Reassure her, ma'am, that it is quite acceptable for a lady to handle the ribbons provided she has a reliable groom in attendance, and that for Barbary to do so will cause no one to hold up their hands in horror.'

Hebe cast him a quelling look. 'It is the danger of such an undertaking, sir, which concerns me, not its propriety.'

'Not concerned with propriety?' he repeated, shaking his head. 'Madam, you shock me!'

'Impossible!' she retorted, and then coloured slightly, glancing uneasily at Lady Hendreth. 'I beg your pardon, ma'am.'

'Not at all, Lady Roxwell.' Lady Hendreth seemed amused. 'You are quite right, of course. He is not in the least shocked, and said that only to be provoking. But I believe you need have no apprehension on Miss Roxwell's account. In competent hands, these sporting carriages are not nearly as dangerous as they look.'

'Oh, Aunt Hebe, of course they are not,' Barbary put in impetuously, 'and it is something I have always longed to do, ever since Mr Lorde took me up once in his curricle when I was quite a little girl. I thought *he* might teach me, and last summer asked him if he would, but he said he could not spare the time.'

Hebe was so appalled by the narrowness of this escape, and by the thought of what the Misses Nidwell would have had to say if Barbary had been seen driving about the countryside with Robert Lorde, that she could not summon up the spirit to make any further protest. Encountering Hendreth's ironic glance, she knew he had guessed what she was thinking, and she wondered if he had agreed to teach Barbary to drive in order to forestall any attempt on her part to persuade some future admirer to do so. She could think of no other reason for him to be so obliging.

When they returned to the drawing room after dinner, Lady Hendreth began to describe some of the entertainments she had in mind for her guests. The season, she said, was only just beginning, but Hebe, listening to the various events which her ladyship was so tranquilly enumerating, could only marvel at the stamina which the supposed invalids who frequented the spa apparently possessed. Hendreth, watching her from beneath lazily drooping eyelids, presently intervened to say in an amused tone, 'Be careful, Mama! I should have warned you that I experienced the greatest difficulty in persuading Lady Roxwell to emerge from suclusion and widen her horizons to include Bath and, eventually, London. We don't want to frighten her.'

Hebe looked indignant and Barbary giggled, but Lady Hendreth shook her head reprovingly.

'Her ladyship has been in mourning, Blaise,' she said quietly. 'A widow grows accustomed to living retired, and it requires a certain effort to take up the threads of one's social life again. And am I not correct, Lady Roxwell, in thinking that you had only emerged from a previous period of mourning shortly before your husband's death? I am sure Mr Fernhurst, whom you may remember calling upon you when he was in Rome last year, told me that you travelled to Italy with your brother, who had died there.'

The moment had come, far sooner than she had expected. She was not ready for it! Could not sit there speaking calmly of Geoffrey as though he were a casual acquaintance whom it required an effort to remember. She could not—yet even as her panic-stricken thoughts scurried to and fro like startled rabbits, and her heart thudded somewhere in the region of her throat, she found herself doing exactly that, while one corner of her mind was absurdly recalling Hendreth's words to her a few days before '. . . whatever your inward misgivings, you will always appear at ease . . .'

'Yes, that is true. Felix was mortally ill before we left England, but he was so eager to visit Greece, which, thanks so Sir Hugo's kindness, we were able to do, that I never regretted making the journey.'

Except that it brought me to an empty marriage and a forbidden love, brief happiness and enduring pain, and now, in the course of time, has brought me here, to this drawing room in Bath, and perhaps to an answer to the question which has tormented me for a year . . .

She heard herself say quite calmly, 'I believe Mr Fernhurst told me that your ladyship is a close friend of one of his aunts, who also resides at Bath. I trust all is well with him? He left Rome, I was told, only a few days after Sir Hugo died, at which time, of course, I was not receiving callers.'

'I believe he is very well,' Lady Hendreth replied. 'He called upon me last summer, shortly after his return to England. He has not been in Bath since then, though his aunt, Mrs Barrington, tells me she expects him to bring his wife to visit her later in the spring.'

It was strange, Hebe thought with an odd sense of detachment, that a mortal blow could strike yet inflict no pain. Just a numbness, a stillness, as though life itself had been halted by those two brief words, 'his wife'. She felt as though she was suspended in a cold, dark emptiness, and though she knew she ought to make some response, her wits seemed as numb as her emotions, utterly paralysed. Then gradually she became aware again of her surroundings, and found she was looking straight into Hendreth's eyes. He was sitting beside his mother on a sofa facing the one occupied by Hebe herself and Barbary; lounging there with one arm stretched casually along the sofa's back, yet there was nothing casual in his hard, faintly questioning gaze. That realization jerked Hebe into a sense of self-preservation, for among all the people she would not wish to guess her secret, Blaise Hendreth held pride of place. She managed to say with tolerable composure, 'I was not aware that Mr Fernhurst was married. His wife was not with him in Rome.'

'No, their wedding only took place last autumn,' Lady Hendreth explained, apparently unaware of any oddity in her guest's manner, 'although the marriage was arranged years ago by their respective families. Mrs Fernhurst is very young. They were married on her eighteenth birthday.'

'She is also very rich,' Hendreth added cynically. 'A great heiress, and her father so morbidly afraid of her falling victim to a fortune-hunter that he arranged this marriage with Fernhurst—the two families are neighbours—before she was out of the nursery. A queer start, I've always thought, for the

Fernhursts are by no means plump in the pocket, and Geoffrey Fernhurst certainly has an eye to the main chance.'

'He was only a schoolboy when the marriage was arranged,' his mother reminded him. 'In any event, I am not entirely sure that you are right about him.'

'Good God, Mama! Of course I am right,' he said impatiently. 'You have only to see how he toadeats Mrs Barrington. You surely don't believe he would dance attendance on her as he does if she were not a rich, childless widow?'

Hebe sat with bent head, staring down at her hands clasped tightly together in her lap. She was still numb with shock, so that though she heard Hendreth's strictures upon Geoffrey they made very little impression on her at the time, her whole attention being concentrated upon not betraying herself. She was profoundly grateful when Barbary drew their companions' notice towards herself by saying suddenly, 'Well, I think it is horrid! Horrid, and quite abominably Gothic! *I* would not submit tamely to being handed over like—like a parcel, to some man my father had chosen for me. This young lady must be very poor-spirited!'

'It is possible, of course,' Hendreth said scathingly, 'that she is merely obedient, and imbued with proper respect for parental authority. What would *you* do, if I decided to arrange a marriage for you?'

Barbary hesitated, looking consideringly at him, a mischievous little smile tugging at the corners of her mouth. 'I don't think I will tell you,' she said candidly at length, 'for then you would know what to expect and how to stop me. Besides, you are not going to arrange a marriage for me, are you?'

'I might,' he retorted, 'if I could think of anyone I dislike sufficiently to inflict you upon. And that was not meant to be a compliment, you baggage!'

Hebe listened with determined attention to this exchange. She knew she must not allow herself to think. Not now. Not until she was safe in the privacy of her bedchamber. If she concentrated only upon what was being said, closing her mind to the bitter thoughts clamouring just beyond the edge of consciousness, she might be able to get through the rest of the evening without giving her secret away.

Get through it she did, though the effort required was so great that by the time she found herself alone she felt exhausted. When Lucia finally left her—for not even Lucia must suspect anything amiss—Hebe lay staring into the darkness and faced the fact that there had been no misunderstanding, no malicious intervention. Her first, instinctive reaction to Geoffrey's abrupt departure from Rome had been the right one.

The numbness of shock had passed by that time, and now that she had acknowledged the truth she waited for the pain to come, the familiar, remembered anguish which ought to be so much sharper now that the last hope had been slain. She felt nothing. No, that was not true. Emotion of some sort was kindling within her, though it was a little while before she realized what it was. Anger. Anger at Geoffrey for his heartless, calculated betrayal; anger at herself for being so gullible, and even more for cherishing a foolish, sentimental hope that matters were as she wished them to be rather than as they were. A hope which—she could admit it now—she had been using simply to try to restore to life feelings which had perished in misery and humiliation more than a year ago. Now she could come to terms with what had happened. Her anger was a cleansing, cauterizing emotion, and though the experience would leave a lasting scar, the wound itself would soon heal. The sense of release was overwhelming.

She slept well, and woke in a purposeful frame of mind, surprising Lucia, when asked what she wished to wear, by saying briskly, 'A walking-dress. It does not matter which. I am going out to buy some new clothes, for if I am to chaperone Miss Roxwell to parties it is time I put off my blacks. I will ask Lady Hendreth where the best shops are to be found.'

Her ladyship, warmly commending Hebe's intention, suggested Milsom Street, and also furnished her with the name and direction of her own modiste. Hebe invited Barbary to accompany her, but was not in the least surprised when this was declined in favour of going out with Hendreth in the curricle for a first lesson in handling the ribbons. What did surprise Hebe was his lordship's prompt redemption of a promise which she had supposed he had made reluctantly, for she had never expected to see him in the role of indulgent guardian.

She spent a pleasurable morning, and made so many purchases that the footman provided by Lady Hendreth to attend her, since in the steep, cobbled streets of Bath carriages were seldom used, could carry only a small proportion of them. There were enough, however, for her to discard her mourning as soon as she returned to Laura Place, and, on being informed that a light nuncheon was about to be served, to go down to the breakfast parlour in an elegant gown of silver grey silk and a lace cap far more frivolous than anything she had worn since returning to England. She was pleased with the effect, but even so was mildly surprised when her altered appearance won typically outspoken praise from Hendreth, whom she encountered at the head of the stairs. He looked her over with a critical eye and then said approvingly, 'Oh, very becoming! Young Barbary will have to look to her laurels, or she will be quite outshone.'

'Pray do not be absurd!' Hebe spoke sharply, annoyed by her own satisfaction at this improperly worded compliment. 'I have no intention of trying to compete with Barbary. That would be quite ineligible!'

'Quite!' he agreed sympathetically. 'You know, that's a devilish fetching cap! Much more appealing than the turban you were wearing last night. That made you look like a dowager.'

'That turban, my lord,' Hebe said coldly, beginning to descend the stairs, 'is in the very latest mode.'

'I dare say it is—for a lady well past her prime. You'll need many more years in your dish, my girl, before you have to take to headgear of that sort.' Hebe cast a very speaking glance at him over her shoulder, but he only grinned unrepentantly. 'No need to give me dagger-looks! That was meant as a compliment.'

'I am so glad you explained that,' she said brightly. 'Your lordship's mode of expression is so original that one sometimes has difficulty in distinguishing compliments from insults.'

'Vixen!' he remarked affably, following her down the stairs and then going ahead to open the door of the breakfast parlour for her, adding provocatively as she went past him into the room, 'At least that is an accusation which can never be levelled against your ladyship.'

His mother's presence prevented her from replying in kind, so she loftily ignored both words and speaker as she went to take her place at the table. Lady Hendreth regarded her approvingly and remarked that she had obviously spent a successful morning, while Barbary, staring in astonishment, so far forgot herself as to say badly, 'Aunt Hebe, how different you look! And so much younger!'

'Don't tell her that!' Hendreth said urgently, feigning alarm. 'Lady Roxwell sets great store by her advanced years, and may imagine she has fallen into the error of dressing too youthfully. Some elderly ladies, you know, are unwise enough to do that, but I am sure she would not wish to be one of them.'

Barbary broke into a ripple of laughter, but though Lady Hendreth smiled, she said in a tone of mild reproof, 'I feel quite sure that Lady Roxwell, when at last the time comes to consider herself elderly, will not be guilty of such an error of taste.' To Hebe she added, 'Do not regard his nonsense, my dear. I have told him more than once that levity sometimes carries him too far.'

'I do not regard it, ma'am,' Hebe assured her lightly. 'I believe I am now sufficiently well acquainted with Lord Hendreth to have grown accustomed to his orignal manner of expressing himself. It is a trifle disconcerting at first, of course.'

'*You* were never disconcerted,' Blaise said cheerfully. 'From the moment of our meeting you gave me my own again in no uncertain fashion, and have continued to do so ever since. It is one of the things I particularly like about you.'

Hebe was vexed to feel her cheeks growing warm, but retorted with spirit, 'That, my lord, was due to nothing more than an instinct for self-preservation, for had I *not* retaliated in kind, I would have been completely overborne. I had never in my life addressed anyone in that fashion, and still am not certain which shocked me more, *your* extraordinary remarks or the replies I was goaded into making.'

'Come, come, my lady!' he admonished her, with a laughing look in direct contrast to his tone. 'My mother will be wondering in just what kind of verbal fisticuffs we engaged at that first meeting.' He lifted a quizzical eyebrow at his parent, and added reassuringly, 'Her ladyship expressed herself with considerable force, Mama, but only within the bounds of propriety, I promise you.'

'It is quite unnecessary, Blaise, for you to tell me *that*,' Lady Hendreth informed him, 'and I only wish I could be certain that the same applies to you. Now that is quite enough! I am accustomed to your teasing, but Lady Roxwell is not!'

He laughed, but said no more, allowing Barbary, who was bursting with eagerness to describe her morning, to do so without interruption. Hebe listened with only partial attention, for she was pondering Lady Hendreth's last remark. Were Hendreth's provocative remarks no more than teasing? Hebe did not know, for she had no previous experience on which to draw. Felix had been of too serious a turn of mind to indulge in elder-brotherly banter, while any tendency to levity on Hebe's part had been kindly but instantly repressed. It occurred to her now, for the first time, that until just lately laughter had played very little part in her life.

That afternoon Lady Hendreth received a visit from an old friend, Mrs Delaford; a visit which Hebe suspected had been prearranged for Barbary's benefit, since the caller was accompanied by her daughter, Amy, a pretty, fair-haired girl of eighteen. To Hebe's relief, for she had been uncertain how well Barbary, accustomed to the rule the roost in her own family, would get on with other girls of her own age, the young ladies took to each other immediately, and were soon chatting animatedly on a sofa a little removed from where their elders were sitting. Lady Hendreth regarded them indulgently, and confirmed Hebe's suspicion by saying indulgently, 'Very promising! It will be an excellent thing for Miss Roxwell to make friends, for as I told you, Maria, for most of their lives, she and her brothers and sisters have had only each other for company.'

Mrs Delaford nodded understandingly. 'I can imagine nothing more daunting for a girl than to be thrust into her first season, knowing no one.' She added to Hebe, 'Amy, too, is to make her come-out this year, Lady Roxwell. We remove to London just before Easter.'

'Do you live in Bath, ma'am?' Hebe inquired politely.

'No, in Wiltshire, but my mother resides here and we are all accustomed to making frequent visits. That is why Amy has such a large circle of acquaintances in the town.'

'Lady Roxwell is in need of a governess for Miss Roxwell's younger sisters,' Lady Hendreth put in, 'and it occurs to me, Maria, that Miss Stillwood will soon be seeking a new situation.'

'Yes, indeed,' Mrs Delaford agreed, and turned to Hebe. 'Miss Stillwood has been with me twelve years, ma'am, but Amy is the youngest child and so her duties are coming to an end. She is an excellent woman, highly qualified and, I may add, held in the greatest affection and esteem by all my family. I feel sure you would find her eminently suitable.'

Hebe thanked her, and before the visitors took their leave it was arranged that Miss Stillwood should wait upon her the following afternoon. It was also arranged between the two girls that they would meet next morning at the Pump Room, where Amy expected to be in attendance on her grandmother.

On the following morning, therefore, Hebe and Barbary, escorted by Hendreth, walked to the Pump Room, while Lady Hendreth was conveyed there in her sedan-chair. Hebe had been considerably surprised to find his lordship prepared to accompany them, for she had supposed him to have little patience with such tame proceedings, but when she ventured to say so, he replied that since he had many acquaintances in Bath, it behoved him to pay his respects to as many as he might encounter at the Pump Room. He could not imagine, he added in a saddened tone, what had led Lady Roxwell to suppose him to be rag-mannered.

Hebe gasped, turning an indignant glance towards him. 'Well, upon my word! What reason, my lord, have you ever given me to suppose otherwise! You insulted me the very moment we met, you boast that you are uncivil to everyone—!'

'Not boast,' he interrupted reproachfully. 'I *told* you so, I admit, but only because you questioned me on the subject. That cannot be described as boasting.'

'Well, perhaps not, but you seem to take pride—!' She detected a quizzical look in his eyes, and checked for a

moment before adding in a scolding tone, 'You are quite
abominable!'

'I know,' he agreed sympathetically, 'but how can I resist
it when you *will* persist in taking me so seriously? Come,
now! Confess that you were on the point of apologizing to me
just then for having accused me of anything as ill bred as
boasting.'

Since she had been about to do exactly that, Hebe bit her
lip in mortification, but after feeling totally nonplussed for a
moment or two, was inspired to retort sweetly, 'Oh, no, my
lord, not ill bred! Only an excessively *well*-bred person could
be as uncivil as you are, and still be received.'

He gave an appreciative chuckle. 'You know, that's very
good! You have a waspish tongue yourself at times, my
lady.'

'Only, I trust—I most devoutly trust—when you, sir, are at
hand to provoke me. I have a lowering suspicion that your
incivility is infectious.'

He nodded understandingly. 'Like measles! Do you think
there is any hope that we shall spread an epidemic?'

The picture thus conjured up was so ridiculous that Hebe
burst out laughing, though she informed him severely that he
ought to have said 'danger' instead of 'hope'. He would not
agree, and only their arrival at the Pump Room rescued her
from an argument which she did not think she could win.

Hebe had supposed, though without giving it a great deal
of thought, that all the habitués of the Pump Room would be
elderly or invalids or both, but though the larger proportion of
the company could be so described, there were a number of
persons present who were neither. Most of them were females,
but Hendreth was by no means the only younger man to be
seen; there were, in fact, several a good deal younger, either
acting as escorts to the older ladies, or paying court to the
young ones.

Amy Delaford was soon discovered, seated beside an old
lady wearing a yellow wig. Lady Hendreth's party joined
them, introductions were performed and chairs procured for
their ladyships, and then Hendreth went to obtain for his
mother a glass of the hot spring water from the pumper whose
duty it was to dispense it. Before doing so, he asked Hebe if

he could perform the same service for her, assuring her
earnestly that the Bath waters were held to be of the greatest
benefit to those no longer young. She politely declined, though
with so flashing a glance from her fine blue eyes that he went
away chuckling.

Amy, released by their arrival from her grandmother's
side, had taken the opportunity to lead Barbary away to meet
some of her own friends, and Miss Roxwell was soon drawn
into an animated group. Hebe, mindful of her responsibilities,
cast frequent, rather anxious looks in her direction, and this
watchfulness did not go unremarked in one quarter. A little
later, when they had left Amy's grandmother and were making their way across the room towards some other of Lady
Hendreth's friends, Blaise said softly in Hebe's ear, 'Relax
your vigilance, ma'am! You are the girl's chaperone, not her
gaoler.'

She looked quickly up at him, torn between vexation and
anxiety. 'I cannot help being uneasy. Recollect that she has
never before been into company.'

'I see no cause for alarm. Her manners now leave nothing
to be desired—something which scarcely seemed possible, six
months ago.'

'Her manners are charming, I agree, but her nature is
unchanged, and I fear that if she is put out, her temper may
betray her into unbecoming conduct.'

'Never!' he said decisively. 'That little minx is too clever
to do anything to spoil her own chances.' He saw that Hebe
looked doubtful, and added with what she considered to be
odious assurance, 'Don't believe me, do you? Just wait and
see.'

It seemed, in the days which followed, that his lordship's
confidence was justified. Barbary was much admired, but
though most of the young men, and some older ones, were
soon competing for her attention, she somehow avoided alien-
ating the other girls. It seemed to Hebe, torn between pride
and uneasiness, that only she could see that Barbary did
nothing spontaneously. She had selected a role for herself and
was playing it with the skill of a born actress, captivating
young and old alike; growing a little more confident each day;

practising the part which would be hers in London. Yes,
Hebe thought, Barbary was clever. She wished that she could
rid herself of the conviction that Barbary was calculating.

Yet in spite of this vague disquiet, Hebe found to her
surprise that she was enjoying her stay in Bath. Her immediate liking for Lady Hendreth deepened as they came to know
each other better. She felt that here was a woman whom she
could truly regard as a friend, and, insensibly reassured by
her ladyship's tactful support, found her introduction into
Bath society less of an ordeal than she had anticipated. Even
Hendreth himself, in spite of his unpredictable and usually
maddening ways, proved an unexpected source of encourage-
ment, though Hebe was never quite sure whether this was
intentional or accidental.

She was astonished at the fullness of her hostess's social
round, for as well as the Pump Room, and the fashionable
libraries which were as much places to meet one's friends as
to borrow books, there was the theatre to visit, the Sydney
Garden with its grottoes, labyrinths and waterfalls to walk in
when the weather was fine, and private parties to attend.
Dinner parties, rout parties, informal dances for the young
people (it was not considered proper for girls not yet 'out' to
attend public balls at the Assembly Rooms) and, during the
day, riding parties to places of interest in the surrounding
countryside. To the latter, Hebe was naturally unable to
accompany her charge, and this caused her such misgiving
that, the first time such an expedition was proposed, she felt
reluctantly obliged to admit his lordship to her confidence.

He brushed her qualms aside without ceremony. 'No reason in the world why you should accompany her if you don't
wish to. My mother will send a trustworthy groom, and I dare
say Mrs Delaford will do the same.' He saw the relief which
for an unguarded moment Hebe had allowed to show in her
face, and added abruptly, 'Don't you care for riding?'

She hesitated, reluctant to reply with an untruth in which
she might later be caught out, and equally unwilling to confess her inability. The hesitation was her undoing; Hendreth
said shrewdly, 'Or don't you ride at all?'

'No,' she said crossly. 'I have never learned how.' He

looked astonished, and she added defensively, 'I always lived in a town, and my father kept no stable. I had no opportunity.'

'Well, if you are to live in the country you will need to learn. No point in starting before you go to London, but when you return to Astington in the summer, I'll see about finding a suitable mount for you. And don't talk any flummery to me about being too old,' he added warningly as she opened her lips to protest.

'I *am* too old,' she retorted. 'I quite see the advantages of being able to ride, and indeed, since coming to Astington I have frequently wished that I could, but if you imagine that I will allow myself to appear ridiculous by engaging someone to give me lessons in an accomplishment which all my neighbours appear to have acquired in the nursery, you are very far out in your reckoning.'

'Oh, I don't propose that you hire a riding-master,' he said calmly. 'I'll teach you myself.'

'You?' she said blankly. 'Why in the world should you do such a thing?'

He grinned at her. 'Would you believe me if I said it would give me great pleasure?'

'No,' she replied baldly, then, changing her mind, added bitterly, 'Yes, I would, for it would give you an unrivalled opportunity to berate and bully me.'

'Lady Roxwell!' he said reproachfully. 'When have I ever done such a thing?'

'When have you ever done anything else? Oh, I know you say you are no more uncivil to me than to anyone else, but if that is true, my lord, I am astonished that anyone of your acquaintance still acknowledges you!'

He knit his brows in apparent perplexity. 'I don't follow your reasoning, ma'am. *You* still do so.'

Hebe did not deign to reply.

Lady Hendreth, besides taking her guests to parties in other people's houses, had already begun making plans to hold one of her own. She described it as a rout-party, but since a small orchestra had been engaged and the guests included most of the young people with whom Barbary had become acquainted, it was taken for granted that dancing would play a large part in the evening's entertainment.

Her ladyship compiled her guest list with a skill which left Hebe lost in admiration, for it encompassed, in the number of some fifty persons, not only Barbary's contemporaries but also their parents' and even grandparents' generation. Hebe wondered how so varied a company could be entertained, but Lady Hendreth had no such doubts. The two drawing rooms, with the doors between them set wide, would accommodate the main part of the company, supper would be taken in the dining room, and there would be card-tables set up in the library for those whose tastes lay in that direction.

'Though I trust, Blaise,' Lady Hendreth warned her son at breakfast that morning, 'that *you* do not intend to spend the whole evening there. It would present a very odd appearance.'

'The appearance presented would be even more odd, Mama, if I were to join in the dancing with a set of boys and girls barely out of the schoolroom,' he replied dryly. 'I will engage, however, to do my duty by helping to entertain the dowagers.'

Barbary made a little grimace of disappointment, and said coaxingly, 'Will you not dance even *one* dance with me, sir? Lady Hendreth has been kind enough to say she is giving this party for me. It is my very first, and, after all, you *are* my guardian.'

'Least of all with you, my child,' he replied coolly. 'I make it a rule never to dance with ladies whose heads do not reach as high as my shoulder.' He glanced at Hebe. 'Now, if Lady Roxwell will be kind enough to stand up with me—?'

Hebe shook her head. 'I fear I must decline, sir. Your lordship will have observed, as I have, that chaperones do not dance.'

'Tonight my mother will be Barbary's chaperone, so for once you may consider yourself released from your duties.'

'I will do no such thing!' she said indignantly. 'It would be quite infamous to expect Lady Hendreth to burden herself with *my* responsibilities in addition to her obligations as hostess. I am astonished that you should suggest it!'

'Are you, ma'am?' he replied curtly, 'I was under the impression that no lack of consideration on my part could astonish you.'

She looked up in quick surprise, for he seemed genuinely annoyed, and so in place of the sharp answer she might have returned, she said placatingly, 'Even though I cannot feel it would be proper for me to dance, I do understand what you mean. I can well remember how uncomfortable it is to stand up with a partner shorter than oneself.'

'From the far-off days of your youth, no doubt,' he agreed caustically. 'How glad you must be that advancing years and the responsibility of your adoptive family now make it unnecessary for you to endure such embarrassment.'

'May I remind you, my lord,' Hebe replied stiffly, vexed to find her tentative olive branch so brusquely spurned, 'that it was your lordship who was obliging enough to point out that I stand to your wards in the relationship of a great-aunt?'

'Oh, good God! Am I never to be allowed to forget that singularly inept jest?' he exclaimed angrily. He thrust back his chair and got up, adding curtly, 'Ladies, I must beg you to excuse me. I have matters to attend to which will occupy me all day.'

He went out. There was a little silence, and then Barbary asked in a subdued tone if she, too, might be excused. She had promised to go walking with Amy Delaford. Hebe agreed absently, and then, when the door had closed behind the girl, said in the tone of one anxious for reassurance, 'I fear I have vexed Lord Hendreth, but I *am* right, am I not, in thinking it would be improper for me to dance tonight?'

Her ladyship shook her head. 'Not improper,' she said judiciously, 'though among so youthful a company it might, as Hendreth himself pointed out only a few minutes ago, present a somewhat odd appearance. You reminded him of that, which is probably why he was so vexed.' She hesitated for a moment, and then went on, 'I trust, though, that you will not take it amiss if I say that, however improperly expressed, there is a good deal of truth in what he says. You *are* too young to regard yourself as nothing more than a duenna for Barbary Roxwell and her sisters.'

'They have no one else,' Hebe said pleadingly, 'and it was Lord Hendreth's own wish that I should chaperone Barbary. I begged him to find some other lady to do so, but he said he knew of none.'

'That is quite true,' Lady Hendreth admitted, 'and it is also true that as their great-uncle's widow, you are the most proper person to have charge of them. That is not quite what I meant.' She hesitated again, obviously choosing her words with care. 'I hope, my dear, you will not feel, if I venture to offer you a little advice, that I am busying myself in matters which are not my concern. My only desire is to stand your friend.'

'No, indeed!' Hebe said vehemently. 'I shall be most grateful. I *told* Lord Hendreth I did not know how to go on in fashionable society!'

Lady Hendreth smiled. 'My dear Lady Roxwell,' she said with some amusement, 'I would not venture to presume to criticize your conduct, even if there were any cause for criticism. No, the advice I wish to give you is this. When you go to London, do not feel, just because Miss Roxwell is in your charge, that you are obliged to confine your own circle of acquaintances to the parents of her contemporaries. You will meet many congenial persons far nearer to you in age.'

'Will I, ma'am?' Hebe said doubtfully, 'I dare say you are right, and yet I have a melancholy suspicion that I shall fit in nowhere.'

'Now that,' Lady Hendreth said firmly, 'is a great piece of nonsense! I shall write to Lady Felchester—who, I may say, knows *everyone*—and beg her to make certain that you do not dwindle into a mere duenna. After all, if you were Miss Roxwell's elder sister, even a *widowed* elder sister, you would neither expect, nor be expected to consort only with dowagers and middle-aged matrons. You have as much right as she has to enjoy the coming season.'

Hebe, somewhat taken aback by this novel point of view, said with an ingenuousness which made the elder woman smile, 'I have no expectation of *enjoying* myself, ma'am.'

'Why not?' Lady Hendreth asked unanswerably. 'I flatter myself that you are finding a certain degree of enjoyment in the very mild entertainment I am able to offer you.'

'Yes, indeed,' Hebe assured her emphatically. 'Your ladyship is everything that is kind, but—!'

'Yet I believe,' her hostess continued inexorably, 'that you had as little expectation of enjoying a visit to Bath as you appear to expect in London.' She saw that Hebe looked conscience-stricken, and added in explanation, 'Hendreth told me that he experienced the greatest difficulty in persuading you to come.'

Hebe reflected that 'persuade' was not the word she would have used to describe his lordship's methods, but one could scarcely tell Lady Hendreth so. She said uncomfortably, 'I *was* unwilling to leave Astington Park, but not because I was ungrateful for your very kind invitation. And I was *not*, whatever Lord Hendreth may suppose, endeavouring to renounce the world.'

'Is that what he said?' His lordship's mother sounded amused. 'That was too severe, for in the first year of widowhood it is not permissible to do anything but live very quietly, but it would not do, you know, to bury yourself in the country for the rest of your days. Though I understand from my son that you enjoy country life?'

Hebe nodded. 'Yes, I do. I have been very happy at Astington.'

'It is an excellent thing,' her ladyship admitted cautiously, 'if one *can* enjoy living in the country. I fear I always detested it, even as a girl, and when my late husband took me to Abbotswood for the first time, I knew at once that I could never be happy there. That great, gloomy house—parts of it, you know, are nearly *six hundred* years old—and the dreadful winters! And each year only a scant six weeks in London during the season! I cannot tell you how much I hated it! With Hendreth, of course, it is quite otherwise, but in that respect he is very like his father.'

Hebe looked puzzled. '*Is* Lord Hendreth so deeply attached to his home? Forgive me, but I understood that he spends much time travelling abroad.'

'Too much,' Lady Hendreth agreed emphatically, 'but his estates mean a great deal to him none the less. Of course, I know that once he is married he will settle in England for good, for he has told me so.'

Hebe blinked at her in astonishment. '*Is* Lord Hendreth to be married, ma'am?'

'Not that I know of,' his mother admitted sadly. 'I *do* wish he would, for I long to have grandchildren, but to tell you the truth, Lady Roxwell, I am beginning to despair of his ever finding a bride.'

'But surely,' Hebe was puzzled, 'a man in Lord Hendreth's position would have no difficulty in arranging a suitable marriage?'

Her ladyship sighed. 'None whatsoever, but unfortunately my son holds very strong views on the subject of marriages arranged solely for practical reasons, with little or no affection upon either side.' She hesitated, as though debating how far to confide in her companion, and then added in a deliberately colourless tone, 'My own marriage was of that kind and it was—not happy. Blaise does not forget that.'

Hebe digested this in silence, thinking that this must be the reason for Hendreth's contemptuous dismissal of her own marriage, and intrigued by the novel view of him presented by his mother's words. He was right, of course, as she knew from her own experience, but he was the last person she would have expected to remain single unless he could marry for love. She found it almost impossible to picture him paying court to a girl, or competing successfully against gentlemen with more engaging manners and greater address, for though Hebe was not naive enough to suppose that a man in his thirties had had no amorous adventures, in affairs of that kind his wealth and rank must have been of greater importance than his manners to the women concerned. They would probably be of greater importance to most gently bred females as well, but if his mother were to be believed he would not, in marriage, be content with that. Would he ever find his bride, she wondered, and just what sort of woman would be able to capture the heart of this odd, abrupt, exasperating man?

PART
═══════*SIX*═══════

THE HOUSE WHICH Mr Benchley had found for the Roxwells was situated in Brook Street, only a stone's throw from Lord Hendreth's town residence in Grosvenor Square. His lordship, who had preceded them to London, had assured Hebe before she left Bath that she need be in no worry over servants, since she would find the house fully staffed. Hebe, though a little doubtful, took him at his word, and brought her charges from Gloucestershire accompanied only by Lucia and Barbary's abigail, with Miss Stillwood in charge of the schoolroom party. The new governess was a pleasant, sensible woman in her late forties who managed successfully to combine firm discipline with a genuine understanding of her pupils, and to Hebe's relief, after a difficult but mercifully short period of adjustment the girls had settled down with her happily enough.

The dependence upon Lord Hendreth proved justified. There was a full complement of servants, from butler and housekeeper to kitchen-boy, and Hebe was astonished, on the morning after her arrival, to be informed by the butler as she sat at breakfast with Barbary and Sybilla that the coachman had presented himself to receive her orders. She stared blankly at the man, and said in a bewildered tone, 'But I have no coachman in London, Wrightson, and no carriage either.'

'Begging your ladyship's pardon,' Wrightson replied imperturbably, 'the man was engaged, and the barouche acquired, at Lord Hendreth's orders. His lordship himself, I understand, selected the horses.'

'Well!' Barbary exclaimed buoyantly before Hebe could reply. 'I will say this for Hendreth—he thinks of everything! And if *he* chose the horses, we may depend on it that they are prime 'uns.'

Hebe directed a reproving look towards her, and said rather doubtfully that she did not suppose the carriage would be required that day, but this would not do for Barbary.

'Oh, Aunt Hebe, yes! We *must* drive in the Park this afternoon. Amy says that *everyone* goes there on fine days, at about five o'clock.'

Sybilla stared. 'Whatever for?'

'To see each other, of course, stupid!' Barbary replied impatiently. 'To show off their clothes, and their carriages and their horses. It is the Promenade, and the *height* of fashion!'

'You mean they just drive round and round the Park?'

'Not only drive. One can ride, or even walk. Aunt Hebe, do let us go this afternoon!'

Hebe, who after two full days spent traveling, would have preferred to pass her first day in London quietly in her own house, stifled a sigh and told Wrightson to instruct the coachman to bring the carriage round at half past four. Barbary was clearly eager to plunge headlong into fashionable life, and though it now seemed unlikely that she would fly into a tantrum if her wishes were thwarted, Hebe was sufficiently apprehensive of the immediate future to wish to keep her charge in a sunny mood.

Fortunately for this desire, they had not long risen from the table when Mrs Delaford and Amy called to welcome them to London, and to invite Barbary to go shopping with them in Bond Street and then accompany them home to eat a nuncheon before being restored to her chaperone in the early part of the afternoon. Hebe, silently calling down blessings on Mrs Delaford's head, readily gave her assent, and, having seen them off, sent for the housekeeper and started to acquaint herself with the house and the servants. An hour or so later she was in the linen room when Wrightson came to tell her that Lord Hendreth had called.

Delaying only long enough for a brief visit to her bedroom mirror, Hebe made her way to the drawing room, where she found his lordship flicking over the pages of a periodical. He laid this aside and came forward, and Hebe, as they shook hands, was astonished how pleased she was to see him. He might be impatient, unmannerly and quite odiously autocratic, but he was a known and familiar figure, and it was curiously comforting to know that he was within reach.

'You will be wishing me to the devil, I dare say,' was his characteristic greeting, 'for it's not likely you welcome morning callers on your first day in town, but I'll not impose on you for long. I came merely to assure myself that you had all arrived safely, and to ask if it will be convenient for you to bring Barbary to meet my Aunt Felchester tomorrow.'

'Yes, I am sure it will,' she replied, 'but pray do not suppose, my lord, that your visit is an imposition. I am delighted to see you.'

He raised a quizzical eyebrow. 'That sounds ominous! What's wrong?'

'Nothing is wrong,' she replied indignantly. 'I am delighted to have an opportunity to thank you for all you have done. This house, the servants, even a carriage. I would have been in a dreadful worry had I been obliged to arrange all these things for myself from Astington.'

'I know you would,' he agreed cordially, 'but you must not give me too much credit, you know. I simply issued the necessary orders, and they were carried out.'

'Well, I did not imagine that you personally engaged the footmen and chambermaids,' she retorted, 'but you did choose the horses yourself, or so I am given to understand. Thank you!'

'Yes, for there was no one I could trust to do that,' he explained, adding reflectively, 'Except perhaps Barbary, but it would be quite improper for her to take a look in at Tatt's. Females don't, you know.'

'So I should hope! Now do, pray, sit down, and allow me to offer you some refreshment.' She pulled the bellrope as she spoke, adding as they seated themselves, 'No doubt I also have you to thank for the fact that the cellar is well stocked?'

He grinned. 'Pure self-interest! I knew I should be coming to call on you. May I suggest the madeira?'

She choked, tried in vain to look severe, and when the butler appeared said in a colourless voice, 'The madeira for Lord Hendreth, Wrightson, if you please.'

'And two glasses,' Hendreth added. She made a little gesture of protest, which was ignored until Wrightson had left the room. Then Hendreth went on calmly, 'Yes, I dare say you would prefer ratafia, or some similar rubbish, but it is time you learned better, my lady. Now tell me, where are all my wards? The house seems strangely peaceful.'

Hebe decided that it would be prudent to ignore the more controversial implications of his remarks, and explained that Barbary was with Mrs Delaford and Amy while the younger girls had gone out with their governess.

'Fortunately, Miss Stillwood is well acquainted with London,' she concluded. 'She has taken them to walk in the Green Park.'

'They have taken to her, then? I fancy you were a little apprehensive about that.'

'Yes, for Miss Piltbury had been so important to them for so long that I feared they would resent a new governess. I think they did, a little, just at first, but now they go on famously.'

He nodded, but indifferently, and Hebe, who knew he felt no interest at all in the schoolroom party, did not pursue the subject. Instead she told him of the very kind letter from Lady Hendreth which she had found awaiting her, in which her ladyship mentioned that she had kept her promise to write also to Lady Felchester.

He nodded again. 'My aunt told me she had received the letter. I don't know what it contained, but it certainly inspired her with a lively desire to meet you. I was practically commanded to escort you there tomorrow.' He saw Hebe's expression, and chuckled. 'Don't look so alarmed! I won't let her intimidate you.'

'I don't think you can prevent it,' Hebe told him candidly. 'I am intimidated by the mere thought of meeting Lady

Felchester. Is she *very* formidable? But then,' she added without giving him time to reply, 'it is of very little use to ask that of *you*. I dare say you were never intimidated in your life.'

'Well, not for a good many years,' he admitted apologetically, 'and certainly not by Aunt Felchester. Never mind! When she tries to stare you down, as try she will, give her her own again, as you did with me when first we met.'

'That is no help at all,' Hebe said crossly. '*You* made me angry, but I cannot suppose that Lady Felchester will offer similar provocation.'

'Oh, I don't know! She is famous for what *she* likes to call plain speaking, which may be interpreted as an unshakable belief that she knows what is best for everyone, and has no hesitation whatsoever in telling them so. An impossible woman!'

Hebe opened her eyes very wide at him. 'You *do* surprise me, sir! From what you have just told me, I would have supposed you and her ladyship to get along famously.'

'No, no! We are too much alike,' he retorted, spiking her guns. 'Happily, Felchester's place is in Yorkshire, so we meet only occasionally if I happen to be in town during the season, and we usually contrive to brush through without actually coming to cuffs.'

'I am relieved to hear it, but that does not prevent me from being in a quake at the prospect of meeting her ladyship. I am told she is one of the foremost leaders of fashion, and that it is of the utmost importance to win her approval.'

'True, if one cares for such flummery, so you had better impress upon Barbary that she must mind her manners. Aunt is bound to set up her back, and though I wouldn't blame the chit, it won't do for her to be giving the old lady back answers.'

'Thank you,' Hebe said bitterly. 'That was all I needed to complete my discomfiture. However, if you are to escort us to Lady Felchester's, *you* may issue the warning to Barbary. She is far more likely to take heed of you.'

He looked at her rather hard. 'Giving you trouble, is she?'

'No,' Hebe said slowly. 'She behaves very prettily still, but as you know, she made quite a hit at Bath, and the admiration she received there went to her head a little. She found Astington sadly flat by contrast, for the weather was so bad that it kept even her indoors for most of the time. Besides, her younger brothers teased her a good deal, so that between one thing and another she could scarcely wait to get to London. I must admit I am in a little worry in case the excitement of being here leads her to behave unbecomingly.'

'I still think her too shrewd to spoil her own chances, but I will certainly drop a word of warning in her ear if it will set your mind at rest. And it seems to me,' he added, studying her so searchingly that she flushed, and shifted uncomfortably in her chair, 'that it badly needs to be set at rest. You are fretting yourself to flinders—and don't try to hoax me into believing it is all on Barbary's account!'

She was saved from the necessity of an immediate reply by Wrightson coming into the room with the wine. By the time this had been poured and the butler had withdrawn again, she had recovered her countenance a little, but had she been foolish enough to hope that the interruption would divert Hendreth from the subject she was soon undeceived. He reverted to it as soon as they were alone again.

'What can I say to convince you that your fears are groundless? I thought my mother had succeeded in allaying them while you were at Bath, but it seems I was wrong.'

She looked resentfully at him. 'Lady Hendreth was kindness itself, but to be the guest of a lady of the first consideration is a very different matter from finding oneself alone in a world where one knows almost no one, with the responsibility of a young girl to look after. I cannot even be sure whom it will be proper for her to meet.'

He brushed this aside. 'If that were the case I might sympathize with you, but I've told you repeatedly that Aunt Felchester will present you, and if you have *her* sponsorship you will need need no other. As for Barbary, if any loose screws start dangling after her you may depend upon me to send them packing.' He grinned, adding audaciously, 'I'll even undertake to do the same for you!'

Once again she was stabbed by the illogical fear that he somehow suspected the truth of her acquaintance with Geoffrey Fernhurst, and that this was an oblique reference to that unfortunate affair. She still hoped profoundly that no one in

England would ever discover it, but for some reason it seemed particularly important that Hendreth should remain in ignorance. She said angrily, 'That is not in the least amusing! Let me tell you, my lord, that I have no expectation of *anyone* dangling after me, but if anyone were misguided enough to do so, I fail to see what concern it could be of yours.'

'Of course it would be my concern! I have dragged you from your sanctuary and thrust you out into the world, and it is my duty to protect you from it. *You* may regard yourself as an antidote, but let me tell you that any handsome young widow soon has the men of the town casting out lures to her, and since you have no male relatives—!'

'It is quite improper for you to talk to me in this fashion,' Hebe interrupted in a scolding tone. 'I am sure it is all nonsense, and your peculiar idea of a jest, so let me assure you that if I *should* feel myself to be in need of your lordship's protection, I will inform you of the fact.'

'Will you?' There was an ironical note in his voice which did nothing to reassure her. 'I wonder? Never mind! Time will undoubtedly prove which one of us is right.'

Hebe might view with a sinking heart the prospect of meeting Lady Felchester, but Barbary suffered no such qualms. Shyness was an emotion unknown to her. Hendreth, arriving to escort them to his aunt's house, looked her over with a critical eye and said in his usual blunt way, 'Excellent! Just make sure that your manners are as appealing as your appearance, and keep that temper of yours under control no matter how greatly my aunt may provoke you, for if you fall at this fence, there will be no remounting.'

Barbary, accepting this with better grace than Hebe would have expected, assured him that she was well aware of the importance of the occasion. Then, reminded perhaps by her guardian's sporting metaphor, followed this with an urgent request that she be provided with a riding horse, so that she might join the equestriennes she had seen in the Park the previous day.

'Want to take the shine out of them all, I suppose,' he remarked. 'Very well, but remember! No galloping in the Park. It's not considered to be at all the thing.'

'No, no! I promise! Will you choose a mount for me *yourself*, sir? I know I can depend on you to get just what I would like.'

'No need to try to turn me up sweet,' he said sardonically. 'I've said you can have the brute. Just see to it that your anxiety to be all the crack doesn't tempt you to go beyond the line.'

'No, my lord,' she said demurely, adding, with a saucy glance up at him, 'Perhaps you had better ride with me the first time, just to set your doubts at rest.'

'Baggage!' he said dispassionately, but Hebe did not think he seemed displeased. 'Perhaps I will, for I can see from Lady Roxwell's expression that she is about to remind me that you have been accustomed to ride only in the country, and that it is a very different matter to control a spirited mount in busy city streets.' He raised an inquiring eyebrow at Hebe. 'Am I not right, ma'am?'

Since she had been about to voice exactly that protest, she responded only with an affronted look, which made him laugh, and allowed him to escort her out to the barouche. Barbary's delight at having her request so readily granted had made her look quite radiant, and more than one masculine head turned as the open carriage passed by on its short journey to Mount Street. Hebe would have liked to believe that her charge was really as indifferent to these admiring glances as she pretended to be.

No fault, however, could be found with her demeanour as she followed her chaperone into Lady Felchester's impressive drawing room. Her ladyship was equally impressive. A large woman, nearly as tall as Hebe but a great deal stouter, with iron-grey hair, and blunt features in which it was possible to trace a faint resemblance to her nephew. She was very fashionably dressed, and Hebe could only be thankful that her own attire, and Barbary's, were also in the latest mode. Anything less, she felt sure, would have prompted Lady Felchester to dismiss them out of hand as a couple of country dowds.

As Hendreth performed the necessary introductions, she found herself being subjected to a long, hard scrutiny. It made her uncomfortable, but, remembering his lordship's advice, she managed to dissemble this, and met the searching regard coolly, with a faint, inquiring lift of her brows. This seemed to please her hostess, for she nodded approvingly, shook hands with a brisk, firm clasp, and said in a forthright way, 'So you are Hugo Roxwell's widow! How d'you do! I hear you've taken charge of his nephew's brood. This the eldest girl?' Barbary made her curtsy, composedly but at her most demure, and Lady Felchester nodded again. 'Well, miss? My sister-in-law assures me that you are a pretty-behaved young female, so I will do what I can for you, though I'd advise you not to set your hopes too high.'

'No, ma'am,' Barbary replied gravely, 'and thank you. I am very much obliged to your ladyship.'

Lady Felchester half turned, and beckoned forward a girl who had been lingering in the background. She was of medium height but rather thick-set, which made her look shorter than she actually was, with sandy-fair hair and a freckled complexion, and though charmingly dressed appeared to lack animation.

'This is my granddaughter, Caroline Ingham,' Lady Felchester informed Hebe. 'Lady Roxwell, Caroline.'

Miss Ingham curtsied nervously to Hebe, murmured something indistinguishable in reply to her greeting, and cast a glance of pure terror at Hendreth, who nodded indifferently in response. Lady Felchester sighed, made her known to Barbary, and advised them to go away and get acquainted, since they were both making their come-out this season.

'And it is to be hoped,' she added in a lower tone as Caroline obediently led Barbary to another part of the big room, 'that Miss Roxwell will be able to draw her out a little. Her mother and I are at our wits' end! As if being bran-faced, poor child, were not cross enough to bear, she is as shy as she can stare, as well, and practically tongue-tied in company. I do not know what is to become of her!'

'Perhaps,' Hendreth suggested, 'if you and her mother bullied her less, she might show some sign of improvement. I know nothing whatsoever about schoolgirls, but in my experience, no person of timid disposition is ever encouraged to be otherwise by constant exhortations to assert himself.'

'Good gracious, Blaise! If her mother and I did not take Caroline about, and tell her how to go on, she would hide herself away at home with her books and never venture out. They tell me she is clever, but what help, I ask you, is book-learning to a girl desirous of establishing herself creditably? However, that is neither here nor there! I fancy, Lady Roxwell, that you will experience little difficulty in finding an eligible *parti* for *your* charge. An exceedingly pretty girl, and Lady Hendreth tells me she took very well at Bath. You must bring her to the ball I am giving for Caroline the day after tomorrow. Both Lady Sefton and Lady Jersey will be here then, and I can present you to them. They are two of the patronesses of Almack's, you know, and you will be needing vouchers.'

Fully sensible of the favour Lady Felchester would be doing her if she could obtain for her the coveted vouchers, Hebe murmured her thanks, and then went on, with a somewhat defiant glance at his lordship, 'Lady Hendreth may also have informed you, ma'am, that I am not at all in the habit of going into fashionable society. In fact, this is *my* first visit to London as well as Barbary's, and I have almost as little idea as she has how to go on. Lord Hendreth will not admit that this renders me totally unfitted to be her chaperone, but I am persuaded that your ladyship will agree that it is so.'

'No,' Lady Felchester replied bluntly, 'I can't say that I do. Of course, had you simply set up your establishment in London, knowing nobody, it would not have answered at all, but as it is, the only objection *I* can see is that you are far too young and personable, and will probably have your hands full coping with your own admirers, let alone Miss Roxwell's.'

Hebe gasped, and cast so suspicious a glance at Hendreth that he laughed, and then explained to his slightly affronted aunt that he had already warned Lady Roxwell of this possibility, and received a severe trimming for his pains.

'For nothing will convince her, ma'am, that she is not long past her prime, and fitted only to be duenna and adoptive aunt to the Roxwell family. I doubt if even you will be able to persuade her otherwise.'

'Rubbish!' Lady Felchester said robustly, disposing with one word of Hebe's convictions. 'Besides, neither your persuasions nor mine will be needed once she has seen for herself that she is mistaken.' She nodded kindly at Hebe.

'There is no reason in the world why you should not marry again.'

'Lady Felchester, I assure you!' Hebe, scarlet-cheeked, was torn between indignation and embarrassment. 'I have no expectation—indeed, no wish—!'

'No wish, possibly, at this present,' Lady Felchester allowed generously. 'That I can understand. I was, after all, acquainted with Hugo Roxwell from the time we were both in the nursery! It would be a great pity, however, to permit the past to prejudice you against a possible match in the future, and I am strongly of the opinion that you *should* marry again.'

Hebe, with the feeling that she was trying to resist being swept along by an irresistible force, and fearful that at any moment Lady Felchester might start to enumerate possible future spouses for her, cast a harassed, beseeching look at Hendreth. He grinned unsympathetically, but diverted his relative's attention by pointing out that the purpose of the Roxwell ladies' presence in London was to find a husband for Barbary, since she had a younger sister almost, as it were, treading on her heels.

'And lacking both Barbary's looks *and* her charm,' he concluded with brutal candour, 'so if the elder is not off Lady Roxwell's hands by the end of the season, the younger will be cast completely into the shade next year. As for Lady Roxwell herself, whether or not she decides to be married again, and to whom, is for her alone to decide. Though I have assured her,' he added wickedly, 'that I will warn off any really undesirable characters who may come dangling after her.'

'So I should hope,' Lady Felchester said sharply, not giving Hebe time to make any reply, 'and while we are on the subject of marriage, nephew, allow me to point out that it is high time *you* stopped junketing about the world and gave some thought to your responsibilities. The succession ought to have been secured years ago.'

'Your memory, aunt, is not what it was,' he replied sarcastically. 'You have obviously forgotten the existence of my cousin, William, and his two sons.'

'William Hendreth,' stated her ladyship, not mincing matters, 'is a fool, and those boys of his expensive fribbles who have cost him a pretty penny first and last. I should be excessively sorry to see any of *them* step into your shoes!'

'With respect, ma'am,' he retaliated, in a far from respectful tone, 'it is extremely unlikely that you *will* see it—unless, of course, I should meet with some accident. I am not exactly in my dotage.'

'You will be five-and-thirty next month,' his aunt reminded him with merciless accuracy, 'and ought to have set up your nursery years ago. Irresponsibility is the one thing I have no patience with!'

'One of the *many* things,' he corrected her affably. 'Shall we leave this subject, ma'am? We are embarrassing Lady Roxwell.'

'Oh, I see no reason to stand on ceremony with her ladyship,' Lady Felchester informed him in a large-minded way, embarrassing Hebe more than ever, 'but I know it is not of the least use to remonstrate with you. You are as stubborn as your father was, and just as infuriating.'

'I infuriate you, ma'am, because I will allow you neither to dictate to me, nor to saddle me with what you would consider to be a suitable bride. Never mind! Devote your match-making abilities instead to finding husbands for those two,' he nodded towards Barbary and Caroline at the far end of the room, 'and leave me to settle my affairs in the way which seems best to me.'

His aunt uttered a sound which in anyone other than a high-bred lady of fashion would have been termed a snort, but, knowing from experience that nothing was to be gained by arguing with him, abandoned the topic in favour of one more immediately fruitful, and proceeded to question Hebe closely about the other members of the Roxwell family. She then gave it as her opinion that if Clement wished to manage his own estate it would be an excellent thing, but that he must acquire a little town polish before settling down in Gloucester-shire; instructed Hebe whom to engage to give Sybilla singing lessons; expressed a hope that the twins would be taken on some informative and improving visits to places of historical interest while they were in London; and showed an alarming tendency to select careers for the three younger boys. Once again Hebe had the sensation of being swept helplessly along, and could not help feeling that Lady Felchester's patronage might prove to be a mixed blessing.

There was no doubt, however, that to be launched into London society at one of her ladyship's parties was an advantage which could not be denied. Hebe was fully sensible of this, though she could not view the prospect with the same unalloyed delight as Barbary did, and was secretly much relieved when Hendreth announced that he would come to escort them to his aunt's house. She at once invited him to dine in Brook Street on the evening in question; he accepted, and they parted on terms of quite unaccustomed affability.

The next matter of moment was to decide what to wear. Hebe might lack worldly experience, but she was shrewd enough to realize that Barbary must stand out from the crowd of hopeful debutantes who would undoubtedly be present at the ball, and she selected for the girl a charming confection, acquired at Bath but never yet worn, of rose-pink gauze over satin of a paler shade, fastened with tiny satin roses. Clusters of similar roses trimmed the little puffed sleeves, and there was a spray of them to set in Barbary's black curls. She possessed a modest necklace of pearls which had belonged to her mother, and which her Papa had somehow salvaged from the wreck of his affairs to bestow on his favourite child, and with these clasped about her neck, and her toilette completed by pink satin slippers and long gloves of fine pink kid, she looked lovely enough, Hebe thought with a stab of almost maternal pride, to outshine any girl in London.

Hebe herself, feeling that her status as chaperone as well as her widowhood demanded that she avoid light colours, chose deep blue satin, made for her by Lady Hendreth's modiste with the kind of elegant simplicity which most appealed to her. The dress was cut low across the bosom, and after a little heart-searching she decided to wear with it the sapphire set which was among the jewels handed over to her by Mr Benchley. The decision was made with some reluctance, for she could not feel that she had any right to wear the Roxwell jewels, and these scruples had already led to a heated argument with Hendreth, when he discovered that she had not brought the gems with her to Bath. Now, however, her sense of style told her that the gown needed something of the kind to set it off; common sense suggested that such an indication of affluence could only enhance Barbary's prospects; and she felt reasonably certain that if she appeared again before his lordship without any ornaments he would immediately demand why the devil she was not wearing any. In fact, she thought exasperatedly, he was quite capable of marching her back to her bedchamber and rifling the jewel box in search of something suitable.

The set consisted of necklace, earrings and an ornament for the hair, and though the setting was old-fashioned, the stones were particularly fine, and flashed impressively in the candlelight. Hebe, critically studying her reflection, was obliged to admit that they created exactly the effect she had in mind, and added considerably to her self-confidence. What she failed to remark was the way the sapphires reflected and deepened the colour of her eyes, or how dramatically they glowed against her red-gold hair. She allowed Lucia to drape a long scarf of silver tissue across her arms, picked up the silver-embroidered reticule of darker blue satin which matched her sandals, and went down to the drawing room.

When Barbary joined her a few minutes later, she was wearing a slightly smug expression and carrying, as well as her reticule and fan, a posy of pale pink roses tied with long satin ribbons.

'Look,' she said, holding out the flowers. 'From Hendreth, I must say I was surprised to receive them, for I would not have thought him in the habit of making such gestures, would you?'

'No,' Hebe admitted slowly. She was conscious of a tiny, transient prickle of disquiet, and added, more in response to that than to Barbary's question, 'But after all, he *is* your guardian, and this is your first London ball. It is a special occasion.'

'It was clever of him to choose the right colour.'

'Not really,' Hebe said dampeningly. 'He asked me the other day what colour you would be wearing tonight. I could not imagine why he wished to know.'

They were interrupted by the arrival of Hendreth himself. Hebe went forward to greet him, and as they shook hands his glance encompassed her in a swift, comprehensive survey. He nodded approvingly, but she was startled, and very slightly disturbed, to see a glint of rather more than approval in his eyes, though all he said was, 'Good evening. I'm glad to see you have overcome your foolish scruples sufficiently to wear those sapphires. They become you.'

'Thank you.' She answered tartly from mere force of habit, for the look in his eyes had thrown her temporarily off balance. 'I have made up my mind not to disagree with you tonight, so I will refrain from pointing out that those scruples do not seem foolish to me.'

He grinned. 'We *are* going to have an insipid evening, aren't we? No disagreements!' He turned to Barbary, looking her over critically while she, supremely confident of her own beauty, dimpled mischievously at him. 'Well, my child, you certainly *look* ready to play the part of belle of the ball. That's a very fetching gown!'

'Thank you, my lord!' She sketched a curtsy, with a saucy glance up at him from beneath her lashes. 'And thank you, too, for these delightful flowers. They are the first I have ever been given.'

'They won't be the last, if I know my fellow men,' he replied dryly. 'Don't let it go to your head! You are not up to snuff yet, my girl, although you may think that you are.'

Lady Felchester's ball proved to be less of an ordeal than Hebe had feared. For one thing, the Delafords were there, and since they had arrived before the Roxwells, Mrs Delaford was on watch for them and took them under her wing as soon as they arrived, while the fact that Hendreth was their escort was equally reassuring. He might not be popular, but he knew almost everyone, and made a point of introducing Hebe and her charge to as many people as possible. Lady Felchester, too, once she was released from the obligation of receiving her guests, was seen to be singling out Lady and Miss Roxwell with especial kindness. Hebe might feel a trifle overwhelmed by the sheer size of the gathering—there were more than five hundred people thronging Lord Felchester's spacious residence— but she experienced none of the panic she had anticipated.

Barbary, of course, was in her element. Hendreth, casting a speculative glance over the company when they first entered the ballroom, buttonholed a nearby sprig of the nobility and sought leave to present 'Lady Roxwell, and Miss Roxwell, my ward.' The young Viscount, who had looked rather wary when first addressed, brightened perceptibly at sight of Barbary, and, having obtained permission, led her to join the country dance which was just forming.

'And that, I fancy,' Hendreth remarked in an undervoice to Hebe, 'is all which will be necessary.'

His confidence was justified. It very soon became obvious that Barbary was assured of no lack of partners, and even before the first dance was over had promised Viscount Linwood the privilege of taking her in to supper. Hendreth, when these gratifying tidings were conveyed to him by Hebe, received them with maddening calm, and merely said, 'Then I had better take you in, ma'am, so that we may station ourselves nearby in case her triumphs go to her head. I trust you warned her against drinking too much champagne.'

This remark put her quite out of charity with him, and since by that time she had found that the people she met, far from regarding her with contempt, seemed bent on pursuing the acquaintance, she turned her shoulder to him in a very pointed way and embarked on an animated conversation. His lordship grinned, and strolled off to the card-rooom.

An hour or so later Hebe was seated at the edge of a group composed of Mrs Delaford, her daughter, Amy, Barbary and several gentlemen, when her attention was caught by a young woman sitting alone a short distance away, beside one of the long, curtained windows. The girl—for she looked to be no older than Barbary—was a colourless little thing, with mouse-brown hair twisted into a complicated arrangement of braids and curls, an elaborate gown of straw-coloured lace and a necklace and earrings composed of rubies so large that Hebe wondered for a moment if they could possibly be real. It was these overpowering jewels which first caught her eye, but then she noticed that their wearer was exceedingly pale, and fanning herself with a desperation scarcely justified even by the warmth of the room. As Hebe watched, she pressed the back of one gloved hand to her lips, then, letting the fan drop, rose to her feet and took an uncertain step towards the window, clutching at a fold of the heavy curtain. Hebe, assuring herself by a quick glance that she was momentarily unobserved, got up from her chair and moved quickly but unobtrusively to the girl's side, slipping a supporting arm about her waist and saying softly, in a matter of fact tone, 'I fear you are unwell. Can I be of assistance to you?'

The girl turned her head towards her, but blindly, as though she could not focus her eyes. Her face was very white, beaded with perspiration. She whispered disjointedly, 'So hot—and I feel so sick! Oh, I am going to faint!'

'No, you are not,' Hebe said reassuringly, and reached out her free hand to twitch aside the curtain. To her relief, the window beyond was unlatched, and gave on to a tiny, ornamental balcony balustraded with wrought iron. 'All you need is a breath of cool air.'

She pushed open the window and guided her companion through, letting the curtain drop back into place behind them. The girl drooped against her so that Hebe was obliged to hold her up, but since she was very small and slight this presented little difficulty, and after a minute or two the beneficial effect of the cool night air made itself felt. The sufferer drew a long, shuddering breath, and the weight upon Hebe's supporting arms grew less.

'Oh, I am better now,' she murmured. 'Forgive me, and thank you, thank you! It would have been so mortifying—! I could not have borne it!'

'It would have been very natural,' Hebe said calmly. 'The ballroom is excessively hot. I felt it myself. We will wait here for a few minutes more, until you feel stronger, and then I will take you to find your mama. I am sure she will feel that you ought to go home without delay.'

'Oh, yes, but I did not—! I came here with my husband.'

'Oh!' Hebe said rather blankly, for the girl seemed so young that it had not occurred to her that she might be married. 'I beg your pardon. I did not realize—but it makes no difference, you know. We will send someone to find him, and then you may be comfortable.'

There was no immediate response, but after a moment or two the girl said wretchedly, in a conscience-stricken tone, 'I am so very stupid! I do not like big parties, or hot, crowded rooms, and the lights and the music make me dizzy—though I perfectly understand how fortunate we are to be invited by Lady Felchester, and that it is important we should be seen here—!' Her voice quivered and she broke off, but added apologetically after a brief pause, 'You must think me a very poor creature, ma'am, but you see, I—I am increasing, and it makes me feel so dreadfully unwell.'

Hebe, already suspecting that the unknown husband was selfish and inconsiderate, found her suspicion confirmed by this confidence. Any man, she thought with strong indignation, who would insist upon an unwilling and pregnant child-wife accompanying him to a ball simply because it would be socially inadvisable not to be seen there, must be utterly unfeeling. She was obliged to make a deliberate effort not to let her voice betray her thoughts as she said decidedly, 'In that event it would certainly be better for you to be at home and in your bed. Do you feel able now to go back into the house? Since you are in a delicate situation, it may perhaps be unwise to linger too long in the night air.'

'I think so,' the girl said reluctantly, 'but I—I do not know precisely where my husband is, and there are so many people—!' Please—you have been so kind—will you help me to find him?'

'Certainly I will help you. We will find somewhere quiet to sit until he can be brought to you, only—' she hesitated '—it seems quite absurd, but we do not know each other's names.'

'Oh, how stupid of me! You must think me quite idiotish! I am Aurelia Fernhurst.'

There was a tiny pause. Hebe stood for a moment, rigid with shock, and then said with some difficulty, 'Mrs *Geoffrey* Fernhurst?'

'Yes.' Aurelia sounded frightened. Hebe was aware of it even through her own dismay. 'Do you know my husband, ma'am?'

The effect of the shock was passing now, and feeling coming back. Hebe was not at all sure what those feelings were, but she managed to say, in a gratifying normal tone, 'I was a little acquainted with him in Rome, when I lived there with my late husband. My name is Hebe Roxwell. Come now, let me take you back into the house.'

She turned as she spoke, drawing the curtain aside, and the

first person she saw was Lord Hendreth, standing almost at the spot where she had been when she first noticed Aurelia Fernhurst, and looking about him with a faint frown. He caught sight of her as she came through the curtains, and his expression changed to one of astonishment as he saw her companion. Hebe observed this almost without noticing it, and beckoned imperiously. He came, looking amused now.

'How fortunate that you are here, sir,' she greeted him, 'for you must be familiar with this house, and able to take us somewhere where we may be quiet. Mrs Fernhurst is unwell and would like to go home, but we are not quite certain where her husband may be.'

'By all means,' he replied promptly. 'Will you take my arm, ma'am? I know of an anteroom which is probably unoccupied.'

Aurelia murmured timid thanks, took his proffered arm without looking at him, and then, with Hebe following, let him guide her round the edge of the ballroom, across a broad landing and into a small—empty room. Leading her to a sofa, he said as she sat down, 'I believe I saw Fernhurst in the card-room not long ago. I'll fetch him to you.'

He went out. Hebe placed a cushion behind Aurelia's head and made her lean back against it, and then sat down beside her, taking one of the girl's limp hands and chafing it gently between her own. She acted automatically, aware only that in a few minutes she would be face to face with Geoffrey for the first time since that day in the villa garden, for though she had known that such an encounter would almost certainly occur sooner or later, she had never envisaged the possibility of being obliged to confront him in the presence of his wife and Blaise Hendreth. It was a daunting prospect.

Yet whatever her feelings were towards Geoffrey, for Aurelia she felt only compassion, and when the door opened again, and she saw the girl turn her head apprehensively towards it, the little colour which had returned to her face draining out of it, she felt a rush of angry protectiveness. Then she was confronting Geoffrey, and her first feeling was utter astonishment that he looked so different from her memory of him. In Rome he had seemed to her the embodiment of a masculine ideal, but now she saw merely a slim, foppish young man, too dandified in his dress; handsome, certainly, but weak, with an unappealing peevishness in his expression. Had he changed so much, or had she? Or—the thought came unbidden—did he merely appear ineffectual by contrast with Hendreth?

It was immediately apparent to her that although she had been prepared for this encounter, he had not. He was looking annoyed as he came into the room, but when he caught sight of Hebe, annoyance gave place to a look of profound consternation. He changed colour, and checked for an instant, staring, then with a visible effort moved forward again, saying uncertainly, 'Lady Roxwell! I was not informed—! I had no notion—!'

'Indeed, why should you?' Uncertainty at an end, Hebe spoke coolly, aware that she was maliciously enjoying his discomfiture. 'I am sure Lord Hendreth thought it necessary to tell you only that Mrs Ferhurst is unwell. In fact, it probably slipped his mind that you and I have met before.'

Geoffrey was staring at her as though he could not believe that they had; as though this self-possessed young woman with her air of well-bred indifference was a total stranger to him. Which, in a sense, she was. The Hebe Roxwell he had known, the girl, innocent of the ways of the world, who could be thrown into confusion by a well-chosen compliment or a meaning look, had vanished as completely as though she had never existed; destroyed, though he was incapable of realizing it, by his own betrayal of her. With the Hebe Roxwell into which the intervening time had transformed her he was completely at a loss.

Hebe herself, discerning something of his feelings, found that revenge was sweet. She turned the knife a little, saying briskly, 'However, this is scarcely the time to renew our acquaintance, for though Mrs Fernhurst is somewhat recovered, she is still far from well and should be conveyed home with the least possible delay. It was, if you will forgive me for saying so, unwise in the circumstances to allow her to attend such an occasion.' She glanced at Hendreth. 'I think Mrs Fernhurst's carriage should be sent for.'

'Already done, ma'am,' he responded. 'I gave the necessary orders on my way to the card-room, and it will be at the door by the time Mrs Fernhurst has been taken downstairs.' He encountered Geoffrey's affronted and far from grateful look, and added ironically, 'I felt certain, Fernhurst, that you would not wish your wife to be kept waiting.'

'No,' Geoffrey agreed reluctantly, and looked at Aurelia. 'That is, if you really wish to go home so early, ma'am?'

'Yes, if you please,' she murmured timidly. 'If *you* have no objection.'

'Of course he has no objection,' Hebe said bracingly. '*Your* comfort and well-being, my dear Mrs Fernhurst, must naturally be his first concern.' She rose, and set a hand under the girl's elbow to help her to her feet. 'Would you like me to come downstairs with you?'

'Oh, no, thank you! I am better now, truly, just very tired, and I have been so much trouble to you already.' She clasped Hebe's hand between her own and squeezed it convulsively. 'Thank you so very much! So kind—!'

Her voice becoming suspended by tears, she released Hebe, set a hand on the punctiliously proffered arm of her set-faced spouse, and with a stifled murmur of thanks to Hendreth, went with him out of the room.

'Poor little thing!' Hebe remarked compassionately when Hendreth had closed the door behind the Fernhursts. 'It was bad enough to drag her here when she is terrified of such occasions, but to abandon her and go off to play cards—! Infamous!'

He grinned. 'As you had no hesitation in making plain to him, in the most civil way possible, of course. Poor devil! I have seldom seen anyone quite so thunderstruck.'

He spoke lightly, but there was a certain intentness in his eyes which Hebe was too preoccupied to perceive. She felt extra-ordinarily elated, for the dreaded encounter with Geoffrey had come and gone, and it was he who had been at a disadvantage, not she. Now her liberation was complete.

Her triumphant reflections were interrupted by Hendreth, who said ironically, 'Well, ma'am, now that we have succoured Mrs Fernhurst, and her husband has been put firmly in his place, isn't it time you returned to the ballroom, where your charge has been left unchaperoned for the past half-hour?'

'Oh, good heavens!' Brought abruptly down to earth, Hebe

stared at him in dismay. 'I had forgotten all about her! But I *had* to assist that unfortunate girl, and Mrs Delaford was there—! Surely Barbary could not get into a scrape in just half an hour?' She added doubtfully, 'Could she?'

'I should imagine,' Barbary's guardian replied consideringly, 'that that little minx could get into a scrape in half a minute if she chose. The last I saw of her, she was dancing the waltz with Hatherley. The Earl of Hatherley,' he added in explanation.

'Oh, dear!' Hebe looked worried. 'Is he not quite the thing? Who presented him to her?'

'I did. Known him for years, and he's not only all the crack, but devilish eligible into the bargain.' He chuckled at the look in Hebe's face. 'Did I give you a fright? You deserve it! Only a very poor sort of chaperone, let me tell you, deserts her charge in the middle of a party.'

'Yes, I know,' she admitted guiltily. 'I am truly sorry, and I'll not do it again, for it was shockingly thoughtless of me. I do trust that no tongues have been set wagging because of it.'

'Not about Barbary, but there's every chance they will soon be wagging about *you*, if you are discovered alone with me in this secluded spot.' He shook his head sadly. 'It's a censorious world, m'dear!'

'Really, you are too absurd! Hebe said indignantly, rearranging her silvery scarf across her arms. 'Anyone hearing you would think me a mere girl, instead of a widow and duenna to your ward.'

'Yes, wouldn't they?' he agreed cordially. 'And anyone looking at you would think precisely the same.' She uttered an impatient exclamation, but he took her lightly by the shoulders and turned her to face a mirror on the wall nearby. 'Take an impartial look at yourself, my girl, and let me hear no more nonsense about widows and duennas. The fact that you are both will no more stop the tabbies' tongues than it will prevent the men from admiring you.'

Hebe stared resentfully at her mirrored image. Apart from the fact that she was now able to dress in the first style of elegance, she could find no more in her appearance to admire than she had in her girlhood, for in her opinion she was far too tall and too slender, her features were too strongly defined and her hair too nearly red, to permit her the smallest claim to good looks. With the intention of administering a snub, she transferred her gaze from her own reflection to her companion's, and the unexpected thought darted into her mind that beside Hendreth, she did not seem particularly tall; that, in fact, they made a very satisfactory couple. Furious with herself for entertaining, even for a moment, so unbecoming a notion, she turned abruptly away, saying with dignity, if a trifle obscurely, 'Fine feathers, my lord, cannot transform a barnyard hen into a peacock.'

He gave a snort of laughter. 'It would be a damned queer set-out, m'dear, if they could.'

'I mean a pea*hen*!' She broke off, remembering too late what a drab creature a peahen was. 'No, I don't! I mean—!' She encountered a look of expectant mockery, and added bitterly, 'You know very well what I mean!'

'Yes, and that's as big a piece of nonsense as all the rest,' he said frankly, 'but I see that nothing *I* can say will convince you. You will just have to learn from experience—but don't make a habit of being private with a man in a secluded little room like this, or you may experience more than you bargain for.' Ignoring Hebe's outraged gasp, he walked back to the door and opened it. 'Shall we go, ma'am? I believe supper is shortly to be served, and you must be reunited with your charge before then.'

In the ballroom, Barbary, under the indulgent eye of Mrs Delaford, was discovered in animated conversation with a gentleman Hebe had never seen before. She looked round as the latter came up to them, and broke off what she was saying to exclaim, 'Oh, there you are, Aunt Hebe! I wondered what had become of you. May I present Lord Hatherey? Lady Roxwell, my lord.'

The Earl of Hatherley blinked, but excused his obvious astonishment with well-bred ease, saying with a humorous look, 'I am enchanted to make your ladyship's acquaintance. Pardon me for appearing nonplussed, but when Miss Roxwell spoke of her aunt, I must confess I pictured a much older lady.'

Hendreth nodded understandingly. 'In a turban,' he murmured.

Hebe gave him a quelling look. 'My late husband, sir, was Miss Roxwell's great-uncle,' she explained with a smile, 'so I suppose I should be thankful that she did not describe me to you as her great-aunt.'

He laughed. 'Ah, that would have been daunting indeed! I have two great-aunts of my own.'

Hebe laughed, too, deciding that she liked him. He was, she thought, a few years younger than Hendreth, a moderately tall man with a lean, mobile countenance and hazel eyes, very fashionably dressed. Yet there was nothing of the fop about him, for he had a look of physical toughness which was enhanced rather than diminished by the flawless cut of his coat and the exquisitely intricate arrangement of his neckcloth. Had Hebe been more familiar with the *ton,* she would have recognized him instantly for what he was, a top-of-the-trees Corinthian, member of a set who prided themselves as much on their sporting prowess as their sartorial elegance.

Supper was announced. Viscount Linwood appeared to claim his partner, and Lord Hatherley turned to Hebe.

'May I have the very great pleasure, ma'am, of taking *you* in?'

Hebe was given no chance to reply. Hendreth said casually, 'Too late, Charles! Lady Roxwell is engaged to take supper with me. We have a joint responsibility, you know, to look after my ward.'

He proffered his arm, and Hebe, with a smiling word of regret to Hatherley, laid her hand upon it and allowed him to escort her from the ballroom. As they descended the stairs, however, she said meditatively, 'It did not occur to you, I suppose, that I might have wished to accept Lord Hatherley's invitation?'

'Not for a moment,' he agreed. 'You promised two hours ago to have supper with me.'

Hebe sighed. 'No doubt it is useless to remind you that I did nothing of the kind. You stated that we would take supper together.'

He nodded. 'To keep an eye on Barbary. Of course, if you are so lost to all sense of responsibility as to prefer carousing with Charles, I'll take you back to him, but don't blame *me* if that young minx indulges too freely in the champagne and ends the evening thoroughly foxed.'

She tried unsuccessfully to stifle a chuckle. 'Oh, you are

too absurd! I can imagine nothing more unlikely, and in any event, *my* presence is not needful to restrain her. You, I am sure, are far more capable than I of checking any folly on her part.'

'Quite,' he replied, 'but you may not be aware that Barbary and Linwood have arranged to join a party composed of Amy Delaford, my cousin Caroline, two other girls whom I do not know, and the boys who are partnering them. If you imagine that I am going to spend the whole of supper presiding over a table occupied only by the infantry, you are very much mistaken. Besides, the unknowns' mamas would not like it above half.'

'Oh, I see! I am to be there to lend *you* countenance. What a good thing you explained that to me.'

'No, you hornet, you are to be there to provide the leaven in some singularly uninteresting dough. Don't you know that you are the only female of my acquaintance, with the sole exception of my mother, who does not bore me to distraction?'

She was startled, and cast a quick, questioning glance up at him to see if he were serious, and although his gaze met hers sardonically, she had the impression that he was. Secretly a little flattered, she contrived to dissemble it, and replied in her usual manner, 'I am obliged to your lordship, and since I know that you are not in the habit of making pretty speeches, can only assume that this encomium is earned by the fact that I am usually prepared to stand up to your overbearing ways.'

He appeared to give this his consideration. 'Oh, I don't know about that! Aunt Felchester invariably stands up to me, and I find *her* excessively boring.'

'Oh, pray hush!' Hebe cast a guilty look around to see whether anyone within earshot was attending. 'I know it is useless to remind *you* how improper it is for you to speak so of your aunt, particularly in her own house, but you might spare a thought for me.'

'My dear girl, I do! You would be astonished, I dare say, to know how frequently.' He paused just inside the supper room, scanning the throng in search of his quarry. 'There they are! Young fools! They have even left empty seats at their table. Let's go and put a damper on their high spirits before it occurs to any of them to forestall us.'

Barbary and her companions did indeed seem taken aback, and even a little dismayed, to find Hebe and Hendreth taking the vacant seats at their table, but Hebe herself was too busy pondering his lordship's words to be greatly amused by their chagrin. She would have liked to pursue the subject a little further. To get to the bottom of the mystery, for had his manner been other than it was (and if the idea had not seemed so absurd) she could almost suspect him of trying to flirt with her.

PART
SEVEN

Yet in the days and weeks which followed, although they were a great deal in each other's company, she had no cause to entertain such a suspicion again, and finally came to the conclusion that imagination had for a moment got the better of her. Lord Hendreth flirted with no one, but as time passed he was seen to be paying more and more attention to his ward. Not that there was anything in the least lover-like in his attitude towards her, but he regularly took her out in one of his sporting carriages, allowing her to drive his high-bred horses; acquired for her, from Lord Hatherley, a beautiful and spirited black mare, bred in the justly famous Hatherley stables; escorted her and Hebe to the theatre, to military reviews and balloon ascensions, and even to Almack's; and astonished society hostesses by accepting more of their invitations than he had done for years.

He was not a comfortable guest, for his abrasive manners, and inability to suffer fools gladly, set up more than one back, while most of the younger people were terrified of him; but since, with all his faults, he possessed those two essential qualities of the matrimonial prize, irreproachable lineage and a large fortune, the mothers of marriageable girls neglected no opportunity to bring their nervous daughters to his attention. Hebe, watching, as it were, from the wings, found this hugely entertaining, and on one occasion, having seen a determined matron ruthlessly routed, could not resist saying to him. 'Have you *no* mercy? That poor child is now utterly in disgrace with her mama for failing to capture your fancy. You might at least have aked her to dance.'

His glance mocked her. 'What, and raise utterly unfounded hopes in her mama's bosom? You shock me, ma'am! Besides, I am waiting for *you* to stand up with me.'

Hebe sighed. 'As I have several times reminded you, sir, propriety forbids me to dance.'

'Only propriety? This is most encouraging! I imagined that you totally disapproved of such a frivolous pastime.'

'You imagined nothing of the kind,' she said indignantly, 'for I told you how horridly conspicuous I used to feel, dancing with a partner shorter than myself.'

'So you did! Come and dance with me, then, and you will not feel in the least conspicuous.'

Hebe looked at the couples beginning to circle the room in a waltz. It was out of the question, of course, but just for a moment she wondered what it would be like to glide across the floor with Hendreth towering over her, her hand in his, his other arm around her waist—! Thrusting such unseemly thoughts aside, she said in a tone of strong common sense, 'You are very much mistaken, my lord! I have not danced for years, and the waltz only in the schoolroom, so would undoubtedly make such a mull of it that I would be *odiously* conspicuous. A laughing-stock, in fact, especially if compared, as I undoubtedly would be, with Barbary. She dances exquisitely. Her feet scarcely seem to touch the floor.'

Barbary was at that moment dancing with Viscount Linwood, who had been one of her most fervent admirers ever since their first meeting at Lady Felchester's ball, and Hendreth's glance followed them as they whirled past.

'Yes,' he remarked ironically, 'I have heard her compared variously to a piece of thistledown, a fairy, a rose-leaf blown by the wind and numerous other unlikely objects, each one more nauseating than the last. Young Linwood yonder is one of the worst offenders.'

Hebe looked indignantly up at him as he stood beside her chair. Lord Linwood was her favourite among Barbary's many admirers, and she secretly cherished hopes of a happy outcome.

'It is most unfair to poke fun at him on that account,' she said sharply. 'The compliments he pays Barbary may be extravagant, but there is no doubt that they are sincere. He is quite desperately in love with her.'

'Very likely!' Hendreth's tone was mordant. 'And this time next year he will be just as desperately in love with another reigning beauty. He is still in his salad days.'

'How odiously cynical!'

Hebe, too, was now watching Barbary and her partner, and thinking what a charming couple they made, the Viscount's fair good looks a perfect foil for the girl's dark beauty. She was unaware that Hendreth had transferred his own regard to her, and only became aware of it when he said with some amusement, 'Take care! You have the look of fond complacency I have seen in the face of many a matchmaking mama, and it will not do to pin your hopes on *that* marriage.'

She flushed and averted her gaze, but said with a hint of tartness, 'It is *my* belief, my lord, that Linwood will make Barbary an offer.'

'I am quite certain that he will. I am equally certain that I shall refuse my consent.'

'You will—?' She looked up at him again, torn between disbelief and anger. 'Why? What have you against him?'

He shrugged. 'Against the boy himself, no more than against any other untried cub. As a husband for Barbary, a great deal.'

'I do not see what objection you can possibly have! He is well born, with excellent manners and a most amiable disposition—!'

'Too amiable!' he broke in curtly. 'He could never manage Barbary! The minx would bring him around her finger until she grew bored with his devotion, and then toss her bonnet over the windmill just to relieve the tedium. My strongest objection, however, is that Linwood is the eldest of a large family, his father's estates are grossly encumbered, and *he* would dislike the match for his son as greatly as I would dislike it for my ward. He is on the lookout for an heiress for the boy. Some nabob's daughter, like your young friend, Mrs Fernhurst.'

The mordant note was still in his voice, and Hebe experienced again the uneasy qualm which always assailed her whenever Hendreth referred to the Fernhursts. It was true that a certain degree of intimacy had developed between her and Geoffrey's wife, for Aurelia, pathetically grateful for Hebe's kindness at their first meeting, showed an embarrassing tendency to cling to her, and though Hebe had done nothing to encourage this, she had not the heart to rebuff one for whom she felt sincere sympathy. It was more than disconcerting, however, to know that Hendreth had been observing them. She said, trying for a light note, '*Is* she a nabob's daughter? I did not know.'

'Lord, yes! The old man made a fortune in India. He's the younger son of some north-country squire, but by the time he settled again in England, his health was broken and he was advised to live in the most temperate climate he could find. He bought a property in Devon which as luck would have it—Fernhurst's luck, that is—adjoined Fernhurst's father's place.'

'Mrs Fernhurst, I believe, is an only child?'

'The only surviving one. Her elder brothers and sisters were all born, and died, in India, so the girl is her father's sole heiress. Fernhurst has done very well for himself.'

Hebe regarded him rather suspiciously. 'You appear to know a great deal about his affairs.'

Hendreth shrugged. 'From my mother. As you are aware, Fernhurst's aunt, Mrs Barrington, is one of her bosom-bows. As his wife appears to be becoming one of yours.'

'I am sorry for her,' Hebe said defensively. 'She is such a timid little thing, and not at all well just at present. Someone should tell her husband that what she really needs is to be living quietly at home in the country, with her mama close at hand, instead of racketing about town as she is obliged to do.'

'Why don't *you*?' Hendreth suggested calmly. 'Tell him, I mean. After all, you have been acquainted with him for some time.'

Hebe's startled gaze flew up to meet his. He met it blandly, and she said with an effort, 'I have been acquainted for some time with a number of persons, my lord, but I would not dream of meddling in their private concerns, no matter what my opinion of their conduct might be.' Then, partly to change the subject, and partly because she was genuinely concerned, she went on, 'This is a nonsensical conversation! We were speaking, my lord, of Barbary.'

'I know we were,' he agreed sympathetically. 'I had just pointed out to you the impossibility of a match between her and Linwood, and you were about to advance some revoltingly sentimental reason why I should consent to it.' He shook his head. 'No, ma'am! I know you have a *tendre* for the boy, but it will not do. Besides, I have something different in mind for Barbary.'

More than that he would not say, but Hebe was left in no doubt that he was wholly in earnest about the Viscount. She began to worry in case Barbary had formed an attachment in that quarter, for it occurred to her that just lately the girl seemed to have changed. There was a softer quality about her now which made her more enchanting than ever, and though she still dispensed her favours impartially among her many admirers, Hebe felt that she was no longer being ruled entirely by practical considerations. At the first opportunity she tried tactfully to discover her charge's feelings towards the Viscount, and was only partially reassured when Barbary said cheerfully, 'Linwood? Oh, I like him very well, but he is only a boy, after all! I think I prefer older gentlemen.'

Since her suitors ranged from Sir Matthew Dodington, a widower in his forties with daughters nearly as old as herself, to the inarticulate, nineteen-year-old brother of one of her intimates, it was to be supposed that she had had ample opportunity to arrive at that conclusion. Hebe would have liked to inquire further, but did not feel that she and Barbary were upon sufficiently close terms for her to do so.

To her astonishment, Hebe had found that she, too, was not without a little group of admirers, and though it was galling to have to admit that Lord Hendreth had been right, she was feminine enough to be secretly flattered by their attentions. Yet though the wound dealt by Geoffrey Fernhurst had long since healed, she was wary of risking such unhappiness again, and withdrew behind a barrier of quiet dignity which, though she was always pleasant, encouraged no man to suppose that he found favour in her eyes. Only one person was able to breach her defences, for no matter how often she resolved to treat Hendreth with the same reserve, he invariably contrived to provoke her into crossing swords with him. He was, she told herself frequently, the most exasperating, autocratic person she had ever known; she would not admit, even to herself, that she found their encounters a stimulating change from the endless exchange of civilities which fashionable life seemed to demand.

One day towards the end of May, Hebe received an unexpected morning visit from Lady Felchester. Barbary was out, and Hebe, in the back drawing room where the pianoforte stood, was listening to Sybilla's most recently learned song. From where she sat she saw the door of the front drawing room open and Wrightson usher in Hendreth's aunt, but before she could rise, or the butler announce the visitor, Lady Felchester lifted an imperious finger to prevent them. She then waved Wrightson away, advanced into the middle of the room and stood listening until the song came to an end. Sybilla, seated at the instrument, remained unaware of her arrival until the last note had died away and Hebe got up and went to greet the caller. Then, flushed with embarrassment, she rose and came reluctantly forward to make her curtsy.

Lady Felchester smiled kindly at her. 'Delightful!' she said briskly. 'You have a remarkably fine voice, child. Cultivate it! She turned to Hebe. 'I am happy to find you alone, Lady Roxwell. There is a matter I wish to discuss with you.'

Hebe's heart sank, for these words sounded ominous, but she hid her misgivings, saying with a smile, 'Pray be seated, ma'am. Sybilla dear, will you be good enough to tell Wrightson to deny me to anyone who may call while Lady Felchester is with me?' She waited until the girl had left them, and then said bluntly, 'Is something wrong, ma'am?'

'Most certainly it is,' Lady Felchester replied trenchantly, 'and, as usual, it is my nephew's doing!' She then interrupted herself to ask abruptly, 'Where is Miss Roxwell?'

'She has driven out with Lord Hatherley,' Hebe faltered. 'To Richmond Park.' A pang of uneasiness assailed her. 'That is unexceptionable, is it not?'

'Oh, quite! Hatherley, you say?' She paused, apparently giving the matter her consideration. 'Thought he seemed taken with her! Would have been a capital thing for her, too!'

'Lord Hatherley?' Hebe was taken aback. 'Surely he is a great deal older than she?'

'Ten or twelve years, no more! I doubt if he is very much over thirty.' She added meaningly, *'Hendreth* is thirty-five.'

'Yes, I know, but what has that to do with—!'' Hebe broke off as the import of Lady Felchester's words dawned upon her, and then, after a moment of stunned disbelief, said incredulously, ''You cannot be serious?'

'Question is, is Hendreth serious?' Lady Felchester demanded unanswerably. 'And, my dear Lady Roxwell, it's a question more and more people are asking! Some of them have even had the impertinence to ask it of me.'

Hebe became aware of a most curious sensation. She felt as though the bottom had dropped out of her world, that there was no longer any sure foundation, any support to which to cling. She tried to draw a deep breath to steady herself, and could not because her heart was thudding so painfully and there was a strange tightness in her chest, as though all the tears in the world were gathering there. It's shock, she thought muzzily. Shock at the idea that anyone could give credence to a thing so manifestly absurd. Barbary and *Hendreth*—?

'I found it impossible to believe,' Lady Felchester was saying, 'though it cannot be denied that he has singled her out for a degree of attention I have never before known him to bestow on a female. A respectable female,' she added as an afterthought.

There was a pause. Hebe could think of nothing to say, and in any case was not at all sure that her voice would work if she did. Two names were repeating themselves stupidly and endlessly in her mind. Barbary and Hendreth! Barbary and Hendreth . . .!

'Remaining in town for weeks on end!' Lady Felchester was enumerating instances of her nephew's uncharacteristic conduct. 'Letting her drive his horses. Squiring you both to parties and theatres and to Almack's. *Almack's*! He had never set foot in the place before!'

Hebe moistened her lips. 'She *is* his ward,' she offered feebly.

'Precisely! It cannot look well, if he does want to marry her. Better to delay until she is full age, but I cannot see Hendreth having the patience to wait nearly two years for his bride. The girl either, if she favours him.' She looked sharply at Hebe. 'Do you think she does?'

Hebe shook her head helplessly. Disjointed sentences flashed through her mind. 'I think I prefer older gentlemen.' 'I have something different in mind for Barbary.' Was it possible? It was incredible, unthinkable, but—was it possible?

'She does not confide in me,' she managed to say after a moment. 'There is no closeness between us. Not as there is between Sybilla and me. I know nothing of Barbary's real feelings.'

'Does her sister?'

'I should not think so,' Hebe said doubtfully, 'and even if she does, I could not ask her to betray a confidence.'

'Very true,' Lady Felchester conceded regretfully. 'However, the matter will have to be cleared up one way or another. Can't have him ruining the girl's chances by being so particular in his attentions, if he *don't* want to marry her.'

'Do you—!' Hebe was still having trouble with her voice, and had to start the question over again. 'Do you *really* believe, ma'am, that such a thing is possible? I remember that you told Lord Hendreth it was high time he married—!'

'Been telling him so for the past five years,' Lady Felchester replied bluntly, 'and much heed he has paid to me! No, Lady Roxwell, I did not believe it! When it was first hinted to me, I said it was a bag of moonshine. Couldn't see Hendreth marrying a chit out of the schoolroom, no matter how pretty and spirited she might be. But this morning I received a letter from my sister-in-law.' She added abruptly, 'You know he posted down to Bath a few days ago?'

Hebe nodded. 'Yes, he told me that it was Lady Hendreth's birthday this week and that it is his custom to spend it with her.' She paused, realized that her hands were gripped so tightly together that it hurt, and deliberately relaxed them. 'Did—did her ladyship's letter give you reason to alter your opinion?'

'It most certainly did,' Lady Felchester said decisively. 'Oh, not in so many words, but I could tell from the whole tone of it that she is in the high gig, and she writes that she has every reason to believe that he will now remain fixed indefinitely in England. That can mean only one thing. He assured her years ago that once he married, he would give up his nonsensical travelling. Good thing, too!'

'Yes,' Hebe said in a low voice. 'Yes, her ladyship told me that.' She drew a long breath. 'It would seem that it is certain, then!'

'Nothing,' her ladyship declared forcefully, 'is certain where my nephew is concerned, except that he will set the world by the ears if he can. The most we can hope for is that since he has informed his mother of his intention, she will prevail upon him not to delay the announcement of his engagement any longer.'

'Perhaps,' Hebe suggested reluctantly, 'that is the reason for his reticence. Would he not wish Lady Hendreth to be the first to know, and to tell her himself, rather than by writing to her, before making the engagement public?'

Lady Felchester looked much struck. 'Now why did I not think of that? You are right, of course! He *would* not for the world let *her* learn of it in any other way. Dare say that was why he had you take the girl to visit his mother before bringing her to London. Wanted her to meet his intended bride!'

She got up, rearranged her silk shawl about her shoulders, and nodded in a satisfied way at Hebe, who had also risen. It was clear that the matter was now satisfactorily settled in her mind, at least.

'Depend upon it, we may look for an announcement any day after his return,' she continued cheerfully. 'Foolish of me not to have realized how things were, for then I need not have troubled you, Lady Roxwell. Still, there's no harm done! Quite the reverse, in fact, for it's as well for you to know what's in the wind, and I fancy you had no suspicion?'

Rather faintly, Hebe admitted it, and Lady Felchester then shook her hand briskly and went away, leaving her hostess a prey to the most profound agitation. Hebe was not sure just why she was agitated; why the thought of Hendreth marrying

Barbary should have turned her whole world upside down. It could make little difference, surely? She would still be the mistress of Astington Park, in charge of Sybilla and the twins; he would still be their guardian, and the younger boys'; in fact, it would make everything easier, since he would be in England, within reach if any sudden crisis occurred. There was no reason in the world for this feeling of hollow emptiness, or for the prospect of a return to Astington later in the summer, which had seemed so enticing, suddenly to lose all its appeal, just because it now seemed more than likely that at the same time, Barbary would be going to Abbotswood as Hendreth's bride.

Later in the day, when Lord Hatherley brought Barbary home, Hebe found herself studying the girl, searching for something which might confirm or deny what Lady Felchester had told her. Barbary was certainly looking exceptionally radiant. There was a kind of glow about her which might well, Hebe thought wretchedly, be the sign of a girl happily and confidently in love and certain that her love was returned.

They went to Almack's that night. Barbary danced every dance; gathered her usual court of admirers about her; seemed not in the least disconsolate because Lord Hendreth was not there. Yet why should she be disconsolate? In a few days he would return, and no doubt claim her as his own. Hebe, seated among the chaperones, exchanging platitudes with the mothers and aunts of Barbary's friends, felt for the first time that she belonged irrevocably there. Her head began to ache, and she wished with all her heart that she could have stayed at home.

Next morning brought a letter from Clement at Oxford. He had paid a brief visit to Astington, and wrote to assure Hebe that all was well there, and to recount such items of local news as might be supposed to interest her. Old Mr Nidwell had died, characteristically at a time and in a manner calculated to cause his daughters the maximum inconvenience and distress; General Gaynes and Mr Lorde had fallen out yet again over the question of a boundary fence; Abbotswood was a hive of activity, because Hendreth had given orders that all the rooms which for years had stood closed, the ornaments packed away and the furniture swathed in holland covers, were to be made ready for use again. Curiosity was rife in the neighbourhood, and speculation that at last his lordship must have decided to marry and settle down.

Feeling more depressed than ever, and totally disinclined to share the contents of the letter with Barbary and Sybilla, Hebe put it away and tried to divert her mind by dealing with various domestic matters. These occupied her for an hour or so, by which time Barbary had gone out with Amy Delaford and Amy's elder, married sister, and Sybilla, presumably, joined her little sisters and Miss Stillwood in the schoolroom. Hebe, still possessed by an unaccountable desire to keep herself occupied and not have time for reflection, decided to write an overdue letter to Mrs Hallam, but she had scarcely seated herself at the writing-table in the drawing room and picked up a pen when the door opened and Wrightson came in.

'Pardon me, my lady,' he said apologetically, 'but a Mr Murslowe has called, and begs that your ladyship will be gracious enough to grant him a few minutes of your time. I would have informed him that you are not at home, but he assures me that he was for many years in the service of the late Sir Hugo Roxwell, and so I thought that your ladyship might wish to see him.'

Her ladyship, half turned from the table but with the pen still between her fingers, did not present the appearance of one eager to interview her late husband's old retainer. There was dismay as well as astonishment in her face, and Wrightson thought she had even turned a little pale. Several moments passed before she replied, but then she said in an expression-less voice, 'Yes, he was Sir Hugo's valet. I cannot imagine why he should wish to see me, but you had better show him in.'

The butler withdrew, and Hebe got up and walked across to the fireplace, an unpleasant and irrational tremor of apprehension running through her. What, in heaven's name, could Murslowe want? She thought she had seen the last of him when she sent him home from Italy, and her first, instinctive reaction had been to refuse to receive him, for to do so could only revive unwelcome memories. Then she had realized that if she did refuse, she would always wonder uneasily why he had asked to see her, for he never had, and never would, wish her anything but ill, and it was better to meet such animosity face to face than to risk increasing it by denying herself.

She was still standing by the fireplace when Murslowe was shown in, and as she watched him come towards her she saw how his sly glance darted over his surroundings, making a swift, assessing survey of the style and comfort of the drawing room itself and of the back drawing room partially visible through the archway at its far end. Then he paused in front of her, and the same assessing look flickered over her from head to foot, taking in the elegant morning-dress of pale green cambric, the fashionably dressed hair beneath the frivolous scrap of a cap, and only when he had assimilated every detail of her appearance did his eyes briefly meet hers. Then he bowed to exactly the proper depth, just as he had always done, with the deference which was somehow insulting in its studied correctness. Irritation overcame uneasiness, and she said coldly, 'Well, Murslowe? I did not expect to meet you again.'

'No, my lady, and I am deeply grateful to your ladyship for consenting to see me, when you have, I am sure, so many pressing engagements, so many calls upon your time.'

His tone was as correct as his manner, but none the less Hebe felt certain that he was mocking her. His eyes were discreetly lowered, his sour, pale face wore a respectful expression, but she knew, as surely as though she could see into his mind, that he was remembering a previous confrontation, in her dressing room at the villa when he had brought her the fragments of Geoffrey's letter. She felt herself go hot with humiliation, and, fearful that he might detect it, turned away to sit down.

'Yes,' she said coolly, disposing her skirts about her, 'I have a great many things to do, so perhaps you will tell me without delay what you wish me to do for you. You do, I presume,' she added ironically, 'wish me to do *something?*'

'I *hope* that you will, my lady,' he admitted apologetically. 'The truth is that I find myself in somewhat unhappy circumstances.'

Her brows lifted. 'Indeed? I am sorry to hear it. Have you no present employment?'

'I have, my lady, but it is not what I have been used to. My employer is Sir Barnaby Kyte, a merchant knight of the City. A worthy person, but vulgar.' He sighed. 'Your ladyship will recollect that Sir Hugo dressed always in the styles prevalent in his youth, and my long association with him had left me ill equipped to minister to today's gentlemen of high fashion. Sir Barnaby was a last resort, but beggars, you will agree, cannot be choosers.'

Hebe regarded him with a little frown. The air of humility did not deceive her. Murslowe hated her as much as ever, but if, as she suspected, he was leading up to asking her for money, she could not imagine why he should expect her to give him any. Yet he did expect it. His humble, apologetic air was the thinnest of veneers over supreme self-confidence.

'This is very regrettable, Murslowe,' she said with assumed indifference, 'but I fail to see what it has to do with me. You cannot be foolish enough to imagine that *I* am in a position to help you to more congenial employment?'

'Oh, no, my lady,' he assured her promptly. 'That would be beyond anything foolish! The truth is—if your ladyship will permit me to explain—that although I have been in service since my early youth, it has always been my ambition eventually to retire, and acquire an establishment of my own. An establishment in a select part of town which would provide accommodation for single gentlemen of *ton*. I could achieve that ambition, my lady, if I came into possession of, let us say, five thousand pounds.'

Hebe stared blankly at him for a moment, and then she laughed. His meaning was clear, but the suggestion was so outrageous, so fantastic, that she was unable to take it seriously.

'I should think you very well might,' she said dryly. 'I should think you might as well live in comfort and idleness for the rest of your days, but even supposing that I could raise such a sum—which is, of course, out of the question—why in heaven's name should I make *you* a gift of it?'

He moved his hands in a deprecating gesture. 'Oh, not a gift, my lady! A gift implies nothing in return. No, no! It would be a price. A purchase price.'

'Would it, indeed?' She still could not believe that he was serious, and her tone was sceptical. 'And what would I be purchasing—for five thousand pounds?'

There was the tiniest pause before he replied. He lifted his gaze to meet hers—it was the first time he had looked directly at her since that one fleeting glance when he entered the room—and his eyes were cold and vindictive and utterly without mercy. He said, softly and triumphantly. 'My silence, Lady Roxwell. My silence concerning what happened in Rome.'

For a few seconds shock held her silent, all feeling suspended, and then anger at his effrontery began to take possession of her. So he was threatening to make public her supposed *affaire* with Geoffrey Fernhurst. A year, even six months ago, she might have believed that such a disclosure would do harm beyond repair, but she was by now sufficiently well acquainted with the standards of the *ton* to know that such lapses on the part of married women were by no means uncommon, or even, if discreetly conducted, very much frowned upon. A single girl's reputation must be jealousy guarded, but once the protection of the marriage ring was hers (and she had provided her husband with an unquestioningly lawful heir) very few people condemned her if she took a lover.

'I do not like being threatened, Murslowe,' she said coldly at length. 'Nothing of which I have cause to be ashamed happened in Rome, but even if I *had* betrayed my husband, the disclosure now of my infidelity could not do me so much harm that I would feel constrained to pay *you* a small fortune to keep it secret. If you believe that it would, you know very little of the world.'

Murslowe continued steadily to regard her. He did not seem in the least put out by her contemptuous dismissal of his threat, for the mean lines of his mouth widened in a smile which did not alter the coldness of his eyes. He said, in the same softly triumphant voice, 'Your ladyship is, of course, perfectly right. Fine. ladies commit adultery every day. It is less common, however, for them to commit murder also.'

Hebe gasped, and the thought flashed into her mind that the man must be mad. She glanced swiftly at the bellrope hanging beside the fireplace, and wondered if he would try to prevent her if she tried to summon Wrightson. As though reading her thoughts, Murslowe said contemptuously. 'No, I am not deranged, and it is useless to try to convince yourself, or anyone else, that I am. You murdered your husband, Lady Roxwell, because he had found out that Mr Fernhurst was your lover, and meant you to pay dearly for your faithlessness. You murdered him because you knew that never again, as long as he lived, would you make any move which was not watched, have any acquaintance, man or woman, whom Sir Hugo did not know and approve. That you were to be kept as close as any prisoner, and would be unable henceforth to enjoy the wealth for the sake of which you had married an old man. You could see no way to loosen your bonds, and so you severed them.'

Hebe listened to his accusations with growing alarm, for if he believed what he was saying, he could not be completely sane. She said in a reasonable tone, seeking to humour him, 'How am I supposed to have committed this crime? You were present. You know how Sir Hugo died.'

'Yes, I know! I saw him die in agony, of the poison which for days you had been administering to him in the guise of medicine. You did not even summon a doctor until you knew he was beyond all help.'

Hebe rested her hands on the arms of her chair and gripped hard, as though by the action she could retain, too, a grip on reality, and with a tremendous effort kept her voice calm and reasonable.

'If you believed that, Murslowe, why did you not accuse me then?'

A sneer twisted his lips. 'In a foreign land, where I knew only a few words of the language while your ladyship spoke it as fluently as any native? Where every servant in the house except myself was of *your* choosing, and obedient to your commands? No, no, my lady! I did not even dare to betray my suspicions, for fear that you would find the means to send me the same way as my poor master. When you arranged for me to return to England I looked upon it as a deliverance, and was thankful to make my escape.'

Hebe continued to stare at him, fighting a rising sense of panic. On the face of it, Murslowe's threat seemed absurd, to accuse her of an imagined crime committed a year before in a foreign land, with no evidence to support the charge. Yet would he make the threat if it were as empty as it seemed? He was no fool, and she had rejected by now the thought that he was the victim of some wild delusion concerning Sir Hugo's death. This was a deliberate and carefully calculated attempt to exort money from her, and to make such an attempt at all, with the inevitably unpleasant consequences to himself if it failed, he must be confident of the outcome. That was what frightened her.

It was vital not to let him recognize that fear. She said in the same calm way, 'I have been back in England, Murslowe, for nearly a year. If you entertain such suspicions, why have you not come forward before? And why not make your accusation in the proper quarter, instead of offering to condone my supposed crime by keeping silent—at a price?'

He lifted his shoulders and spread out his hands in mock regret. 'Madam, I am a poor man, in uncongenial employment and approaching old age. I cannot afford the luxury of seeing you brought to justice.'

She raised her brows. 'Indeed?' she said ironically. 'Are you sure it is not because you know that such a charge, supported by your word alone, would be received with derision and disbelief?'

'My word alone?' he said softly. 'I think your ladyship has forgotten Lucia, your maid. She, too, was in Rome.' Hebe made an impatient movement, but he continued smoothly, 'Oh, at first she would undoubtedly range herself with your ladyship against me, but would her loyalty survive questioning under oath in a court of law? Remember, she is in the same unfortunate position that I occupied in Rome. She is a foreigner in a strange land, and a papist to boot. I think fright and self-interest would eventually overcome any feelings of loyalty.'

Hebe knew that he was right. Lucia, like Murslowe himself in similar circumstances, had made no attempt to master her employer's language, and Hebe could imagine how terrified she would be if she were questioned by lawyers or magistrates, much less be required to give evidence before judge and jury.

Murslowe saw the dismay in his victim's face, and smiled thinly with unconcealed satisfaction.

'I do not say,' he went on consideringly, 'that your lady-ship would be convicted upon such evidence, but to be brought to trial at all would be enough to ruin you, and I am confident that I can arouse enough suspicion against you to ensure *that*.' He sighed. 'What a sensation it will cause! You have been, in vulgar parlance, cutting quite a dash in fashionable circles since coming to London. You *and* your charming young charge! You might be acquitted, but mud sticks, Lady Roxwell, even when it is spattered on the innocent as well as the guilty. You would be very well advised, you know, to agree to the arrangement I suggest.'

He paused, letting the implications of his words sink in, letting her imagination fill in the appalling details of the picture he had so roughly sketched. And fill them in it did, more luridly than anything he could have said. Hebe saw herself suddenly as the centre of ever-widening circles of scandal and disgrace, circles which spread outwards like the ripples caused by a stone cast into water until they touched everyone with whom she had the least degree of intimacy; and just as the ripples nearest to the stone were deepest, so the trouble would most grievously afflict those to whom she was most closely bound.

She felt as though she were in the grip of a nightmare, which was made all the more horrible by its prosaic background. Her pleasant drawing room, with the sunlight of early sum-mer slanting between the curtains to lay patches of brightness on the floor; the everyday sounds from the street below; even the neat figure of Murslowe, with its air of mock deference, standing before her as though awaiting some trivial domestic instruction. As though he were not holding a pistol to her head.

Her terrified thoughts scurried to and fro, but after a minute or two, out of the welter of dismay, fear and helpless anger, one idea slowly emerged. She must play for time. There was not the smallest hope that she could raise the sum Murslowe was demanding, but she had to make him believe that she might; had to gain a respite in which to seek a way of escape from the trap closing about her.

'If I did agree,' she said slowly at last, 'you must realize that I would need time. Such arrangements cannot be made at a moment's notice.'

'My lady, I am aware of that.' Murslowe bowed slightly, outwardly the perfect servant. 'I shall naturally wait upon your ladyship's convenience. Shall we say—a week from today?'

'A week?' Hebe exclaimed in consternation, but then broke off, checked by the mockery in his eyes. After all, why not? She had as much hope of raising the money in a week as in a month, or three months, or a year. She shrugged. 'Very well, though I promise nothing.'

Murslowe bowed again. 'I shall wait upon your ladyship a week from today.'

'No!' Hebe spoke sharply. 'I have to wish to arouse curiosity in my household by repeatedly receiving you. As soon as I have anything to tell you, I will send you word.'

'I am at your ladyship's service,' he said mockingly, 'and shall await your summons with no common degree of anticipation. The house of Sir Barnaby Kyte, my lady, in Russell Square. I do trust, though, that your ladyship will not be foolish enough to delay our next meeting *too* long, for that, you know, would have the most unfortunate consequences.'

He left her with that implied threat ringing in her ears, and for several minutes after he had gone, Hebe remained motionless in her chair, contemplating with despair the inevitability of disaster, for though she had gained a breathing space, she could see no way out of the impasse confronting her. Her widow's jointure was ample to maintain her in a considerable degree of luxury, but it was provided out of the Roxwell estate and she had no capital on which to draw. The modest house in Cambridge, at present hired out to a tenant, was worth not one tenth of the sum Murslowe had demanded. A money-lender was out of the question, even if she knew how to find one, since she had no adequate security to offer against so substantial a loan.

Hendreth! The thought was instinctive, and so was the almost overwhelming desire to turn to him for help. He

certainly possessed the means to rescue her, and no doubt, for
Barbary's sake, would also have the will, since even his
profound disregard for public opinion could scarcely accept
with equanimity the prospect of his bride's step-aunt and
chaperone being charged with her husband's murder. Hebe
toyed with the idea for a moment or two, imagining the relief
of placing her difficulties in his more than capable hands, yet
knowing all the while that she could never bring herself to do
it. She was not quite sure why. He would rake her down
unmercifully, but she was not afraid of his blunt tongue; it
would mean confessing her brief infatuation with Geoffrey,
but the humiliation of being known for a romantic fool would
surely be a small price to pay for escape from her present
perilous situation. For Barbary's sake, and for the sake of
Barbary's brothers and sisters, she knew that she ought to
ask Hendreth's help, but she also knew that, for reasons into
which she instinctively shrank from probing, she would do
anything in the world rather than seek it.

Yet what *could* she do, to avert the disaster with which
Murslowe threatened her? Such a scandal would bear most
heavily on the young Roxwells, but they would not be the
only people harmed by it. There was Hendreth himself; Lady
Felchester, who had sponsored Hebe's entry into the world of
fashion; Lady Hendreth, who had been so kind and for whom
she had conceived so sincere an affection; even poor little
Aurelia Fernhurst, who was bound to feel she had been
callously betrayed by one whom she regarded with respect
and gratitude; and Lucia, a loyal servant who did not deserve
to be hounded and harassed by the Law.

For a little while, in her utter despair, Hebe even contemplated suicide, yet that, even supposing she could find the
courage and the means to do it, would create almost as great a
scandal as being accused of murder. Speculation as to the
cause of so desperate an act would run riot and make life
intolerable for all those whom she was most concerned to
protect. She could not leave them so bitter a legacy.

Somehow she got through the rest of the day, though she
could never afterwards remember how she had passed the
time. She must have done everything that was expected of
her—received callers, driven with Barbary in the Park, accom-

panied her during the evening to various social engagements—
yet no recollection of these things remained. threats, and the
utter impossibility of meeting his demands, and found no
room in her mind for anything but the frantic, futile search for
a way of escape.

It was early the next morning, after a sleepless night
which had left her almost lightheaded with worry and fatigue,
that the idea of flight occurred to her. Murslowe could hold
his threat over Lady Roxwell's head because she had become
a familiar figure in the world of fashion, but if her ladyship
were to disappear, to vanish completely, not merely from
London but from all contact with her friends and acquaintances,
that threat would be rendered wholly ineffectual. It was a plan
which could only have been born of desperation, fear and
exhaustion, but to Hebe in her extremity it seemed entirely
feasible. She must, of course, be gone from London before
Hendreth returned, since he would feel no compunction about
probing into reasons which everyone else would accept without question, and she must think of some way of covering her
tracks to preclude any possibility of pursuit. It was a measure
of the state of mind to which the past hours had reduced her
that this seemed a reasonable solution to all her problems.

It was no more than a vague, general idea at first, but when
letters were brought to her as she and the two girls sat at
breakfast, and she saw that one of them was from a friend at
Cambridge, it crystallized suddenly into a plan of action.
Reading the letter without absorbing one word of its contents,
she uttered an exclamation compounded of dismay and
annoyance, adding, as Barbary and Sybilla turned inquiring
faces towards her, 'Oh, how vexing! My dears, I shall be
obliged to leave you for a day or two. Something has occurred which makes it imperative for me to visit my old home
without delay.'

They stared. Sybilla said blankly, 'Leave us? Leave us
alone in London?'

'You will not be alone, love. Miss Stillwood is here, and I
shall, of course, inform Lady Felchester and solicit her good
offices on your behalf.'

'Aunt Hebe, you *can't* go away!' Barbary broke in
indignantly. 'Tomorrow is the Allingtons' Venetian breakfast!'

'Yes, Barbary, I know! I will send a note to Mrs Delaford, asking if you may go with her and Amy.' Barbary looked sulky, and she added with a touch of sharpness, 'I am exceedingly sorry, but it cannot be helped, and I am quite sure that matters can be arranged so that you do not lack *someone* to chaperone you to all your engagements while I am away. Now I must go. I have a great many things to attend to.'

She pushed back her chair and got up. Sybilla sat staring down at her plate with a troubled expression, but Barbary looked decidedly put out, and as Hebe went towards the door said pointedly, though with apparent irrelevance, 'Hendreth will be back in town any day now.'

Hebe, feeling unequal to an argument at that moment, pretended not to hear, but the reminder filled her with a strong sense of urgency. That it filled her also with a feeling of the utmost wretchedness and desolation she did her best to ignore.

The next few hours were crowded, and left her no time for reflection, but at last the post chaise and four was at the door, and the family, shepherded by Miss Stillwood, assembled in the hall to bid her goodbye. As Hebe shook hands with her, the governess said a little anxiously, 'Forgive me, Lady Roxwell, but it is already past two o'clock. You will never reach Cambridge today.'

'No, but I shall be able to reach Bishop's Stortford, which is a little more than halfway,' Hebe replied with a calmness she was far from feeling, 'and if I set forward early tomorrow morning, it should be possible to arrive at Cambridge by noon. It is of the utmost importance that I get there as soon as I can.'

Except that I am not going to Cambridge, she thought wearily. From Bishop's Stortford I shall go to Harwich, cross to the Continent from there, and then—where? It does not matter, as long as I can lose myself in an anonymous obscurity.

She turned to embrace the twins, holding each of them close for a moment and thinking with anguish that this was the last time she would ever do so. When she kissed Sybilla's cheek, the girl suddenly flung her arms around her, clinging tightly and saying in an urgent undervoice, almost as though she suspected something amiss, 'Aunt Hebe, you *will* come back soon?'

'Dearest, what a foolish question! Did I not say I must leave you for a *few days*?' Hebe released herself gently and turned, almost with relief, to brush her lips against Barbary's cool, dutifully offered cheek. No fear of any emotional farewells there. 'Remember, Barbary, should any gentlemen call, you may receive them only if Miss Stillwood or your sister is present, and do not go out without your maid or a footman to accompany you, or your groom if you are riding.'

Barbary assured her indifferently that she would, and Hebe, unable to find any further excuse to linger, and fearful that if she did she might betray her emotion, went quickly out of the house and climbed into the waiting chaise. Lucia followed her, since to set out unattended by her maid would certainly arouse suspicion, and as the carriage moved off Hebe's last glimpse of her 'family' was Kitty and Jane waving goodbye from the doorstep. She fluttered her handkerchief in response, and then averted her face to stare fixedly through the window beside her so that Lucia would not see that she was blinking away tears.

Lucia, in fact, presented a problem. Since she spoke so little English it was unlikely that she would realize for some time their change of destination, but once they arrived at Harwich it would be necessary for Hebe to take the maid into her confidence to a certain degree. What she would make of her mistress's sudden decision to abandon a luxurious and privileged way of life in favour of precarious independence abroad Hebe could not tell, but she hoped, once they were in Europe, that by making Lucia a generous present of money and setting her on her way to her native land, she could prevail upon the woman to accept that decision without question.

Lucia might be persuaded to accept it, but Hebe had an uneasy suspicion that there were those in England who would be less complaisant. It had occurred to her during the morning that simply to disappear without a word would not do; it would create a mystery, and the sort of sensation she most wanted to avoid, so it was essential that some sort of explanation should be left behind. In the end, she had written to Hendreth, informing him that she had tired of a life of

fashionable idleness, and the responsibility of an adoptive
family, and so was going away; he would oblige her by
making no attempt to follow or find her. Hebe did not expect
for one moment either that his lordship would believe her, or
be prepared to oblige her in this fashion, but as she had
directed the letter to him at Abbotswood she hoped that by the
time it caught up with him she would be beyond the reach of
any inquiries he might set afoot.

For the whole of the journey to Bishop's Stortford she
remained sunk in abject misery, as indifferent to the busy
City streets as to the leafy solitudes of Epping Forest. Contem-
plation of the unknown future filled her with misgiving, for
though she had a considerable sum of money with her it
would not last indefinitely, and by the time it was gone she
would have been obliged to find a way of earning her living.
She could teach, she supposed, since she was fluent in three
languages, or she could become a housekeeper, but neither of
these prospects did anything to raise her spirits.

Even more lowering, however, was the thought of those
left behind, and of the way in which they would come to
regard her. If Murslowe's object were revenge rather than
profit, he had achieved greater success than he knew, for all
those to whom she had become attached since her return to
England must surely remember her, if they remembered her at
all, with bitterness and contempt.

She spent another uneasy night, sleeping little, and set out
in the morning with a throbbing headache and a growing
conviction that she would be better dead, or else ought never
to have been born at all. The journey seemed endless, yet
when at last the chaise rolled into Harwich she felt she could
have wished it to last twice as long, so that she could have
deferred just a little the final, irrevocable step of leaving
England.

She found that this was to be deferred whether she would
or no, for the weather had worsened as they travelled eastwards,
and they reached the coast to find a violent summer storm
scourging the North Sea. Until this had blown itself out, Hebe
was told at the busy posting-inn where she was set down,
there was no possibility of any vessel leaving the harbour.

She bespoke bedchambers for herself and Lucia, and a

private parlour, reflecting ruefully after she had done so that this was an extravagance she would probably never be able to afford again. One became too easily accustomed, she thought, to the privileges of wealth. As Miss Cullingworth, she had readily accommodated herself to using the public rooms of inns; as Mrs Cameron (her mother's maiden name, which she intended to assume) she would have to learn to do so again.

By the time Hebe had eaten her dinner, Lucia had overcome the barrier of language sufficiently to discover the truth of their present whereabouts, and came to her mistress in considerable agitation. Hebe's explanation did nothing to soothe her, for she was too intelligent to accept it at face value, and she alternately begged Hebe to return to London or to confide to her the truth of whatever trouble was driving her away. It took a long time to convince her that her mistress could not be persuaded to do either, and to reconcile her to the idea of separating once they had crossed the sea, the argument continuing right up to the moment that Hebe climbed into bed. It left her exhausted, and with a horrid suspicion that the respite was only temporary, until the argument could be resumed in the morning.

So worn out was she that at last she slept heavily, and woke to hear the gale still rattling the windows and driving intermittent rain against the panes. This did not augur well for her escape, and later, when she went into the parlour for breakfast, the waiter who served the meal confirmed her worst fears. There was no hope of a passage that day, and even the prospect for the next was uncertain.

Hebe began to feel uneasy. There was no reason in the world why anyone should suspect she had not gone to Cambridge, but she could not rid herself of an uncomfortable feeling that something might yet happen to bring all her desperate plans to ruin.

The foreboding was to prove justified. Midway through the afternoon she was trying to occupy herself with a piece of needlework, though for the most part her hands lay idle in her lap as she sat lost in unhappy thought, while Lucia, seated by the table, plied a needle more diligently, repairing a torn flounce on the dress Hebe had worn the day before. Contrary to the latter's expectations, the maid had not repeated the arguments of the night before; she had spoken no more than was necessary, but her very silence was eloquent of deep disapproval and ill-usage, and did nothing to raise her mistress's spirits.

The parlour was at the rear of the inn, and though this circumstance rendered it quiet and secluded, it denied its occupants the diversion of watching the comings and goings in the busy yard and the street beyond. It also prevented them from watching any new arrivals, so when a familiar voice spoke in the passage outside, saying impatiently, 'In here, is she? No, don't trouble! I'll announce myself,' Hebe had only a few seconds of startled, horrified disbelief before the door was flung open and Lord Hendreth stood grimly regarding her from the threshold.

He looked a menacing figure as he loomed there in the doorway, his height and his breadth of shoulder exaggerated by a long, many-caped driving-coat of white drab, but Hebe's first reaction at sight of him was a surge of pure joy. This was succeeded an instant later by alarm and dismay, but it showed her, in a blinding flash of self-knowledge, the source of her deepest and most painful sorrow during the past few days. Revealed to her the extent of her own hitherto unsuspected folly.

Lucia was gaping at him, her sewing fallen from her hands. Hendreth glanced at her and said briefly—his Italian was as fluent at Hebe's, 'Leave us. My business with your mistress is private.'

'At once, my lord, and very gladly!' Lucia jumped up, bundling her work together anyhow and adding darkly as she made briskly for the door, 'Now perhaps there will be an end to this foolishness!'

He nodded. 'You may be sure of it. Occupy youself by packing your mistress's gear. We shall be leaving shortly.' He moved aside to let her go out, remarking sarcastically in English to a waiter lingering outside, 'Wasting your time, my friend! I doubt your ability to understand Italian.'

The man retreated in disorder, followed by Lucia. Hendreth closed the door and advanced into the room, removing his hat and shaking the raindrops from it before placing it, with his gloves, on the table. The driving-coat, also glistening with rain, was stripped off and flung down beside them, while Hebe watched with a sort of paralysed fascination. Then he turned to face her, and she saw with a little jolt of dismay that in spite of the deliberation of his movements he was thunderously, blazingly angry. She swallowed, and said in a voice which in spite of all her efforts emerged faint and quavering, 'What—what are you doing here?'

'Simple, my girl! I have been following you,' he replied shortly. 'The question would appear to be, what are *you* doing here? If your destination is Cambridge, you are a damned long way off course!'

She could find no answer to that, and instead said defiantly, 'Where I go, and why, is no concern of yours. You had no right to follow me!'

'No right?' He spoke quietly, but the tone bit. 'I return to town to find that you have abandoned your charges on the flimsiest of pretexts, run away from London like a panic-stricken schoolgirl, and you say I have no right to follow you? Good God! Did you suppose I would permit such hare-brained folly?'

His choice of words struck a spark of indignation which helped to bolster her flagging courage. She said more sharply, 'I am not accountable to you, sir, for my actions. If I choose to visit Cambridge, or—!'

'Cambridge?' he interjected with savage irony. 'You lack a sense of direction, my lady, as greatly as you lack common sense!'

This annoyed her more than ever, and she went on with considerable emphasis, '*Or* Harwich, or any other place in this country or out of it, that is *my* concern, and mine alone!'

'Wrong!' he said curtly. 'When you chose to take charge of my wards, you made yourself answerable to me. If the responsibility of them has grown irksome, I would expect you to inform me of it, not take yourself off and leave them to their own devices.'

'I did nothing of the kind! They are in Miss Stillwood's care, and Mrs Delaford said that she would chaperone Barbary.'

'Yes, for the few days she expected you to be away,' he replied scathingly, 'but *you* intended your absence to be permanent. Well, it won't do! There's no reason in the world why you cannot come back to London, and you may as well know that I've no intention of listening to any excuses.'

'There is every reason—!' Afraid of disclosing too much. Hebe choked back what she had been about to say, and after a second or two added desperately, 'Would not Lady Felchester—!'

'Aunt Felchester has already put herself to the trouble of presenting Barbary, and I can see no reason to burden her also with the task of arranging and acting as hostess at the party which must be held to mark Barbary's engagement.' He paused, narrowly studying Hebe's face, and then went on in a sardonic tone, 'Never tell me you did not suspect that *that* was imminent!'

'No.' Hebe spoke faintly, for she had the curious impression of having received a violent physical blow; she realized that she was trembling, and gripped her hands tightly together so that they would not betray her. 'I mean, yes! I was aware—but I did not know it would be so soon.'

'The sooner the better! The wedding will probably take place at the beginning of July, when young Clement comes down from Oxford—Barbary naturally wants him to give her away—so there will be a devil of a lot for you to attend to. Bride-clothes, and the like.' He paused, raising a sardonic eyebrow. 'You are singularly lacking in enthusiasm! What's the matter? I thought all women loved a wedding.'

'Lord Hendreth!' Hebe spoke as steadily as she could, her gaze fixed resolutely on her hands, still tightly clasped together in her lap. 'It is quite impossible for me to return to London, or even to remain in England. You cannot know my reason for this decision, and I can only entreat you not to inquire into it—!'

'I know precisely what your reason is!' he interrupted furiously. 'You are running like a frightened rabbit because Roxwell's crafty rogue of a servant tried to extort a sum of money you don't possess by threatening to have you charged with poisoning the old man. And you were fool enough to believe he could do it!'

The shock was so great that Hebe felt certain she was going to faint. There was a rushing sound in her ears, her surroundings faded into whirling darkness, and only a blind determina-

tion not to succumb to such weakness in front of Blaise
Hendreth enabled her to cling grimly to the edge of consciousness. After a little the weakness receded somewhat and
she was able to say faintly, 'How did you—?' You could not
possibly know about that!'

'Sybilla!' he replied shortly. 'By God, how I have misjudged that girl! It seems she was going through some music
in your back drawing room when the enterprising Mr Murslowe was admitted, and by the time she realized what was
happening, it was too late to disclose her presence. She heard
everything, and after the fellow left, slipped out by the other
door so that you wouldn't know she had been there.'

'Sybilla!' Hebe covered her eyes with her hand, remembering the girl's preoccupation, her anxiety as they said goodbye. 'Oh, poor child! I had no idea—I thought she was in the
schoolroom.' Another thought occurred to her, and she lifted
a puzzled face towards him. 'Yet that does not explain—did
she confide in *you*?'

He nodded. 'You seem as surprised as I was! I arrived in
London only a couple of hours after you left, and as I was
about to go into the house, Hatherley drove by with Barbary
in his curricle. They halted to exchange greetings, and Barbary mentioned the encounter to her sister when she got
home. Early yesterday morning, Sybilla came to my house in
the devil of a pucker.'

Hebe gasped. 'Sybilla did—what?'

He laughed shortly. 'You may well stare! No doubt you
always supposed she was scared to death of me. You're right!
She was, but, by God! It didn't prevent her from coming.
That, my lady, is the measure of her courage and of her
regard for you. And of her good sense! It's a pity you haven't
as much. Why the *devil* didn't you come to me yourself?'

'Oh, how could I? How could I tell *anyone*? And for
Sybilla to—! I would not for the world have had her hear
such things as Murslowe said!'

'Don't worry!' There was a jeering note in his voice that
made her flinch. 'She didn't believe a word of it, and in any
event I have the impression that she had not understood the
full implication of Fernhurst's part in the affair.'

'Thank heaven she did not! Overcome by mortification,

Hebe spoke in a whisper, her head bowed. 'Though it was not as you suppose. I was never—! Murslowe was lying, just as he once lied to Sir Hugo, for he always hated me.' There was no response to this, and a fleeting glance at his face showed her that it still wore that look of bleak anger. A sob rose in her throat, and she added with difficulty, 'I suppose I cannot expect you to believe that.'

'Why not?' he said in a hard voice. 'You don't doubt I believe he was lying about the cause of Roxwell's death.'

She made a little gesture of dismissal, not looking up. 'That is quite different.'

'Is it? You imagine that I can swallow without difficulty the notion that you are an adulteress, but choke on the suggestion that you have committed murder? For what kind of credulous fool do you take me? Knowing Fernhurst, I would be astonished to learn that he did not try to seduce you. Knowing you, I would be even more astonished to learn that he succeeded.'

'Thank you!' Relief that he did believe her caused the tears to brim over. She averted her face, saying in a stifled voice, 'I fear, though, that the rest of the world will be less charitable. I *must* go away! I cannot involve you all in so ugly a scandal.'

'I swear,' Hendreth said between his teeth, 'that if you do not stop talking fustian I'll treat you as you deserve, and beat you soundly! There will be no scandal. I have dealt with Murslowe. He will not trouble you again.'

'What?' She was sufficiently startled to look up. 'How can you say so?' An unwelcome thought occurred to her. 'Oh, heavens! You have not paid him the five thousand pounds?'

'You may be damned sure I have not!' He saw that she looked frightened, and added sardonically, 'Neither did I wring his neck, though the temptation to do so was almost irresistible. I simply made it plain to him that if one word of his lying accusation is ever heard, the consequences to himself will be so unpleasant that he would be well advised to blow his brains out rather than experience them.' He laughed shortly. 'You seem doubtful, ma'am! Do not be! Once he found he had me to deal with, instead of a hen-witted female, he sang a very different tune.'

Hebe had no difficulty in believing this, and was so thankful that she was able to ignore the insult implicit in those latter words. She knew now that her original impulse to seek his lordship's help had been the right one, and that had she yielded to it, she could have spared herself days of sickening anxiety. Even now it was difficult to realize that the threat no longer hung over her.

She said in a low voice, not looking at him, 'I am very grateful to you, and to Sybilla, and I see now that I was foolish to be so frightened, but it was not only myself I was trying to protect. Please do me the justice of believing that.'

'I do!' he replied dryly. 'I never doubted it for a moment. It is not your motives, but your methods which infuriate me. Did you really imagine that to vanish without a word of explanation would not cause just the sort of sensation you were anxious to avoid?'

'I am not *that* stupid,' she said indignantly. 'I wrote a letter to *you,* informing you that I was going away and asking you not to try to find me.'

He looked sceptical. 'I've not received it.'

'Of course not! I sent it to Abbotswood, so that by the time it did reach you I would have left the country.'

'You know,' he said longingly, 'you do deserve to be beaten. Did you honestly believe that *that* would be sufficient to prevent me from posting after you?'

'You would not have known where I had gone.'

'No?' he retorted crushingly. 'How do you suppose I was able to follow you here, when you had given out that you were bound for Cambridge? I suppose you thought you were being very clever, but I had only to inquire for a very tall lady with copper-coloured hair, attended by an Italian maid, and you should be gratified to know how many people remembered seeing you.' He saw that she was looking crestfallen rather than gratified, and added consolingly, 'Never mind! There's no harm done, and since you didn't put me to the trouble of pursuing you to the Continent, I'll spare you the beating. Just spare *me* any of these high flights in future.'

The change in his voice, and the return to his customary manner, encouraged her to raise her eyes to his face, and she saw with relief that he seemed to have recovered his temper.

The relief however, was short-lived, for he continued briskly, 'Well, ma'am, bestir yourself! Your maid should have your gear packed by now, so go and put on your hat while I pay your shot and have the horses put-to, and then we can be on our way.'

'On our way?' she repeated blankly. 'Where to?'

'To London, of course,' he replied impatiently. 'We can put one stage of the journey behind us, and rack up at Colchester for the night. Then tomorrow we can reach town early in the afternoon.'

Hebe made no attempt to obey these peremptory commands. She sat looking at him, thinking of all that a return to London would mean. The announcement of his engagement to Barbary; the party of which he had spoken; the preparations for the wedding, and then the wedding itself. She could not do it. Could not stand by, playing the part of duenna—almost, she thought hysterically, the part of mother of the bride—when the bridegroom was this impossible man whom she herself had come to love so much. A love, she knew, which was no transient emotion, no romantic infatuation such as she had felt for Geoffrey. It was something which would be part of her until the day she died.

'I do not intend to return to London for the present,' she said at length. 'I shall remain here tonight, and tomorrow set out for Cambridge.'

'Oh, ye gods!' he exclaimed exasperatedly. 'I thought we had heard the last of Cambridge. Weren't you attending just now when I said I wanted no more of these high flights? Why the devil do you want to go to Cambridge, anyway?'

'It is my home,' she replied indignantly. 'I have friends there whom I have not seen for nearly three years. Is it so strange that I should wish to visit them?'

'In the middle of the London season, and with Barbary's engagement about to be announced,' he said curtly, 'it's not merely strange, it's out of the question. What maggot has got into your brain? If that rogue Murslowe had not come threatening you, it would never have occurred to you to leave town at all.'

Hebe drew a deep breath and rose to her feet, calling upon all her reserves of dignity, all the gentle hauteur with which she had successfully discouraged unwanted admirers. Facing him with a calmness she did not feel, she said quietly, 'Lord Hendreth, I am fully sensible of the great debt I owe you, and pray believe that I shall be eternally grateful to you for rescuing me from a horrid situation, but that does not bestow upon you the right to tell me what I may or may not do. As you are aware, until the past few months I had been used to live very quietly, and that is what I truly prefer. I do not feel that I *can* return to London. I fear this may prove a trifle inconvenient for you, but—!'

'Damned inconvenient!' he interrupted. 'In fact, totally unacceptable, so if you have now sufficiently unburdened yourself, we'll be on our way.'

'No, we will not,' she said crossly, losing a little of her calm detachment. 'I am trying to tell you—!'

'Tell me in the chaise,' he recommended. 'There will be plenty of time between here and Colchester.'

'My lord, I am not leaving this inn.'

'My lady,' he retorted mockingly, 'you are leaving it as soon as the chaise is at the door, so let us have no more argument on that head.'

Hebe clenched her hands, clinging desperately to her hard-won dignity and doing her best to speak in a reasonable tone. 'This is quite absurd. You cannot compel me to go with you.'

'No?' He strolled forward until less than a yard separated them, and stood looking down at her with a glint of devilment in his eyes. 'Would you care to make a wager on that?'

Hebe, acutely aware of his closeness, and of the tumultuous effect this was having upon her senses, tried to retreat, but the chair from which she had risen was too close behind her. Finding herself trapped, she resolutely avoided looking up at him, and instead said as distantly as she could, addressing a point a few inches away from his left shoulder, 'This is a public inn. What do you suppose the landlord and his servants would do, if they saw you trying to compel me to enter your carriage?'

'Very little, I imagine,' he replied with a grin. 'You see, I had a notion you might prove intractable, so when I found that I had run you to earth, I told the landlord, to whom my inquiries had been addressed, that you are my wife.' Her gaze lifted sharply, incredulously, to meet his, and the grin broadened as he added with relish, 'My *runaway* wife!'

'You told him—!' Between astonishment and anger, Hebe could scarcely get the words out. 'You *dared* to say—! Oh, you are mad!'

'Not at all! I know, you see, how obstinate you can be at times, and guessed you might have some ridiculous notion that because of what has occurred you cannot go back to town, so I took the precaution of cutting the ground from under your feet.'

'You *are* mad,' she said with conviction. 'You know very well that I will deny it.'

'Deny it as much as you like, but I fancy you won't be believed. The man's sympathy is all on my side. Perhaps he has a troublesome wife himself.'

'Lucia will tell him—!'

'Lucia does not speak enough English to tell him anything, and besides, *her* sympathy is with me, too. You heard what she said before she left us.'

Hebe glared at him in frustrated silence, recognizing the truth of what he said. She could imagine how convincingly he had told that blatant lie, and how impossible it would be to disprove it with only Lucia to bear out what she said. Her hands clenched, and Hendreth, observing this with an amused, perceptive eye, deliberately added fuel to the fire by saying softly, 'Of course, you *might* be able to convince me that we should remain here for the night, but don't you feel that, in the circumstances, that might place you in a somewhat equivocal situation?'

It was too much. For an instant Hebe forgot all the rules of proper conduct, all the tenets of her upbringing, and her hand flashed out to deal the blow which she had so often in the past been tempted to deliver, but before it could reach its goal her wrist was caught and held. Simultaneously his other arm went round her waist, pinning her left arm to her side and gripping her hard against him, holding her effortlessly in spite of her struggles to break free.

'Let me go!' she panted. 'Oh, you are abominable! Let me go *at once*!'

'Quiet, woman!' he said calmly, and ensured her obedience

to this command by kissing her in a way which deprived her of all opportunity to say anything.

For a few moments, all her struggles were stilled. For a few moments, taken unawares, her defences shattered, she surrendered joyfully, held fast in his arms and knowing that this was her right and natural place. Then an accusing image of Barbary flared suddenly against the darkness of her closed eyelids, and with a sound between a gasp and a sob she wrenched herself away from him as far as she could. This was not far, since his arms were still around her, but he had let go of her wrist by now and she fended him off with her free hand.

'Oh, this is outrageous! Shameless! Are you so determined to humiliate *me* that you spare no thought for Barbary?'

'To humiliate!' he began furiously, and then broke off, staring down into her face with a suddenly arrested look in his eyes. 'What the devil has Barbary to do with *us*?'

'Oh!' It was an exclamation of outrage. 'How can you ask that, when you are going to marry her?'

'Marry Barbary?' He repeated, and then added with the most heartfelt sincerity, 'God forbid!'

Hebe was so astonished that she forgot to struggle. 'But you said that her engagement is about to be announced.'

'So it is, but not to me, you bird-witted female! To Hatherley.'

Hebe gasped. 'Lord Hatherley?'

'What is so surprising about that? He's been dangling after her ever since they met, and yesterday, when I got back from dealing with your friend, Murslowe, I found him waiting for me. Apparently he and Barbary came to an understanding that day he drove her to Richmond, and all that was needed was my consent.' He grinned. 'I was so impatient to set out after you that I would probably have given it anyway, but as it happens, it was what I had intended all along.'

'Hebe, utterly bewildered, could only say weakly, 'You *intended* Barbary to marry Lord Hatherley?'

He nodded. 'I saw as soon as they met that he was very taken with her, and it occurred to me then that it would be the very thing. She needs an older man to keep her in check. What nearly floored me, though, was the fact that she fell in love with him.'

'Nearly floored you?' Hebe felt that she was fast losing touch with reality. 'Surely that was the very thing you wished to happen?'

'Not until he had come up to scratch,' he explained brazenly. 'As long as Barbary was just setting her cap at him as her most eligible admirer she was clever enough to hold him at arm's length, but once her feelings became involved, she was too inexperienced to hide them, so *I* had to take a hand in the game. I've known Charles for ten years, and he has never wanted anything that fell too easily into his hands.'

Hebe, still in his arms but apparently unmindful now of the impropriety of her position, was no longer trying to thrust him away, but instead was absentmindedly smoothing the lapel of his coat. This fact, however, did not prevent her from saying severely, 'Everybody supposed that you intended to marry her yourself.'

'I know they did,' he agreed cordially, 'and a prime set of gudgeons I thought them. I've never had any ambition to saddle myself with a troublesome schoolgirl, even one who was not my ward.' He added provocatively, 'I never supposed, though, that you, ma'am, would fall into the same vulgar error.'

'I didn't!' she said indignantly. 'At least, not until Lady Felchester—!'

'So that's it!' he interrupted. 'I might have known my good aunt couldn't resist meddling. Still, it's something to know I was able to pull the wool over even her eyes.'

'I don't think you did, until she received a letter from Lady Hendreth which suggested you were expecting shortly to be married. She decided then that you had had me take Barbary to Bath last spring so that your mother might meet your intended bride.'

'Then for once Aunt Felchester was right, except that Barbary merely provided a convenient excuse.' Hebe looked quickly up at him, found that he was watching her with an expression which quickened her heartbeats, and immediately looked away again. Blaise chuckled. 'Don't try to be missish, love. It doesn't become you.'

Hebe, now apparently engrossed in the elaborate arrangement of his neckcloth, said uncertainly, 'Lady Hendreth could not possibly approve of your marrying *me*. We are for ever at odds with each other.'

'Lady Hendreth,' he informed her, 'is delighted. She had almost despaired of my ever finding a woman I could love enough to make my wife. Besides, she grew very fond of you while you were with her.'

'Oh, and I of her,' Hebe assured him, 'but it cannot be what she would wish for you. A widow—!'

'Widow be damned!' he said with sudden violence, and took her chin in his hand to turn her face up, none too gently, so that she was forced to meet his eyes. 'You've not even been a wife yet, my girl! A state of affairs which I intend to alter with the least possible delay.' He kissed her again; Hebe's hand moved from his lapel and went up around his neck. 'In fact,' he added, after a considerable pause, 'if I had had the smallest degree of forethought, I would have obtained a special licence before I left London.'

'Well, upon my word!' Indignation prompted her to lift her head from the resting-place it had found against his shoulder. 'And you have not even proposed to me!'

'Well, don't fly up into the boughs over it,' he recommended. 'I'll propose now, if we *must* observe the formalities. Though I feel obliged to point out,' he added in parenthesis, 'that if you intend to refuse me, your present conduct, my lady, suggests that you have even less regard for propriety than I.' She made an involuntary attempt to draw away, but his grip tightened so ruthlessly that she gasped. 'Oh, no, you don't! I'm going to propose to you, but I'll do it in my own way. You'll get no formal declarations or bended knees from me, my girl!'

She could picture nothing more incongruous, and was obliged to choke back a giggle, but next moment a worrying thought occurred to her. She said in a tone of self-reproach, 'Oh, what am I thinking of? What would become of the children?'

'The children,' he said firmly, 'will remain at Astington Park, in the care of the Danforths and that very competent governess. I'm much indebted to Sybilla, and I have nothing against the rest of 'em, but I don't intend to have them living at Abbotswood.'

'Blaise!' She lifted an anxious gaze to his face. 'They need me.'

'*I* need you,' he stated unequivocally, 'and you will admit, if there's a grain of truth in you, that *you* need *me*. What neither of us need at this present, my darling, is a crowd of schoolboys and schoolgirls under our feet. Time enough for that when we have a brood of our own.' She blushed and glanced away, and he added unrepentantly, 'Yes, I know I've no delicacy, but you should be accustomed to that by now, and in any event, as you so often remind me, you are not a shy young girl. Now, are you going to marry me, or are you not?'

Hebe, realizing that this was as close to a formal proposal as she was likely to get, abandoned the unequal struggle, and answered in kind.

'Of course I am, you overbearing wretch,' she said contentedly, settling her head once more against his shoulder. 'At my age, you know, I cannot afford to refuse so eligible an offer.'